KT-387-323

Deceive Me

KAREN COLE

Quercus

First published in Great Britain in 2019
This paperback edition published in 2020 by

Quercus Editions Ltd
Carmelite House
50 Victoria Embankment
London EC4Y 0DZ

An Hachette UK company

A CIP catalogue record for this book is available
from the British Library

PB ISBN 978 1 52940 865 2
EBOOK ISBN 978 1 78747 658 5

10 9 8 7 6 5 4 3 2 1

Typeset by CC Book Production
Printed and bound in Great Britain by Clays Ltd, Elcograf S.p.A.

MIX
Paper from
responsible sources
FSC
www.fsc.org   FSC® C104740

Papers used by Quercus are from well-managed forests and other responsible sources.

For Max and Toby with all my love

Monday, 18th September 2017

Chapter 1

I thought that things would be different when we moved to Cyprus. I thought it would be a way to escape the ghosts of the past. A fresh start for me and Chris and a way of stopping our daughter from screwing up her life. But nothing has worked out the way I hoped. I suppose I should have known that it wouldn't. I should have known that wherever you go, you drag your past along with you, whether you want to or not. And whatever you do, you can never stop your children from growing up and making their own mistakes.

Last night I woke in the early hours, as I often do these days, and lay in bed gripped by fear. It was three a.m. My heart was racing in my chest and my thoughts were churning, whisking up the same old worries. I must have lain there for hours sweating under the whirring fan, listening to the dogs barking outside and the beeping of the rubbish truck, until the morning light made its way in through the curtains and Chris's alarm went off.

I was like a zombie this morning, sleepwalking through the

household chores, sweeping the red dust that collects on our veranda, picking up clothes in Jack's bedroom, only to drop them back on the floor a moment later – he needs to learn to do it for himself. It's not much of an excuse, I know, but it was because I was so tired that I fell asleep on the sofa mid-morning in front of *Say Yes to the Dress*.

I only woke up because my phone rang. For a moment, I stared in blank bemusement at the name flashing on the screen. Dave – my stepfather. *Why's he calling?* I wondered. Whatever the reason, I didn't want to know. Dave only ever means trouble. So, I pressed the 'end call' icon without answering and checked the time. It was one fifteen and I was already late to pick up the kids from school.

So here I am, scrabbling around for my keys in a panic, and leaping into my furnace-hot car. I race out of the village, past the Oroklini salt lake, already dry and white as a bone, and I turn the AC up full blast, but I'm still sweating, and the steering wheel is burning my fingers.

What kind of mother misses pick-up because they've fallen asleep in front of daytime TV? I wonder. Not that I'm really worried about Grace and Jack. Jack's nearly eleven now, mature for his age, and Grace has just turned sixteen. They can look after themselves. Besides, everyone keeps telling me how safe Cyprus is and what a great place it is for kids to grow up.

Most of the parents and kids have gone by the time I reach the school. Only Olga is still there wafting around, looking

4

immaculate as usual in a white summer dress and strappy sandals, her two perfect, blonde kids sitting obediently waiting for her on a bench.

'Oh, Jo, I'm so glad I caught you,' she says. 'We're having a PTA meeting on Wednesday this week to plan out some events for the year. Can we count on you to come?'

'Um, sure,' I mutter, unable to think of an excuse on the spur of the moment.

'Good, good,' she beams. 'We were all going to bring something, a cake or—'

'Sorry, but I need to go and find Jack,' I say, escaping as soon as I can. It's not her fault. She can't help being perfect, I suppose, but Olga always manages to make me feel totally inadequate.

Jack's on the football pitch kicking a ball around with some other kids. His ginger hair's not hard to spot amongst the dark heads of his Cypriot friends. He's standing in the far goal, his face bright red. How many times do I have to tell him to wear his hat? He's got his father's pale complexion. He'll burn within seconds in the midday sun.

I pick up his hat from the ground by the goalpost and shout across the pitch.

'Ja-ack!'

'Where's your sister?' I ask, as he comes running up, planting the hat firmly on his head and looking around. Grace should be here by now. She's supposed to walk over from the senior school and meet us.

Jack snatches up his bottle and gulps down water. 'I dunno,' he says. 'She must be in the canteen.'

I try her mobile, but it's out of charge or it's switched off. Unusual for Grace, who normally has to be surgically prised away from her phone. I'm guessing that she's still angry with me over the other day. We barely spoke all weekend – the most I got out of her was a nod or a glare. Maybe she's switched it off deliberately.

'Christ,' I mutter under my breath. Grabbing Jack's sticky hand, we trudge across the car park and the schoolyard. It's not far, but in the midday heat it's a major expedition – like crossing the Sahara.

'You have a good day?' I ask, as we stop, panting like dogs, in the meagre shade of a tree, hiding from the searchlight glare of the sun.

'Sure,' Jack shrugs.

'Learn anything interesting?' I wipe the sweat from the back of my neck. A few strands of hair have come loose and are sticking to my skin.

'Nope.'

We have the same conversation pretty much every day. Jack isn't big on communication, much like his father. In that respect he's very different from Grace. Grace has always been a talker. Since she was little, she always confided every detail of her day: who was being mean to whom, what the teacher said, what marks she got in her tests. At least that's how she used to be. In recent months she's stopped telling me anything at all.

The canteen's nearly empty already. There are just a few kids playing table football outside and a couple of teachers sipping frappes. No sign of Grace. But inside, I see one of her friends sitting in the corner, fiddling with her phone.

'Hey, Maria,' I smile. 'How are you?'

'Oh, hi, Joanna,' she says in her perfect English, flashing me a metallic smile. She's a sweet girl with a thick mane of wiry black hair and large, mild brown eyes. The type of girl who does Duke of Edinburgh, plays in the orchestra and always gets good grades. An 'A star' student. Grace used to be an 'A star' student too. *Until Tom came into the picture*, I think bitterly. But now? Her GSCE results were mixed at best, and her end-of-year report ambivalent. *Grace needs to focus in order to live up to her undoubted potential. Grace seems to lack enthusiasm for this subject. Grace put in minimum effort this term.*

Is she destined to throw away her future like I did? A daughter cursed to repeat her mother's mistakes? It's infuriating – after all the opportunities we've provided and all my warnings to her about throwing her life away on a man.

'Have you seen Grace?' I ask Maria. Until recently Grace and Maria were joined at the hip. But not so much over the past couple of months, not since Tom arrived on the scene.

Maria looks startled. 'Er, no, I haven't seen her since the beginning of the day.' She calls out to a passing boy, lanky and acne-ridden with bushy brown hair. 'Hey, Andreas, have you seen Grace?'

He shakes his head and flushes faintly.

7

'I dropped her off this morning,' I say, feeling a first twinge of concern. I picture Grace as I last saw her, climbing the steps to the main school building, lugging her heavy backpack, her black ponytail swinging. The brief backwards glance of defiant blue eyes; the determination not to smile or wave. Even her back radiated anger. Well, I'm her mum. She will have to forgive me sooner or later.

She must be here somewhere, I think, and I try her phone again. But it's still off.

'Can I have some food? I'm starving.' Jack tugs at my arm and I look down at him, bemused. I'd almost forgotten he was there.

'Okay.' I shove a few euros into his palm. He'll buy Coke and sweets and other unhealthy food, but right now I'm too annoyed with Grace to care. Would she have tried to walk home by herself? It's possible, I suppose, given the mood she was in. But it's a good ten miles and in this heat, thirty-four degrees in the shade – way hotter in the sun – it would be . . . Well, put it this way, it's not something I'd like to try.

'Stay here. Don't move,' I say to Jack. 'I'm going to find your sister.'

I climb the stairs and check the toilets. Empty. I peer into the classrooms on the first floor. Most of them are already locked. In the maths department I bump into Grace's maths teacher – a young man called Mr Nicholaou with a thick Greek accent and a close-cropped beard.

He gives me an uncertain nod as if he vaguely recognises me but isn't sure who I am. 'Can I help you?' he asks.

'Have you seen Grace?' I ask. 'Grace Appleton?'

'Er . . . no.' He scratches his head. 'She wasn't in her maths lesson today. I assumed she was off ill. Have you tried the canteen?'

I head to the main office, feeling panic mounting, but trying not to surrender to it. I won't give Grace that satisfaction.

The office is air-conditioned and almost cold compared to the temperature outside. The secretary, a plump, middle-aged woman with dyed black hair and a sour expression, is even wearing a cardigan. As I enter, she drags her eyes upwards as if just that physical act was an effort.

'Can I help you?' she says reluctantly.

'Yes, I'm trying to find my daughter, Grace Appleton. Can you confirm that she was in school today?'

She taps listlessly at the computer.

'She wasn't marked in the register,' she says.

'There must be a mistake,' I say, a note of hysteria entering my voice. 'I dropped her off this morning.'

That gets her attention. Suddenly the listlessness is gone. 'We can ring her tutor to check if you like,' she says, lifting the receiver.

I wait while she speaks on the phone in Greek. I catch a few familiar words and Grace's name but don't get the gist of what she's saying. Then she cups the phone with her hand.

'No. Grace wasn't in school this morning. Her tutor is sure because she won an award for her painting, but wasn't there to receive it.'

'Thank you,' I say. I'm starting to really panic now. To calm myself, I think of all the other times Grace or Jack have 'gone missing'. There was that time in the playpark when Jack was three and I thought he was playing in the crawl tunnel, but he'd actually slipped out of the gate somehow and was by the lake looking at the ducks. And when she was four, Grace went through a phase of hiding in clothes shops, giggling away to herself inside racks of dresses as I called out hysterically. They always turned up unharmed in the end. I comfort myself with this thought. It will be the same this time, of course. It will be a false alarm. *Silly Mummy, worrying over nothing as usual.* But the fact remains that no one has seen Grace since this morning, and I have no idea where she is.

Back in the canteen, trying to remain calm, I ring Chris.

'Hey, Jo. You okay?' he says. I can hear the radio blaring in the background. He sounds tired and impatient. Not that un-usual lately. The job he's been working on – doing all the wiring for a new development – has been stressful. His boss is erratic and the prospective buyers demanding. Lately he's been coming home in a foul mood, more stressed and tired than he ever was in England. So much for our dream of getting away from the rat race and spending more quality time together as a family.

'Are you driving?' I ask.

'It's okay, I'm stopped in traffic. What is it?'

'Grace didn't go to school today.'

'What?'

'She wasn't in school. I dropped her off, but she's not here now and her teachers say she wasn't in lessons.' My voice starts to wobble, and I bite back tears. 'I don't know what to do. Should I go to the police?'

Chris sighs, with a hint of impatience. 'Have you tried calling her?'

'Yes, of course I've tried calling her,' I snap. Fear is making me angry.

'Okay, take it easy, Jo. She'll be okay. She's probably with Tom.'

Until recently it would have been unthinkable that Grace, my well-adjusted, well-behaved teenager, would have skipped school, but with the advent of Tom all that has changed. Grace has become a person I don't recognise. But Chris is right, of course. She'll be with him. Not ideal, but right now it's better than the alternative. At least if she's with Tom, she isn't in any immediate physical danger.

'Look, I've got to go,' says Chris. 'I'll be home soon. Then we can figure out what to do.' And he hangs up.

Bloody Tom, I think as we head back to the car and drive through the snarled-up traffic to his flat. If I could wish him out of existence, I would.

Chapter 2

Tom's apartment is near the seafront in a fancy, modern complex with a large kidney-shaped pool. Next to the pool a glamorous blonde woman is lounging on a recliner watching her little girl splash around in the water. There are carefully clipped shrubs, flowering bushes and modern architecture with a lot of interesting angles and glass balconies. The manicured lawns are real grass – a sign of luxury in water-poor Cyprus. *Tom's parents must help him with the rent*, I think, because there's no way he could afford this place on his diving instructor's salary alone.

Despite the luxurious appearance, the lift is out of order, so Jack and I climb the three flights of stairs. By the time we reach Tom's flat we're both out of breath.

'Oh,' Tom says as he opens the door. He doesn't look exactly pleased to see me. 'What do you want?' he asks, keeping the door halfway closed.

'I want to speak to my daughter,' I say, pushing past him into the apartment. 'Grace!' I call out. 'Grace! Where are you?'

'She's not here,' he sighs wearily. *The lunatic mother again*, he's thinking. I can hear it in his voice. But I don't really care. He can think what he likes. All I care about is Grace.

She must be here. Where else would she be? I storm through the apartment opening doors: to the kitchen, the bathroom, ripping back the shower curtain, then the bedroom, taking in the neatly made bed and the wetsuit hanging up by the door. I even open the wardrobe as if I'm playing a demented game of hide-and-seek.

'What the hell?' Tom follows me. 'What are you doing?'

'Mum, what are you doing?' Jack echoes. He's standing behind Tom. He looks mortified.

'You can't just barge in here like this,' Tom says indignantly.

'Oh, can't I? My daughter is missing. And I think you know where she is.'

'Missing? What do you mean?' he repeats, staring at me. He's doing a pretty good impression of being shocked.

Grace obviously isn't here. Suddenly all the anger leaves me like air rushing out of a balloon. I close the wardrobe door carefully. 'She didn't turn up to school today,' I say. 'I thought she was with you.'

Feeling confused and foolish, I head back to the living room. *Grace, where the hell are you?* I think, looking around the room as if it might provide a clue. It's a large room, tidy and mostly empty. There's a flat-screen TV on the wall and a modern, gleaming black-tiled kitchen separated by a breakfast bar. There are just two pictures on the walls – a poster of all the different fish you can see in Cyprus and a picture of the wreck of the *Zenobia* and some other diving sites. On the table next to Tom's computer are a couple of framed photos: one of him and two other young men in a pub raising beer glasses to the camera and a picture of a little boy holding a tiny baby in his arms. The baby is staring wide-eyed at the camera, its fist stuffed in its mouth, gnawing its own knuckles. Looking at it, I feel a pang of longing and nostalgia. The picture reminds me so much of Grace at that age – the way she would chew at anything with her toothless gums. And for a second, I'm back there in England in my tiny, damp living room with her in my arms.

'That's me and my baby sister,' Tom says, catching the direction of my gaze. 'It's the only photo of us together. She died shortly after that was taken.'

'Oh.' I'm not sure what else to say. I remember now Grace telling me that he'd lost both his baby sister and his father when he was very young. It's part of the attraction for her, I think. For some people there's something romantic about a tragic past. And the fact that he's damaged goods is irresistible to Grace. She's always bringing home stray dogs, cats and birds with broken wings. In some ways Tom is just another one of her pet projects. Something to fix.

I'm not sure what it is, maybe the heat or stress, but I feel suddenly dizzy and I steady myself against the breakfast bar.

'Mrs Appleton? Are you okay? Sit down.'

'Thank you. I just need something to drink, that's all,' I say, sinking onto the sofa. All this rushing around in the heat has made me incredibly thirsty and I'm getting a migraine – pain pulsing behind my right eye. I can't afford to get one now, not until I know where Grace is. 'Could I have some water, please?'

Tom pours me a glass of water and gets a Coke for Jack then sits down opposite us, drumming his fingers against his knees. I can smell his aftershave. It has a citrussy tang and is making me feel nauseous. His face, swimming in front of me, is full of what looks like genuine concern. I must admit it's not too hard to understand what Grace sees in him. He's a good-looking young man. Twenty years old, square-jawed, with long wavy brown hair, broad shoulders and startlingly beautiful blue eyes.

'She didn't turn up to school this morning,' I say. 'Do you know where she is?'

'I don't, I swear,' he says. 'I haven't seen her since Saturday. I've been trying to ring her, but she hasn't been answering her phone.'

Saturday. I press my temples, trying to centralise the pain. I'd rather not think about Saturday. Grace and I had an epic row – one of the worst ever.

I close my eyes, trying to block out the image of her face twisted in anger and to forget the awful, hurtful things she said to me.

I wish you weren't my mother. You're the worst fucking mother in the world.

It was over Tom, of course. Always Tom. Curse him. Before Tom came into the picture, Grace and I had a pretty good relationship. We obviously had our differences. Grace was always

15

quite independent, and I know I can be overprotective at times, but mostly we got along great. I'm only thirty-three, young to be the mother of a sixteen-year-old, younger than many of the mothers of Grace's friends, and we related in a way that they didn't. We went shopping together, swapped clothes, laughed at each other's jokes.

But then, just over a year and a half ago, all that changed.

It seemed so innocent at first, when she came back from a school trip to France with the school's orchestra, radiating the unmistakeable glow of infatuation. *How sweet*, I thought. *A teenage crush.* She didn't try to hide the relationship. She even proudly showed me the photos of him on her phone over dinner that night.

'Thomas Mitchinson,' she said, trying to sound casual, but the flush that crept up her neck gave her away.

'He's how old exactly?' I asked, squinting at the handsome face on the screen with a first lurch of unease.

'He's only four years older than me,' she said defensively. 'Dad's seven years older than you.'

'That's different. We're both adults. You're only fourteen.'

'Nearly fifteen.'

I put my fork down. I'd suddenly lost my appetite. 'You're not having sex, are you?'

'Mu-um! Don't be gross.'

'Because if you are, you need to use protection. I don't want you making the same mistakes as me.'

As soon as the words were out of my mouth, I knew I shouldn't have said them. Grace was staring at me, eyes dark with anger.

'So, I'm a mistake, am I?' she said, her voice quivering.

'No, of course not . . . It's . . .' But I didn't get to finish my sentence. She'd already stalked off in a huff, leaving her vegan spaghetti bolognese half finished.

It's just a crush, I thought at the time. *An innocent crush. It'll blow over. They never have any staying power, relationships at that age. It'll be finished within a month.*

That was nearly two years ago.

I look over at Tom now, his handsome, tanned face, his frank blue eyes. He's doing a good impression of looking concerned. Either he's a good actor or he really doesn't know where Grace is.

'She wasn't with you on Sunday?' I persist.

'No. I already told you.' He sighs, picks up his phone and taps at the screen. 'What if I try?' He holds the phone to his ear. Then after a few seconds he says, 'Nope. Her phone's still not working.'

So, where was she on Sunday if she wasn't with Tom?

I think back. On Sunday morning she snuck out of the house early, before Chris and I were up, and she didn't return until late in the evening. When she got in, she dumped her bag by the door and stormed up to her room without saying a word. At the time, I assumed she'd been with Tom all day. But, if he's telling the truth, it seems she was somewhere else. Where? With whom? There's so much I don't know about Grace anymore, it's scary. My baby girl has become a stranger.

I sigh and stand up. There's no point in staying any longer.

Tom doesn't know where she is, or if he does, he's plainly not going to tell me.

'Can you do me a favour? Let me know if she contacts you?' I say as I head to the door.

He doesn't owe me any favours, but he nods anyway.

'You too. Can you tell me when she turns up? I'm worried about her now.' He does look worried. In fact, it looks like tears are welling up in his eyes – a reminder that despite his manly appearance, he's really not much more than a boy.

'She'll be at home, I'm sure. I'll get her to give you a call,' I say.

I can't believe *I'm* comforting *him*.

Chapter 3

She'll be at home waiting for us as if nothing has happened.

This is what I tell myself as we drive home, BFBS radio blasting out music from the eighties. I imagine Grace's outrage when she finds out that I went to see Tom. Again.

'What the hell, Mum, what's wrong with you?' she'll say. 'Can't you leave him alone?'

'Well, what was I supposed to do?' I'll answer. 'You weren't in school. What was I supposed to think?'

'I can look after myself, you know. I'm not a child anymore.'

I comfort myself with this imaginary argument, with the thought of Grace's fury. It's so much better than the alternative.

Chris's dusty blue van is in the driveway and Lola, our aging beagle, stands up stiffly and comes to greet me, tail wagging listlessly. But there's no sign of Grace. Her school bag isn't by the door and her shoes are not near the shoe cabinet, where she usually throws them. Maybe she took them upstairs. It would be a first, but you never know.

Jack disappears upstairs to hook himself into his PlayStation and I dash up to Grace's room, knock on the door and open it, without waiting for an answer.

'Grace?' I say, steeled for battle. But she's not there, of course, and my heart plummets.

Her bedroom is a mess as usual. Clothes are strewn across the floor, along with pyjamas and dirty underwear draped over her guitar. Books and papers are piled everywhere, as are old cups and mugs with God knows what congealing at the bottom. A trail of ants is making its way up her desk. You can't leave food or drink out anywhere in Cyprus without attracting an army of insects. I think about Tom's fastidiously neat apartment. *Maybe I should have encouraged her to live with him after all*, I think wryly. A few days in Grace-created chaos might have put him off for life.

'Where are you, Grace?' I say out loud, rifling through the papers on her desk searching for a clue.

There's a maths book open on a page of algebra. Grace has doodled on the side, a picture of a bunny rabbit and someone – not Grace – has written 'fuck you' underneath.

Under the maths book there's an essay about *Romeo and Juliet*, written in Grace's neat, curling handwriting. The title is 'What is the role of fate in *Romeo and Juliet*?'

Grace has written the first three lines then stopped abruptly mid-sentence.

The role of fate is crucial to the story of Romeo and Juliet. From the beginning their love is doomed, thwarted by their families, who care more about their own petty squabbles than . . .

Oh God, I groan inwardly. She really sees herself as Juliet – and I suppose I'm Lady Capulet in this scenario. Why do they have to study this stupid play at an age when they're so impressionable? I remember an argument we had when she first met Tom and I was trying to persuade her she was too young to go out with him.

'Juliet was fourteen when she met Romeo,' she said.

'Yes, well, that's a story and it was a long time ago,' I countered. 'Nowadays Romeo would be arrested as a paedophile. So could Tom. You know we could have him arrested. You don't want that, do you?'

We didn't go to the police. Chris was against the idea from the start and I had my own reasons for not wanting to get them involved. Instead, we emigrated here, to Cyprus, to put a bit of space between them. A bit drastic maybe, but it seemed like a good idea at the time.

I'd lived here before, when I was a teenager and had fallen in love with the place. It wasn't hard to persuade Chris that moving was a good idea. He remembered Cyprus with fondness from his days in the army, stationed at Dhekelia, and he'd been wanting to come back for a long time, fed up with his job and the endless grey British winters. Jack was resistant at first because he didn't want to leave his friends, but he soon came around when we told him he'd have a swimming pool. Grace, of course, was incandescent with rage, but we thought she'd accept the idea too, eventually. We thought that with time and distance the relationship with Tom would gradually fizzle out.

At first, it appeared that our plan was working. She made wholesome new friends like Maria and even seemed to be taking an interest in some of the local boys. But we didn't allow for the intensity of her feelings for Tom, or for modern technology. At Christmas last year, we found out that she had been Skyping and messaging Tom behind our backs all the time. Then, as if that wasn't bad enough, four months ago, Tom decided to drop out of university and move here to Cyprus. It's not that I have anything against him personally, but Grace is way too young to be involved in a serious relationship and I know all too well how easy it is for young girls to throw away their future on older men.

I sigh and place the essay carefully back under the maths book where I found it. Grace will go ape if she thinks I've been nosing around in her stuff. Next, I try her laptop. But, of course, it's password protected. I know the password for her phone, having borrowed it about a month ago, and I try that, hoping it's the same. No luck. Then I attempt several different passwords: the name of our dog, her favourite band, Grace's birthday in various combinations, but it's all hopeless. Nothing works. My headache is getting worse. *Grace still hasn't forgiven me for Saturday*, I think.

She's doing this deliberately to punish me. Anger twists in my belly. I feed it. Anger is so much better than fear.

Downstairs Chris is in the swimming pool doing laps, his head sleek and wet, like a seal. I watch his powerful arms slicing through the water. It takes him about four strokes to get from one end to the other. He doesn't notice me, his head down in the water. How can he be calmly swimming now? Why isn't he looking for Grace, panicking like me?

After another few laps, he stops at the edge, takes off his goggles and rests his elbows on the side.

'No sign of Grace?' he asks. There are red circles around his eyes from where the goggles have been.

I shake my head. 'No, she wasn't with Tom. Should we phone the police?' My head is spinning. My instincts tell me I need to act decisively, but I could just be worrying over nothing – being overprotective as usual. After all, she is sixteen. She can look after herself, as she keeps reminding me.

He shrugs and pulls himself out of the water, wrapping a skimpy towel around his thick waist. 'Let's give it a few hours. She'll be back when she's hungry.'

'She's not a dog,' I snap. Usually I value Chris's calm, unflappable approach to parenting. Right now, it seems like a terrible, unforgivable flaw.

He's right, though, she'll be back. He's got to be. Anything else is unthinkable.

But hours pass and there's still no Grace. I go through the motions, feeding the dog, making walnut and lentil burgers for dinner, her favourite. But all the time I'm getting more and more agitated. What if something terrible has happened to her? The possibilities scurry in my mind like an infestation of cockroaches. What if she went swimming in the sea and drowned? What if she was knocked over by a car? What if she's been abducted and murdered?

We eat dinner, picking at our food in silence. Grace's empty place screams her absence.

'Have you checked Facebook?' Chris suggests as he stacks the dishwasher. It's a good idea. Glad of something positive to do, I switch on my computer and log into Facebook. In the search box I type in 'Grace Appleton'. She hasn't de-friended me yet, amazingly enough. Though I strongly suspect that this account is a decoy – that she has another account under a different name. I read an article about it only last week – how teenagers often have one acceptable social media account for their parents to see and another under a different name where they post naked selfies and other alarming things. Not that Grace would ever do anything like that. Surely.

She has 253 Facebook friends, many of whom I've never heard of. I look at the posts. Her last share was two weeks ago – a picture of an abandoned hunting dog that needs rehoming. More recently she's been tagged in someone else's picture, a group photo of her and some of her drama friends at a rehearsal for their play. I scan the comments – a mixture of mystifying in-jokes and sweet, supportive statements. I contact as many of the people who have commented as possible, informing them that Grace is missing and asking if they know where she is. I receive a couple of replies almost immediately saying sorry and hoping she turns up soon, but nothing helpful.

I keep my phone close, so I can see if anyone else responds, or in case Grace tries to contact us, while I sit on the sofa watching the news with Chris, but I can't focus. I'm too worried. Why do none of Grace's friends know where she is? What if she isn't just staying out late to punish me for the argument the other day? I'm remembering myself at her age, the mistakes I made, and I shudder to think of all the things that could have happened to her. What if she hasn't run away at all? What if she's had an accident of some kind? What if she's been abducted, or worse?

By the time it's getting dark I've worked myself up into a state, convinced that something terrible has happened to her, and I persuade Chris that we should call the police. But there's no answer at the local police station, so I ring the emergency services and choose the English-speaking option. To my relief, they respond immediately, and the woman who answers speaks perfect English.

'We'll send someone round straight away,' she says briskly. 'Can you give us your address?'

While we're waiting for the police, I realise we've forgotten about Jack. It's way past his bedtime and he's probably still playing Fortnite, or whatever it is he's playing nowadays. But when I go upstairs the light is already out in his bedroom and I find him washed, changed and curled up on his bed, crying as if his heart is breaking.

'Oh, Jack, baby. What's up?' I say, turning on his bedside lamp. I can never bear it when Jack is upset because he's usually so stoical.

He turns a tear-streaked face to me. 'Grace is going to be okay, isn't she?' he says between sobs.

'Of course she is,' I say, stroking his head like I used to when he was little. 'She's probably just out with her mates somewhere. She's going to be in so much trouble when she gets home. She's going to be grounded for about a hundred years.'

I make my voice light, humorous even, but as I go to the window to close his blinds, and see the police car roll up outside our house, lights flashing silently, a chill grips my heart.

And I think, *It's happened. My greatest fear has come true.*

Chapter 4

Two police officers are in our living room, a man and a woman. Radios are crackling on their belts, their eyes are curious and probing, questions firing from their mouths. They introduced themselves when they arrived, but they have long Greek names that I was too agitated to take in. I think the man is a detective and may be called something beginning with M, or perhaps D, and the woman is Eleni or Elena something. They sit on our sofa sipping the coffee Chris has brought them and smile in a way that I suppose is intended to be reassuring. Chris is doing most of the talking because I'm finding it hard to focus on what they're saying. I feel sick and dizzy. The light is unbearably bright, and their voices seem to be coming from far away. The presence of the police in our house has brought it home to me. They're taking this seriously. This is real. Grace is really gone.

'Mrs Joanna?'

Suddenly, I realise that they're all looking at me expectantly.

'Sorry?' My voice comes out hoarse and broken.

'What time did you drop her off at school this morning?' the detective says gently. He has grey hair and glasses and his gaze is steady and neutral.

I force myself to look into his eyes. *Don't fall apart now, Jo. You need to stay sharp – for Grace's sake as well as your own.*

'Oh. About seven thirty, as usual.' My hands twist in my lap. 'I dropped her just outside the front entrance and watched her go into school.'

'Does she sometimes stay out late without telling you where she is?'

'Not usually, no.'

'And has she run away before?' Apart from the heavy emphasis on the h, which sounds as if he's about to gob up a load of phlegm, the detective's English is perfect.

She hasn't run away, I want to say. But then I think, *Maybe she has.* Isn't that better than the alternative?

'No,' says Chris decisively. 'This is very out of character.'

The female police officer looks around the room; her blue eyes, lined with heavy black eyeliner, are sharp and suspicious. I can all too easily guess what she's thinking. *What's wrong with the parents? What have they done to their daughter to make her so unhappy at home that she wants to run away?* It's a good question. 'Perhaps she's out with her friends?' she suggests. 'Teenagers. They can be . . . difficult sometimes.'

'Eleni is right. Particularly the girls.' The detective nods sagely. 'I know. I have three.' He holds up three fingers to emphasise the point.

Eleni rolls her eyes, stands up and picks up a photo of Grace from the top of the chest of drawers. 'Is this your daughter?' she asks.

It's an old school photo, taken about six years ago. Grace in her primary school uniform. She must've been about ten years old. She had the same long black hair and huge blue eyes. But she was chubbier then, with round, red cheeks and a snub nose. She's smiling at the camera with an awkward false expression. She's never been any good at posing for photos. You have to take her unawares to capture her real personality, the flashes of sly humour, the true beauty of her smile.

'Yes, that's her,' says Chris. 'But it's old. I can give you a more recent one. Wait a second.' He scrolls through his phone and finds a picture of Grace on her birthday, the 2017 version – all willowy curves and sex appeal. She's laughing confidently at the camera, her face lit up by the light from the candles on her cake. She's perfect, I realise, and something stabs me in the heart. Perhaps I've never deserved anything so perfect.

Eleni cups the phone in her hands and peers at the picture. 'Pretty girl,' she says thoughtfully. 'Pretty' doesn't really go far enough. Grace is beautiful, breathtakingly, head-turningly beautiful. People often comment on it, and then look at me thoughtfully, as if they're surprised that such an ordinary-looking woman could give birth to such a stunning daughter. I don't blame them. It's true I've got the same colouring as Grace, blue eyes and dark hair, but that's where the resemblance ends.

'Here, take a look, Dino,' Eleni says, handing the phone to the detective.

Detective Dino glances at the photo then takes a notepad and pen out of his pocket and leans forward.

'Does she take any medications? Drugs?'

'No . . .' Chris says, then looks at me for confirmation.

I shake my head. 'No, she takes hay fever pills sometimes in the spring, but she doesn't need them at the moment.'

'And she doesn't take any recreational drugs?' He smiles. 'Don't worry, you won't get her into trouble if the answer is yes.'

We both shake our heads emphatically. But how would we know? According to some of the other parents at the Mediterranean Academy, drugs are rife at the school and children even take them on the school campus.

'Not as far as we know,' I say.

Dino directs the next question to me. He clears his throat and flushes slightly.

'I'm sorry that I have to ask this, but do you have any reason to think she would harm herself?'

I inhale sharply. The idea is a punch in the gut. A rogue image breaks free from the place in my mind where I keep it locked — an image of my mother, lying on her bed, her arms flung out, vomit caught up in her hair. I found her when I came home from school one day, after she'd taken an overdose of sleeping pills. One of three suicide attempts. I was ten years old.

But Grace? Surely not. Grace is strong and happy. That's what I tell myself anyway. But there's so much I don't know about my daughter nowadays.

I shake my head. Grace was angry, not depressed. I'm sure

about that. But I think about Mum's therapist when she visited the house once. *Depression is anger turned inwards* – isn't that what she said?

'No, I'm sure she wouldn't do anything stupid. She's happy, isn't she?' I look to Chris. Chris frowns and nods.

'Good. That's good.' Dino coughs and looks down at his notes. 'What was she wearing when you last saw her?'

I close my eyes and picture Grace, ponytail swinging, walking up the school steps. The brief backwards glance. What was the expression on her face? Defiance? Anger? Determination? The more I try to remember, the more elusive it seems to get.

'Her school uniform,' I say out loud. 'The Mediterranean Academy uniform. It's a grey skirt and a white polo shirt with the school logo on it.'

Dino beams. 'Ah, she goes to the Mediterranean Academy? My oldest daughter goes there too. Which grade is she in?'

We're here to talk about my daughter, not yours, I want to snap. But there's no point in antagonising him. He may be one of the few people that can help us. 'Year six,' I answer politely. 'She took her GCSEs last year.'

'My daughter's in year four. Her name is Anna. Maybe they know each other.'

'Maybe,' I murmur. This is the way things work in Cyprus. You have to establish a personal connection before business can be done – even, it seems, urgent business like this.

'Is there any reason why she might have run away?' Eleni asks with just a hint of impatience.

31

And before I can stop him, Chris nods. 'We had a row on Saturday, didn't we, Jo?'

I glare at him. How can he be so stupid? We need the police to take Grace's disappearance seriously. If they think this is a simple case of a teenager running away after a family fight, they won't make her a high priority. Surely Chris must realise that.

'It was with me,' I sigh. There's no point in hiding it now. 'But we've had a lot of arguments over the years. She's never run away before.'

'What did you argue about?' Dino asks.

'It was about her boyfriend. She's been seeing a man – an older man. An English man.'

Both police officers are all attention. 'What's his name, this Englishman?' Eleni asks. She sits opposite me on the edge of the chair, leaning forward.

'Thomas Mitchinson,' I say after a moment's hesitation. Despite the way I feel about him, I don't really want to get Tom in trouble with the police. The age of consent is seventeen in Cyprus. So legally Grace is still a minor here.

Dino taps his notebook thoughtfully. 'Is it possible she's with him?'

I shake my head. 'I went to his flat this afternoon, but she wasn't there, and he said he hadn't seen her.' I chew my lip. 'But I think he knows something.'

Detective Dino sips at his coffee. 'Why do you think that?'

'I don't know. It's just a feeling.'

'Do you have his address? A telephone number?'

I give Dino Tom's number and he taps it into his phone. Then he looks from me to Chris. 'We'll look into it,' he says. 'How about friends? Have you checked with her friends?'

'All the friends we know about,' I say. 'I messaged everyone I could think of on Facebook.'

Dino nods. 'Have you checked in her room to see if anything's missing, like clothes or money?'

'I had a quick look this afternoon,' I say, 'but I didn't notice anything obvious.'

'Can you show us her room?' he asks.

I head upstairs with the detective close on my tail.

He looks around at the disarray in her room without comment. Then he picks up a couple of school books from her desk and flicks through them, a thoughtful frown on his face while I rummage in her drawer trying to find her purse without success. I tip up her piggy bank and a couple of coins spill out. No notes.

'Has she taken any money?' asks Dino.

'I'm not sure, maybe.' The truth is, we stopped giving her pocket money a while ago after she refused to stop seeing Tom, and though she probably had some birthday money left over, I can't be certain about that. Money tends to burn a hole in Grace's pocket until it's spent.

The detective nods and slides open the wardrobe door. 'What about her clothes?'

'I don't know.' I rifle through the random jumble of jeans and skirts and dresses feeling hopeless and inadequate. Grace refuses to throw anything away. She has so many clothes stuffed into the back of the cupboard it's impossible to tell if anything's missing. 'Her black fleece perhaps . . .' I venture. Grace has a fleece she really loves and wears around the house all the time. 'Yes, I'm pretty sure it's gone, unless it's in the wash . . .'

I'm about to close the door and look in the washing basket when I notice something. It's not something that's missing but rather something that *isn't missing*.

'Hold on a minute . . .' I blurt.

'What is it?' asks Dino.

'Her PE kit is still here.' It's neatly folded on the shelf where I left it. 'I'm sure she was carrying her PE bag this morning,' I tell him. 'So, what did she have in the bag if it wasn't her kit?'

Dino lifts up the T-shirt gingerly. 'She doesn't have a spare set?' he asks.

'No, she only has PE once a week.'

There's something else, I realise, scanning the wardrobe. She usually keeps a sleeping bag on the top shelf. It's not there.

'Her sleeping bag is gone too,' I say.

Dino nods as though satisfied. 'Well, it looks likely that she's run away,' he says. 'Where does she keep her passport? You should check it's still there just as a precaution.'

I go to our bedroom and check the bedside drawer to see if Grace's passport is still there, where we keep it along with the others. It isn't.

'It's not there.' I stare at the detective in dismay. 'Jesus. You think she could've left the country?'

Dino frowns and shrugs. 'Maybe. She might have gone back

to England, for example. Does she have friends or family she would go to there?'

'Not really.' Grace has never been very close to my mother and, like me, she's never had any time for her step-grandad, Dave. My younger brothers live in Australia now and I have very little contact with them. Chris's parents are both dead. She gets on quite well with Chris's sister, Katie, though.

'I suppose she could have gone to her aunt's,' I say. But if she was with Katie, I think, surely Katie would have let us know by now.

'You should check with her,' Dino says as we head downstairs to where Chris and Eleni are sitting heads bent together, talking earnestly.

Dino nods towards Eleni.

'Well, we'll leave it at that for the moment.'

Eleni, taking her cue, carries the coffee cups into the kitchen and places them on the draining board.

'Here's my telephone number.' Dino hands me his card as they head for the door.

Larnaca Police Department Detective Constandinos Markides, I read.

'A bit of a mouthful, I know,' he smiles. 'I prefer it if you call me Dino. Please feel free to contact me anytime.

'And try not to worry,' he adds as they leave. 'In most of these cases the child turns up unharmed, usually somewhere close by. She's probably at a friend's house.'

Chapter 5

Try not to worry, he says.

He might as well ask the sun not to shine in Cyprus. It's quarter past two now, Grace has been missing for exactly nineteen hours and I'm in a constant state of intense anxiety. So much can happen in nineteen hours and I'm tortured by a succession of images . . . Grace hit by a car lying injured in a ditch, Grace locked up in a cellar, Grace raped or murdered, Grace overdosed on some drug. My head feels as if it's splitting open. How can this be happening to us? But I know that terrible things can and do happen all the time. Your world can be turned upside down in a matter of minutes.

I tell Chris about Dino's idea that she might have left the country and while Chris rings Katie to find out if she's heard anything, I head upstairs to Grace's room to see if I can find her passport. After rummaging around in her chest of drawers and sifting fruitlessly through the muddle of papers and books on her desk, I finally find it on the floor where it has fallen behind the desk. Feeling relieved, I sit on her bed and run my fingers over the gold inscription on the cover we bought her. 'And so the journey begins', it says. When we bought it, I imagined Grace taking it with her on a gap year. I pictured her with a rucksack on her back travelling off to Thailand, Australia, India, visiting all the places and doing all the things I never could because I was stuck at home with a baby by the age of eighteen. This dream I had for Grace seemed so close and tangible at the time. Now there's a part of me that fears it will never happen.

I open the passport to the back pages and find her photo, taken a couple of years ago. Grace stares back at me, unsmiling, with her implacable blue eyes.

'Katie hasn't heard from her. She has no idea where she is,' Chris says heavily as I come back downstairs.

'I found her passport,' I say. 'She's still in the country at least.'

It's a small consolation. Cyprus is a large island – over a million people live here – and it's not going to be easy to find her unless she wants to be found.

My headache is getting worse. Pretty soon it'll be a full-blown migraine. I take a couple of painkillers and lie on the sofa with a cold flannel on my head while Chris tries calling Grace again. God knows how many times. He rings her over and over, getting more and more frustrated until finally he gives up, flinging his phone down on the sofa.

'Jesus, where the hell is she?' he spits angrily – anger being his default reaction to stress. He stands by the window and pulls back the curtain, staring out at the blackness and the empty house opposite. 'She was so upset on Saturday . . .' he says quietly. 'You don't think you were too hard on her?'

I sit up, bristling, my headache temporarily forgotten. I should have known he would try to turn this on me. 'So, you think this is my fault?'

'That's not what I said.' He leans against the wall rubbing his forehead. 'I just—'

'No, but you implied it. You think I've driven her away.'

There's a tense silence while I stare at him furiously. Finally, he sighs.

'Kids her age, they need a bit of freedom. They don't want someone breathing down their neck, telling them what to do all the time.'

'I don't breathe down her neck!' I say, my voice shaking with rage. I can't believe he's doing this. Now, of all times. Chris, who never usually gets involved in parenting at all.

'You do, Jo, you know,' he says softly. 'I know you don't mean to, but you suffocate her. I feel as if you've made her life your life and it's not healthy. You need an outside interest.'

Work, he means. It's always been a bone of contention. Chris has wanted me to get a job for years – to pull my weight financially. But when the kids were small, I was terrified to leave them, even for a minute. I was always worried that if I left them, something bad would happen. When they were old enough to go to school, I got a job as a teaching assistant, so I could keep an eye on them and be at home when they came home. But in Cyprus teaching assistant jobs for non-Greek speakers are few and far between. Not that I've really tried to find one. There's enough to do in the afternoons, ferrying Jack around to football practice and helping Grace with her revision. I like to get involved in everything they do. *Is it true? Is he right? Have I been suffocating them with attention and care?* I brush the thought aside angrily. It's nonsense. I'm a good mother. How can a child have too much love and attention?

'If you were her real father, maybe you'd feel differently,' I snap.

This is totally unfair, and I know it. Chris has always loved Grace. Ever since our wedding when Grace was a bridesmaid, three years old, traipsing down the aisle, scattering confetti, he's treated her like his own daughter. He's never given any word or sign that he feels any differently about her than he does about Jack.

'Fucking hell,' he says, his eyes black with anger. 'You really are a bitch sometimes, you know that?' And he stomps past me towards the stairs.

'Wait. I'm sorry, I shouldn't have said that,' I say, grabbing his arm. We need each other. My family is all I've got. 'We shouldn't be arguing. Not now. We should be supporting each other. It's just that I'm so worried about her.'

'And you think I'm not?'

'No, I know you are. Please. Let's not fight.'

He sighs and sits down next to me, patting my leg. 'Okay, Jo. I'm sorry too. I shouldn't have blamed you.'

But what if he's right? I think as Chris heads to bed. *What if accidentally he's hit the nail on the head? What if this is all my fault?*

★

39

Once Chris is upstairs in bed, I go to the kitchen and climb up on a chair. Right on top of the kitchen cabinets is a cardboard box. On the side I've written in green marker pen *Grace and Jack Memories*.

I hoist the box down, dump it on the floor and brush off the dust. It hasn't been opened since we moved here, and dust collects quickly in Cyprus. My hands are shaking as I rip off the tape and start unpacking objects, excavating layers of our own personal history. On top are Grace's GCSE results and a photo of her as Violet Beauregarde in a school production of *Charlie and the Chocolate Factory*. In the middle layers, reports, photos, paintings, cards that they made for me. *To the best Mum in the World* Grace has written, aged eight. I delve deeper and pull out a purple handprint (Jack's when he was two years old). There's a baby tooth in an envelope, I'm not sure whose, and a lock of silky black hair saved from Grace's first haircut. Right at the bottom of the box I find what I'm looking for, wrapped carefully in tissue paper. A tiny white bodysuit with a giraffe on the front. I threw out all of Grace's other baby clothes, but I couldn't bear to part with this.

'Gracie,' I whisper, burying my face in the soft material and bursting into tears. 'I'm so sorry, Gracie. I'm so, so sorry.'

Chapter 6

2000

'So, why do you want this job, Joanna?'

I'm sitting in this large, elegant living room trying not to get swallowed up by the sofa. I was so nervous before the interview I took two of Mum's Valium. On reflection, that might have been too many, because I'm finding it hard to sit up straight and keep my eyes open. Everything is so remote and hazy, it's hard to focus on what the lady just said. I think it was something about the job. Why do I want this job?

Good question. Why do I want it? Escape is the first word that springs to mind: *escape from our tiny house that always smells of damp, dogs and cigarettes; escape from Dave's stupid fish in their murky, green tank; escape from Mum and her moods and Dave and his drug-fuelled rages.* I don't say any of that out loud, of course. I've got an answer all prepared. I straighten my back, smiling, and try to channel my inner Mary Poppins.

'I want to travel, see a bit of the world, and of course, I've always loved children . . .' My voice tails off unconvincingly. I've never been very good at lying. If I ever did love children, it's been sucked out of me by the twins, with all the tantrums, snotty noses and dirty nappies.

'Good, good,' says the man. Hakan is in his thirties, I guess, good-looking, with dark curly hair and big, liquid brown eyes like Omar Sharif in *Dr Zhivago*. He seems nicer and more approachable than his wife, who's giving off an ice-queen vibe, so I address most of my answers to him.

He glances down at my CV. 'You got good grades in your GCSEs. Why not stay on and finish your A levels, Joanna?'

'Maybe I will later. I want to get some life experience first.'

He smiles approvingly. 'Good girl. I like that. More people should do that.'

Helen, his wife, gives me a sharp look through narrowed lids. 'Have you ever been to Cyprus before?'

'Well, no . . .' The truth is, I wasn't even sure where it was until I looked it up in the atlas last night. Before that, all I had was a vague notion of a place somewhere in the Mediterranean. I found out last night that it's a large island shaped like a stingray in the eastern Mediterranean between Turkey, Syria and Lebanon.

'How do you think you'll handle being so far away from home in a strange country and a strange culture? Don't you think you'll be homesick? Won't you miss your family?'

Ha! That's a joke. I'll miss them like a hole in the head.

'Oh, I think I'll handle it,' I say chirpily. 'I'm a very

independent person.' This is true. I've had to be independent. Your mother being suicidal half the time and your stepdad being a violent drug addict tends to help you grow up fast.

'Do you know much about the history of Cyprus?' Hakan asks, leaning forward and clasping his hands together in his lap.

I shake my head mutely. I'm feeling a bit out of my depth.

He sits back, putting his hands behind his head. 'Cyprus is a divided nation, did you know that?'

Again, I shake my head.

'Oh, she doesn't need to hear about all that.' Helen flaps a hand at him impatiently.

But Hakan ploughs on, ignoring her. 'It's been divided since the war in 1974. The Turkish Cypriots live in the North and Greek Cypriots in the South. I am a Turkish Cypriot.'

'Oh,' I say. I don't really know what else to say. I've never heard of any war in Cyprus. I didn't know there were different kinds of Cypriots. It all sounds very complicated.

Helen frowns. 'You're still very young, Joanna,' she says gently. 'Do you have any experience of looking after little children?'

I'm on firmer ground here. If there's one thing I know how to do, it's look after young kids. 'Yes, lots,' I say confidently. 'I've got twin brothers. They're seven years old now. My mum was . . . ill for a while after they were born, and I looked after them all by myself. Taking care of one three-year-old will be a piece of cake.'

Hakan throws back his head and laughs. His laugh is loud and hearty like a pirate and takes me by surprise. 'Well, you certainly seem mature for your age, Joanna.'

And I blush a little because no one has ever called me mature before.

'So, you have experience of looking after new-born babies?' says Helen. 'We're expecting in five months.' She places a hand on her belly, smiling faintly, and for the first time I notice a small, neat swelling.

'Like I said, Mum was ill after the twins were born, so I looked after them pretty much from day one.'

In fact, my mother suffered from severe postnatal depression and wild mood swings, which the doctors later diagnosed as manic depression. She has currently committed herself to a mental hospital, but I don't see any reason to tell Hakan and Helen that.

Hakan looks at Helen and slaps his knees. 'Well, what do you think? Don't you think it's time she met his majesty?'

Helen nods and stands up. She's beautiful, I realise, tall and blonde and dignified, like Grace Kelly in *High Society*. They make a handsome couple and suddenly I feel short, plump and awkward as I stand up next to her. 'Why not?' she says, smiling.

In the conservatory a small, dark-haired boy is playing on the carpet with a bunch of plastic dinosaurs.

'This' – Helen stoops and ruffles the boy's hair – 'is Adam. Adam, say hello to Joanna.'

'Hi, Adam,' I say breezily.

Adam glances up, smiles shyly, then continues playing.

I've got this in the bag, I think. I know all about dinosaurs and I know all about three-year-old boys. I sit cross-legged on the floor next to him and pick up the biggest dinosaur.

'Who's this guy?' I ask. 'What's his name?'

Adam doesn't look at me, absorbed in his game. 'That's T Wex,' he says. 'They're having a party.'

'Great,' I say enthusiastically. 'Is it a birthday party? Whose birthday is it?'

Adam frowns. He obviously hasn't considered this. He stabs a finger at a pterodactyl. 'It's him's.'

Soon Adam and I are chatting away like old friends and I can tell that Hakan is impressed. Even Helen seems to be thawing a little.

They ask me a few more questions about school, which I'm happy to answer. I've got good grades and I've got nothing to hide. I give them the name of my form tutor as a reference – he's always had a soft spot for me. He totally took my side when I was accused of stealing Hannah King's earrings from the changing rooms.

'When would you like to start?' asks Hakan, as they show me to the door.

Helen shoots him a warning look. 'We have a couple more people to interview,' she says, giving me a tight smile. 'We'll let you know by the end of the week.'

'We'll let you know very soon,' says Hakan. And then, is it my imagination, or does he give me a wink as he's closing the door?

Tuesday, 19th September 2017

Chapter 7

Somebody must have seen something.

I cling to this thought as I drive Jack to school. I need to hold on to something. It's seven thirty in the morning and there's still no sign of Grace. I can't have slept more than a total of two hours last night. First thing when I woke up, I rushed into her room, hoping rather than expecting to see her in her bed, limbs sprawled everywhere, the way she always sleeps, covers tossed off in the night as if she's been wrestling with the sheets. But her bed was empty. Everything was in the same place as yesterday. Untouched. And my world shattered. Again.

Chris has taken the day off work and we're all driving in together, me, Jack and Chris. I'm on autopilot. I keep reliving the last time I saw Grace over and over in my mind. Black ponytail bobbing, the brief backwards glance she gave me, before she was swept up in a sea of teenagers. What was she thinking then? Was she already planning her escape? Did she wait for me to drive off, and then turn around and walk straight out of school? Did someone call out to her – someone waiting in the street, watching her? Someone she knew or a stranger, biding their time, waiting for the right moment. My blood freezes at the thought.

It must have been someone she knew. Grace would never go anywhere with a stranger. Not my smart, streetwise Grace. Either way, there were lots of people there that morning and someone must have noticed something.

If any of her friends know anything, it'll be Maria. Maria and Grace are close. They hit it off on Grace's first day at the Academy, bonding over a shared taste in music, a love of animals and the fact that they are both outsiders of a kind. Grace because she's English and Maria because she's half Bulgarian, half Cypriot. I don't know if the police have interviewed Maria yet, but I doubt it. Besides, even if they have, there's no harm in us talking to her too.

'Don't you think we should leave the police to do their job?' Chris said when I told him my intentions this morning.

'This is too important to leave exclusively in the hands of people who don't know or care about Grace. Maybe we'll realise the significance of something the police have missed.'

Chris shrugged.

And so, the argument was settled.

Security at the school is amazingly lax, and it's scarily easy for us to walk onto campus and to find out from one of the teachers that Maria is in a PE lesson.

They're playing basketball, trainers squeaking on the wooden floor, shouts echoing around the large sports hall. Maria is too absorbed in the game to notice us. We stand by the sidelines for a moment, watching the teenagers lumbering about, until their coach, Mr Bambos, blows his whistle for a break and I take the opportunity to catch his attention.

'I need to speak to Maria Lambrou for a minute, if that's okay.'

'Sure, Sure. Anything I can do to help,' he says. He lowers his voice. 'I heard about Grace. I hope she turns up soon.'

Mr Bambos knows Grace well. He used to teach her badminton every Tuesday and Friday after school. Until she started skipping lessons to meet up with Tom. It was how I discovered Tom was in Cyprus, and she'd started seeing him again.

It doesn't rain that often in Cyprus but when it does, it really rains, thick silver strands of rain, like wire cables that flood the roads and seep in through the cracks in roofs. That day, about six months ago, it was raining so hard I could barely see out of my windscreen as I parked on the road outside. I was early to pick up Grace. I usually had my Greek lesson at the same time and was a little bit late, but that day it had been cancelled and as I was early, I thought I'd take the opportunity to watch Grace play. I dashed through the rain from the car to the hall and stood in the doorway shaking water droplets from my umbrella and my hair and looked around the room.

No Grace.

Perhaps she was in the toilet, I thought, so I sat on the benches at the side and waited. But after ten minutes there was still no sign of Grace and I began to get worried. When I eventually interrupted the lesson to ask Mr Bambos where she was, he seemed confused.

'Grace? She hasn't been to the lesson for a few weeks,' he said, scratching the bald spot on his head.

I waited in the car and watched as she ran, head down through the rain, her badminton racquet slung over her shoulder.

'Good game?' I asked casually, as she climbed into the passenger seat. There was a devil in me that couldn't resist trapping her in her own lies, seeing how far she would go.

She put her seat belt on slowly. 'Okay,' she said carefully.

'Funny,' I said. 'Because I came early. My Greek lesson was cancelled. I thought I'd watch you play for a bit.'

'Oh,' she started and flushed guiltily. I could see the cogs turning in her mind. I watched her squirm for a bit, trying to think of a way to get out of it. Then I turned on her.

'Where have you been? Your coach says you haven't been coming for weeks. What have you been doing? Why have you been lying to me?'

She sighed heavily, balled up her hands into fists.

'Well, Mother, what else was I supposed to do? You would never have let me see him if I'd told you the truth.'

'Tom?' I said. My heart dropped like a stone in a well. 'Tom's here? What the hell is he doing here?'

'He's got a job. He's going to live here until I finish school . . .'

It was worse than I thought. 'Jesus, Grace. What about his medical degree?'

'Oh, he's dropped that.'

'You realise how mad that sounds? Do you think it's fair to Tom? Do you think it's fair to let him throw away his life like that?'

She flushed red and stared out the window at the driving rain.

'He wasn't enjoying uni anyway . . . We love each other and nothing you can say will change that.'

'Don't give me that crap. He's just using you, you know that.'

'Can we just drive, Mother? This conversation is over. I don't want to talk to you anymore.'

I resisted the urge to chuck her out in the rain and let her walk home by herself. Instead we drove home in angry silence, Grace staring out at the raindrops sliding down the window, refusing to look at me, each of us wrapped in our own thoughts.

Perhaps I should have handled it differently, I think as I sit watching Maria pass the ball to a friend and run up towards me. If I hadn't been so inflexible, maybe none of this would have happened. Maybe Grace would still be here, safe and sound.

'Mrs Appleton,' Maria says as she picks up the water bottle she's left on the bench. She looks wary, almost scared of me. It's not that surprising, I suppose. I probably look terrible. I haven't slept or washed or even brushed my hair. I imagine I look like a madwoman.

'Can I speak to you for a moment?' I say, trying to sound as composed as possible. 'Outside?'

'Of course.' She wipes the sweat from her face with a hand towel, then follows me outside to where Chris is waiting on a bench and we sit next to him in the shade of a fig tree. The sun is still low in the sky but it's insanely hot already and the air is dusty and catches in my throat.

'I'm so sorry about Grace,' says Maria, glancing from me to Chris. 'I'm praying for her. That she'll turn up safe and sound.' She clasps her hands together and closes her eyes as if she's praying right now.

'Thank you, Maria.' Praying's unlikely to help, I think. If God exists, he or she stopped listening to my prayers a long time ago. But I suppose there's no harm in Maria trying, if it makes her feel better.

'You haven't heard anything from her then?' I ask.

'No.' She gazes at me. Her eyes are big and troubled.

'You don't have any idea where she might be?'

She shakes her head. 'I really don't.'

'Is there any place you kids go together?' Chris says. 'A place she likes to hang out?'

Maria traces a pattern with her foot in the dust. 'Sometimes we go down by the salt lake – a whole group of us used to hang out there – but Grace hasn't been there much recently. She spends most of her time with Tom now . . .'

'Whereabouts by the salt lake?' asks Chris, leaning forward.

'There's a kind of hut for watching the birds. Near the park.'

'The hide. I know it,' I say, turning to Chris. 'We went down there in February to look at the flamingos and Jack got his foot stuck in the mud. We had to leave his Wellington boot there, remember?'

Chris smiles, a small sad smile. 'I do.'

54

Despite the lost boot, it was a good day. And my eyes fill with sudden tears at the memory of Jack hopping along, trying not to get his sock muddy, and Grace laughing so hard at him that she too fell over in the mud. We all ended up laughing hysterically and flinging mud at each other. That was the last time I can remember Grace coming with us on a family outing. Simpler, happier times, before Tom reappeared on the scene, before my warm, open daughter became cold and secretive.

'Did you see Grace yesterday morning?' I ask Maria, rubbing my eyes.

Maria hesitates. Then sighs. 'I saw her before school for about a minute on our way to our first class. She stopped to talk to someone. I didn't want to be late. We had biology and Miss Telalis is very strict so I left her to it. I didn't see her again after that.'

'And you didn't think to say anything when she didn't turn up to biology?' Chris's freckled skin flushes red and he leans towards her aggressively, a big hulk of muscle and simmering anger.

Maria flinches and shifts away. 'I didn't want to get her into trouble. I thought she'd gone somewhere with Tom.'

I put a restraining hand on Chris's arm and pull him back. I don't think he realises how intimidating he can be sometimes.

'Has she skipped school before to see him?' I ask Maria gently.

Maria blushes and her eyes flick nervously to the side. 'I don't think so.'

So that's a yes then, I think. Maria is such a bad liar.

'Who did she stop to talk to?' I ask. We're not going to get anything out of her about Tom, that's plain, so there's no point pushing the issue.

'Andreas.'

'Which Andreas?' There are about a million different boys called Andreas in the school. Greek Cypriots tend to name their children after parents or grandparents and the same names, like Maria, Andreas and Eleni, get endlessly recycled.

'Andreas Pavlou.'

'Oh.' I think about this. Andreas Pavlou is the boy with bushy hair that I saw in the canteen yesterday. He's not part of Grace's usual crowd. 'I didn't know they were friends,' I say.

'They aren't really. But he's always hanging round her. I think he's got a bit of a crush on her . . .'

'And Grace?' I lean forward. 'What does she think about that?'

Maria shrugs. 'Not much. She didn't really want to get involved with him. He's bad news that boy. He's a junkie.'

'He's a drug addict?' The words snag in my throat.

'Yes.' Maria lowers her voice. 'And I think he deals them too, but don't tell anyone I told you. I've heard that his brother is mixed up in the mafia.'

'The mafia?' I splutter in disbelief.

The mafia is an almost customary part of life in Cyprus. Everyone knows the name of the current mafia boss, and tales of people having to pay a cut to the mafia for their businesses abound. But I find it hard to associate the harmless-looking teen-aged boy I saw yesterday with organised crime.

Maria nods and frowns. 'Well, at least that's what I heard.'

'Do you know what they talked about?' I ask.

'No. Like I say, I didn't wait, but I think he gave her something.'

'What?' Chris asks sharply.

'I didn't see.' She frowns. 'I think it might have been a phone. She put it in her pocket. There was something . . .' She shakes her head. 'I probably imagined it.'

'What?' I lean forward eagerly. 'It could be important.'

'Well, it's just a feeling, but there was something secretive about it, you know, like in a spy movie when they hand over a package.'

Drugs, I think with a chill.

'Do you have a telephone number for Andreas Pavlou?' I ask. 'I'd like to speak to him.'

'Yes, I think so. Wait a second.'

Chris and I sit in heavy silence as Maria heads back into the sports hall to fetch her phone. A ginger cat slinks past, eyeing us suspiciously, and some kids walk past on the opposite side of the tennis courts, a group of girls tossing their hair and laughing. For a dizzying second, I think one of them is Grace. I'm about to call out to her when I realise it's not Grace, that she doesn't even look very much like her, and it's as though one second, I'm floating in the air and the next, I'm falling, crashing back down to earth.

'Mrs Joanna?' Maria is standing over me with her phone. 'Do you want me to message it to you?'

'Sorry, yes please,' I say, swallowing my disappointment.

My phone beeps as she sends me a contact card and I save it to my phone under the name Andreas P. There's a short silence as I watch the girls skirt the tennis court. I vaguely wonder what they're doing. Shouldn't they be in lessons now? I almost hate them for not being Grace.

'What about Sunday?' Chris asks, interrupting my thoughts. 'She wasn't at home or with Tom. Was she with you?'

Maria frowns and shakes her head. 'No, I wasn't here. I stayed at my cousin's in Limassol at the weekend.'

'She didn't mention anything about what she did at the weekend?'

'No.'

'Really?' Chris gives her a sceptical look. 'I thought you girls talked about everything.'

'She didn't tell me anything about her weekend,' Maria says slightly huffily. 'We barely had time to talk before school started.' She sighs and stands up. 'If there's nothing else,' she says, 'I probably should get back to my lesson.'

Damn you, Chris, I think. *Why did you have to go and offend her?* 'Wait,' I say, grabbing Maria's arm. 'Before you go, I need to know . . . Has she said anything unusual to you recently? Was there anything that she was upset about?'

There's a hesitation. A very slight hesitation.

'No,' Maria says. 'She was fine.'

'Are you sure? It could be important, even if it doesn't seem relevant. You want to help find Grace, don't you?'

'Yes, of course, she's my best friend.' She looks at Chris, opens her mouth as if to say something, then closes it again. And just before she turns away, I think I catch a flicker of fear in her eyes. *What is she not telling us?* I wonder.

Chapter 8

'What kind of friend is she? How come she said nothing when Grace didn't turn up to class? And this fucking school! What kind of school doesn't know when the students are missing?' Chris fumes as we return to the car.

He's lashing out, trying to find someone to blame. I understand the impulse. I just wish that when I try to find someone to blame, I wouldn't always come full circle back to myself.

'You're right,' I say soothingly. 'But right now, we need to focus on finding Grace.'

'Well, what do you suggest we do?'

'Perhaps we should check out the place by the salt lake Maria talked about,' I say.

'How about this Andreas kid? He might know something.'

'Yes, we should definitely talk to him,' I agree. 'But let's wait until school's finished. He might tell us more if he doesn't have to rush back to lessons.'

That's not the only reason I don't want to speak to Andreas

yet. If I can, I want to find a way to meet him on my own. I know I'll get more out of him without Chris's 'help'. I saw the way Maria clammed up in front of Chris and I don't want the same thing happening with Andreas.

'Okay.' Chris shrugs and starts up the engine. 'The salt lake it is then.'

As we're driving along the old airport road towards the lake, my phone rings loudly in my handbag and my heart leaps out of my chest. Chris and I look at each other. I see the sudden flare of hope I feel reflected in his grey eyes and I know we're both thinking the same thing. *Grace. Please let it be Grace. Let it be Grace and let her be safe and well.*

I scrabble around breathlessly in my bag for the phone.

But it isn't Grace, of course, it's Detective Dino. Another piece of my heart up in flames. Disappointment is an inadequate word for the way I feel.

'Mrs Joanna,' he shouts over loud music in the background. Is he in a bar or in his car with the radio on? 'Good news. We checked the hospital and the morgue. There are no unidentified females.'

The morgue? I shiver even though it's baking hot in the car.

'We checked all the flight records too and there's no record of Grace leaving the country either. We did find out that she crossed to the Turkish-occupied area on Sunday morning, but she returned to the Republic of Cyprus that same evening.'

'She crossed to the North?' I repeat, glancing over at Chris, who looks as puzzled as I am.

'Yes.' Dino clears his throat. 'Do you have any idea why she would do that? Does she have any friends there?'

'No . . . unless . . .' An image: dark curly hair, dark Omar Sharif eyes. I shake it out of my mind. 'No, not to my knowledge,' I say.

'Okay,' Dino sighs. 'Well, she hasn't used her passport again since, so I think we're safe to assume she's still in the country.'

'We found Grace's passport last night,' I say, realising we haven't told him. I'd meant to phone him, but I guess with all the worry about Grace it must have slipped my mind.

There's a short silence on the other end of the line. 'That's good. That narrows our search a little. Well, I'll keep in contact and I'll let you know if there are any developments.'

'Yes, thank you.'

The lake is completely dry. The mud where Jack got stuck in February is hard and cracked and the flamingos long gone, off to cooler climes. We park in a layby and walk around to the hide, trying to keep to the shade of the mimosa trees.

'She went to the North on Sunday. Did you know anything about that? Why would she go there?' I ask Chris.

Chris stares at a line of ants scurrying across the path. 'There's only one person she knows on the Turkish side,' he says carefully.

'You mean Hakan.'

'Yes.'

'But why? She's never showed any interest in meeting him before.'

61

We've always been open about the fact that Chris isn't Grace's biological father. As soon as she was old enough to understand I told her all about Hakan – or as much as she needed to know. And when we moved to Cyprus, I made no secret of the fact that he still lived here, on the Turkish side. I even suggested that she might want to look him up, but she dismissed the idea out of hand. 'Chris is my dad and always will be,' she said at the time. 'I don't need another.'

'Yes, but why now?' I say to Chris as we reach the hide.

He doesn't answer. We climb the steps in silence. Inside the wooden shelter there's a crushed can of beer on the floor and graffiti in several different languages: Greek, English, German and Russian scrawled on the walls. There's no sign that Grace has been here. Of course. I should've known that there wouldn't be. I look out across the lake to the old Turkish mosque on the other side, listening to the buzz of traffic from the nearby road.

'What exactly are we looking for?' asks Chris, kicking the can.

'I don't know.' I feel a sudden wave of despair. *This is hopeless. How are we ever going to find her?*

A breeze shakes the trees, and someone somewhere is using a chainsaw. But there's another sound carried on the air, from an open window maybe, a sound that makes the hairs on the back of my neck stand up. Out on the lake all the water has evaporated, exposing the salt underneath and all the ugly things that people have thrown in over the winter: cans, old tyres, bones of dead animals. I hear it again – a loud cry that pierces the air.

'Did you hear that?' I whisper.

'Hear what?'

'I thought I heard a baby crying.'

He shakes his head. 'Nope. Look, I'm not quite sure what we're doing here.' He looks out over the dried-up lake bed, then turns to me and gives an exclamation of concern. 'Jo, what's wrong? Are you okay?' I've sunk down into the corner of the hide. My chest feels tight, almost as if it's going to explode; my heart is pounding, and I can't control the shaking that's taken over my limbs. Even my head is twitching out of my control. Chris takes hold of my arms and pulls me up so that I'm standing next to him. He wraps me in his arms.

'It's okay, Jo,' he murmurs softly, stroking my head. 'You're having a panic attack, that's all. You need to breathe.'

I breathe in deeply through my nostrils and out through my mouth, counting to four each time, and gradually the shaking subsides.

'Come on. Let's go home,' Chris says. 'Grace isn't here, and you look like you could use some rest.'

'Okay,' I sigh. I really do feel close to collapsing. I didn't sleep much at all last night and only a couple of hours the night before. Chris is right. It's obvious Grace isn't here. The lake is exposed and there is nowhere to hide. Unless of course . . . but I refuse to think about that possibility. It's ridiculous and anyway, the ground is too hard and dry to bury a body.

We walk hand in hand back along the path.

'It's going to be okay, you know,' Chris says as he drives us back through town. 'We're going to find Grace, and everything will be okay.'

I can't rest, even though I'm half dead on my feet. Nervous energy propels me. At home, barely aware of what I'm doing, I work frantically, trying to keep the thoughts prowling around my head at bay. I sweep the floor and the yard, put out the bins and I tidy Jack's room and our room, straightening the beds, polishing mirrors. Upstairs, the washing basket is overflowing so I bundle up a pile of clothes in my arms, carry it downstairs and dump it in front of the washing machine.

I stare at all the clothes scattered on the floor and feel a stab of pain so sharp and unexpected it takes my breath away. Grace's clothes are there, mixed up with all the others: her jeans tangled with Jack's T-shirt, a small lacy bra hooked on my dress. I stand there for a second or two unable to move. The clothes are a heartbreaking reminder that just a few days ago everything was normal. Grace was with us and life was okay. I pick up her Little Miss Sunshine T-shirt and bury my face in it, breathing in her scent – the smell of her honey shampoo, her deodorant and something else, something that is purely Grace. I clutch the T-shirt, not sure if I can put it in the washing machine. How can I bear to wash away that smell?

But Grace isn't dead, I tell myself firmly. *There's no need to be sentimental. She'll need clean clothes when she gets back, which will be soon.* With grim determination I place the clothes in the barrel, one by one, checking each of the pockets in turn. In her jeans I find one euro and a chewing gum wrapper. And in her shorts, there's a folded piece of paper. On it she's written the name MARILENA in capital letters. *That's weird*. As far as I know, Grace doesn't have any friends called Marilena. *It's probably nothing*, I think, but I fold up the piece of paper and put it in the pocket of my own shorts. You never know what could be important. Then I load the rest of the clothes into the washer and turn the dial.

'Do you know anyone called Marilena?' I ask Chris five minutes later.

He's lying in the bedroom with the curtains drawn. I think he must have nodded off because he starts when I speak, and rolls over, rubbing his eyes and wiping a tiny bit of drool from the corner of his mouth.

'No,' he says, blinking at me sleepily.

'Has Grace ever mentioned anyone called Marilena to you?'

He sits up, scratching his head. 'I don't think so, why?'

I hand him the piece of paper. 'I found this in her jeans pocket just now. It's probably nothing but . . .'

'One of her school friends?' he suggests, handing me back the paper dismissively. 'I doubt it's important.'

He picks up his alarm clock. 'It's one fifteen already,' he says. 'Someone needs to pick up Jack.'

'Can you go, please?' I say. 'I want to stay here in case Grace comes home or rings the landline. Imagine if she came back and there was no one here.'

'All right,' he sighs and swings his legs round, standing up

65

and stretching. He kisses me briefly on the cheek as he's leaving. 'It's going to be okay, Jo. You'll see,' he says.

I wish I could be so sure. I watch out of the bedroom window until Chris's van has turned the corner. Then I pick up my phone and call the number that Maria gave me for Andreas.

He answers after a couple of rings.

'Hello?' he says. He sounds tired, lethargic, as if I've just woken him up.

'Hello, this is Joanna Appleton, Grace's mother. I'd like to speak to you about Grace, Andreas.'

'Okay,' he says after a pause.

'I mean, I'd like to meet up with you somewhere to talk about her.'

'Okay.' Is it my imagination or does he sound suddenly wary? 'Where?'

'How about Fini's on the seafront? Say, two o'clock?'

'Okay.'

After Andreas hangs up, I go downstairs and outside to check if the clothes on the rack in the shade of the pergola are dry. Lola follows me out, her tail wagging listlessly, getting under my feet. I push her out of the way, feeling annoyed. *Why is she such a useless dog?* I think. *Why isn't she one of those Lassie-type dogs that can find a missing child from just smelling their scent?* The thought gives me an idea. Even though I know in my heart that it'll never work, I take one of Grace's damp T-shirts and shove it under Lola's nose. 'Where's Grace, Lola?' I say. 'Where is she?'

But Lola just wags her tail furiously, puts her head on one side and then leads me across the garden to her food bowl.

'Bloody dog,' I say.

Grace, where are you? I think. *What's happened to you?* I can't shake the feeling that she's in danger. I shiver and start pegging up clothes, but my hands are shaking. My nerves are on edge today. I freeze as I hear a sound, somebody, something, moving behind me, in the bushes in the next-door garden. *It must be Graham*, I think vaguely, our elderly English neighbour, but then I remember Graham's gone to the UK for an operation. There shouldn't be anyone there.

Grace, I think, dropping the dress I'm holding.

'Grace?' I call out.

No answer.

There it is again behind me, louder this time, and it's not in the neighbour's garden. It's closer than that. It's coming from the bushes at the far end of our garden. I whip around, gripped by a hope that's so intense it's almost fear. But it's just Lola, carrying something in her mouth. I'd forgotten she was there.

'Lola . . . you gave me quite a fright,' I say shakily, and she veers away from me, wagging her tail wildly, the way she does when she's picked up something she knows she shouldn't have.

'What've you got there, girl?' I ask. But the words choke in my throat as I get closer.

'Lola! Drop that right now! Drop!'

She drops it immediately. It flops to the ground sticky with saliva. *Grace's doll,* the one Hakan sent her shortly after she was born.

I pick it up and stare at it. It's a mess. One eye has been gouged out and her plastic belly has been slashed. I drop it to the ground as if it's burnt my fingers. Then, feeling foolish, I try to laugh. It's ridiculous to be afraid of a doll. But it's not the doll itself that scares me, it's what's been done to it. It hasn't been chewed by a dog or an animal, but cut with deliberate anger, with a sharp implement.

Chapter 9

2001

When the doorbell rings I'm sprawled in a beanbag watching a nature documentary on TV. It's about a lioness who adopts a baby antelope. Instead of eating the antelope, the lioness treats it as her own baby, protecting it from the other lions and refusing to let it wander far from her side.

I don't want to answer the door. There's nobody apart from Hakan that I want to see, and I don't want to miss the end of the documentary. I want to know what happens to the lion and the antelope calf. But Grace has only just gone back to sleep. I don't want whoever's at the door to ring again and wake her up, so I get up and rush to the door.

It's the postman. Tall and nondescript, with a slight stoop.

'This one's from Cyprus,' he says, smiling and holding out a pen and a clipboard for me to sign. 'You got friends there? 'Cos my sister lives in Paphos . . . She moved there—'

'Thanks,' I say, cutting him off. I don't want to waste any more time talking, because I know who the parcel must be from. I scribble my signature on the receipt, snatch the package from him and close the door in his face before he can bore me with details of his sister's life.

In the living room I sit on the edge of the sofa, my heart hammering with excitement as I weigh the parcel in my hands. I would have known it was from Hakan even if the postman hadn't told me that it came from Cyprus. It's Hakan's handwriting on the front. I trace the letters reverently with my forefinger. I love the way he writes the J in Joanna with such a bold downward stroke and the n's, all sharp, impatient angles. Strange how even something as simple as an address written in blue biro can have such a powerful effect on me because I know that *he* has written it.

I tear off the brown paper, careful not to rip through the writing, and examine the contents. It's a doll, with a plastic face and wide, blinking blue eyes. It's the ugliest-looking doll I've ever seen. But I don't care. I'm not bothered, either, that it's probably not suitable for a child under three. It's from Hakan and that's all that matters. It shows that he cares – that he's thinking of us. As I take out the doll a folded sheet of paper slips out of the packaging – a letter! It's just a single sheet but never mind. It's better than nothing. I can barely breathe as I open it. *This is it*, I think. *He's going to tell me when he's coming to England to see Grace.*

Dear Jojo,
Thank you for the photo of Gracie. She's a beautiful baby and
I will treasure it. Here is a doll for her. Sorry I can't be there
in person to deliver it. Give her a big kiss from her daddy.
Love, Hakan

That's it. No kisses for me. No promise to come and visit. No real sign that he feels any regret for the decision he's made. I feel physically sick as I scrunch up the paper and fling it into the bin. Then, after a couple of minutes, I fish it out again and try to smooth it, poring over his words, searching for anything, the smallest hint of love. But there's nothing.

I watch the end of the nature documentary, tears blurring my vision. It does nothing to cheer me up. In the end the baby antelope gets thinner and thinner as it has no mother's milk to drink and, eventually, one morning when they go to the watering hole to drink, it gets eaten by a male lion.

Chapter 10

Where are you, Grace? Why are you doing this to us?

She has been missing for over thirty hours now. And I know from all the TV dramas I've seen over the years that the first forty-eight hours are the most crucial in a missing person's investigation. After forty-eight hours the trail often goes cold. We need to find her soon.

I park near the marina and walk along on the beach side of the road. The harsh midday sun glares down, reflecting off the sand and the pavement. The sun loungers are full of tourists marinating in their own sweat. Children romp in the water, laughing and splashing. It seems like another world – a world that has no connection to me anymore. The world I live in is a much darker place, a place a million miles from theirs.

Andreas is already at the café, sitting outside at one of the tables, hunched over his smartphone. He doesn't see me immediately. He's absorbed in something on the screen, his face screwed up in concentration. *Could this boy have hurt my daughter?* I wonder. I'm suspicious of everybody and everything lately. But what motive would he have to hurt Grace? And he looks like an ordinary teenaged boy. But sometimes, I remind myself, appearances can be deceptive.

I order a coffee and carry it over to his table.

'Hi, Andreas. Thanks for meeting me,' I say, taking off my sunglasses.

He looks up and twitches nervously. His tongue flicks over his lips. Grace and Maria used to call him Sideshow Bob, I remember – a reference to the character in *The Simpsons*. It's a very apt name for him, I realise, looking at him now, but surprisingly cruel. My Grace can sometimes be cruel. Not intentionally, I think, but cruel, nonetheless. The careless cruelty of the young and blessed. I know that because in recent months I've been her victim. I tell myself that people always hurt those they love the most but I'm not sure that's true and, sometimes, I wonder if Grace loves me at all anymore.

'That's okay.' Andreas shrugs and puts his phone down on the table.

I sit down opposite and smile in a way that I hope is not too intense. 'I'm talking to all Grace's friends to find out if anybody knows anything that could help us find her.'

'Yes, you said,' he replies in a monotone. His eyes are dull and bloodshot like he hasn't had enough sleep and his pupils are small like tiny pinpricks. I guess what Maria said about him being a junkie is probably true. I'm sure he's been taking drugs. I couldn't live ten years with my stepfather and fail to recognise the signs.

'But I don't see how I can help,' he adds. 'I really don't know anything. Grace and me . . . we aren't all that close.'

'Maria said you've become good friends recently.'

He blushes faintly. 'Yeah, well, I suppose you could say that.'

'Grace really admires you,' I try. There's no harm in a bit of flattery to oil the wheels. 'She says you're the cleverest boy in her class.' It's true. She did say that. I don't mention the other things she said about him. That he was weird, that he creeped her out. That he was always staring at her.

'Oh,' he says, bright red now.

'You talked to her on Monday morning. The morning she went missing.'

He starts visibly. 'No I didn't.'

'Are you sure? Maria says Grace stopped to talk to you on their way to the first lesson.'

'Oh yes . . . that's right. I'd forgotten. We only exchanged a couple of words.'

'What did she say?'

'It was about our art homework. She wanted to know what we had to do.'

'That's all?'

'Yes.'

You're lying, I think, *but why?* I lean forward across the table.

'Maria says you gave Grace something?'

'Oh.' He looks upwards, as if trying to remember. 'I took a photo of Grace on my phone and then showed her. Maybe that's what Maria saw.'

'Why did you take a photo?'

This time the answer comes quickly, glibly almost. 'It was for the programme. I'm designing the programme for talent night. We need a photo of all the people taking part.'

'Grace entered talent night?' I say, bemused. 'She never told me. What was she going to do?'

'She was going to play the guitar and sing,' he says, 'along with a couple of other people.'

'Sing?' Grace hasn't got a bad singing voice, but she's always been self-conscious about it. I can't imagine her voluntarily choosing to sing in front of a crowd and I wonder if Andreas is making the whole thing up.

'Can I see?' I ask.

'I haven't finished it yet.'

'No, I mean, can I see the photograph of Grace?'

'Oh, sure.' He shrugs, scrolls through his phone, taps the screen and hands it to me.

I draw in my breath at the sight of her. It's like being punched in the gut. There she is, just a day and a half ago, so alive and vibrant – my beautiful Grace with that slight dimple, the elfin chin. *No wonder Andreas is infatuated with her*, I think. *No wonder Tom gave up his degree and his life in England just to be close to her.* I peer at the photo. In it, Grace is fiddling with the gold pendant around her neck, the pendant with the aquamarine stone that Tom gave her for her sixteenth birthday. I'd forgotten she was wearing that. I zoom in on her face, searching for a clue to what she was thinking, but her expression doesn't give much away. There's a sort of ironic half-smile on her lips, the kind of smile she gives when she thinks you're trying to trick her.

What were you thinking at that moment, Grace?

'Where are the photos of the other kids?' I ask. *If he's telling the truth*, I think, *there will be photos of the other people taking part in the talent show.*

Andreas seems unphased. 'If you scroll back, you'll see them,' he says coolly.

I swipe left and sure enough, there are pictures of other children: a group of long-haired teenaged boys posing with guitars, a graceful-looking girl balancing on one leg, toes pointed, arms outstretched. Funny, I could have sworn he was lying. I swipe further back through his pictures and come across a series of photos of crumbling buildings, an empty guard post and a photo of a house which must have once been beautiful, blue shutters hanging off their hinges, peeling plaster and ornate railings along the balconies. There's something about the photos; maybe it's the light or the angle they're taken from, but they manage to convey a feeling of desolation.

'These are good,' I say.

He smiles and suddenly looks handsome. 'I'm doing an art project about Cyprus as a divided island. You know, after the Turkish invasion a lot of the land was left empty when people evacuated their homes.'

I nod. I've been to Varosha, the ghost city in the no man's land between the North and the South. I've seen the miles of deserted sandy beaches and empty hotels, abandoned after the invasion in 1974. But, as far as I remember, entry is strictly forbidden, and there are signs prohibiting the taking of photographs near the checkpoints.

'Are you even allowed to take these?' I say.

He grins and pushes his hair behind his ears. 'No. It's not allowed. I have to be careful not to be seen.'

'Do you often go there?' I ask thoughtfully, handing his phone back.

He shrugs. 'Sometimes.'

'According to the police, Grace crossed over to the North on Sunday. Do you know why?'

He looks genuinely surprised, shakes his head and slips his phone into his pocket. 'No, she didn't say anything about that . . .' He blinks and chews his fingernails. 'Like I said, we're not all that close.'

'So, you have no idea who she might have gone to see there?'

He shakes his head and looks down into his Coke. I scrabble in my bag and pull out the scrap of paper I found in Grace's pocket.

'Do you know someone called Marilena? Is it someone at school maybe?'

'No . . .' he says. But there's a flicker of something in his eyes.

I lean forward, convinced I'm on to something. 'Are you sure? Because you seemed to react, just then, when I said the name.'

He shrugs. 'It's just that my mum was called Marilena. But Grace didn't know her. Why would she write my mother's name down?'

'Was?' I say, without thinking. 'Your mum *was* called Marilena?'

'Yes,' he says bluntly. 'She's dead. She died in a car crash three years ago.'

There is no emotion in his voice, as if it's a totally normal thing to lose your mother when you're . . . what? He must have been just thirteen at the time. Nearly the same age as Jack. I shudder. But Jack will never lose me . . . I won't let that happen.

'I'm so sorry,' I say, and my eyes mist up, because I know what it's like to lose your mother at such a young age. Even if my mother didn't actually die, she might as well have for all the use she was.

'Thanks.' Andreas looks down at the ground and shrugs.

'What about your dad?' I ask gently.

'Oh, he left years ago.'

'So, do you live alone?'

'No. I live with my older brother.'

That must be the older brother Maria mentioned, I think — *the one she said was involved with the mafia.*

I look around the café. There's a man hunched over a cigarette and an espresso and a couple of young mothers chatting, their babies asleep in prams. My heart goes out to this boy who has lost so much at such a young age and has somehow found the strength to carry on. But I can't forget that he could have had something to do with Grace's disappearance.

'Did you see which direction Grace headed after she spoke to you yesterday morning? Because she didn't turn up to her biology lesson.'

He frowns. He looks down, his eyes not meeting mine. 'I don't know. I think she said something about going to the toilet.'

Why is everyone lying to me, I think. *First Maria, now Andreas. Or is it me? Am I becoming paranoid?*

Chapter 11

It's seven thirty. Grace has been missing for thirty-three hours and I've been awake almost as long, running on pure adrenalin. My head is buzzing, and I keep seeing lights flashing in front of my eyes. On the drive home, I black out for a moment at the traffic lights and when I come around there's a long queue of cars behind me hooting angrily.

'Where've you been?' Chris asks curiously when I get home. 'I thought you wanted to stay here in case Grace turned up.'

'I did,' I say. 'But that boy, Andreas Pavlou, got in contact. Maria must have told him we wanted to speak to him. I thought it was too good an opportunity to miss.'

'Oh? And?' Chris stares at me. 'Did he have anything useful to say?'

'Not really. He claims she just asked him about homework and that was the last he saw of her.'

'Claims? You didn't believe him?'

'No, I'm not sure.' I try to put my finger on exactly why I

had the impression that Andreas was lying but I find it hard to put it into words.

'He said that Grace was taking part in the school talent night. Did you know anything about that?'

'Sure, she was going to sing that Carole King song, you know the one – "Killing Me Softly With His Song".'

I do know the one. I can hear her now in my head, strumming her guitar in her room, struggling over the higher notes. *Why didn't she tell me?* I think sadly. I suppose it's just another sign of how far apart we've grown over the past few months.

'Oh, I don't fucking know . . .' I say, suddenly feeling totally overwhelmed and exhausted. 'I don't know anything anymore.'

'Shh.' Chris presses his finger to his lips and tilts his head over to where I notice Jack for the first time, sprawled on the sofa. With the exception of a couple of road rage incidents, I don't think I've ever sworn in front of him and he's put down his phone and is staring at me, eyes wide with shock.

'Hey, Jack. Sorry, I'm not myself at the moment,' I say, sinking into the sofa next to him and ruffling his hair. 'You okay?'

He nods and looks up at me, but there's so much sadness in his face that I want to weep. I gaze into his grey eyes and notice the dark shadows under them. I notice too his unbrushed hair and the black dirt in his nails. He looks like a neglected child and I feel a pang of guilt. I've been so caught up in worrying about Grace I haven't been thinking about Jack at all and I've forgotten about the impact that all this must be having on him.

Since his tears on the night Grace went missing, he hasn't really shown any obvious emotion and he hasn't spoken about her at all, but I know that he must be taking this hard.

'We've been busy while you've been out, haven't we, Jack?' says Chris with false heartiness. 'Jack's been helping me make some posters. We were just about to go into the village with them when you got back.'

He fetches a large pile of papers from the top of the dresser and hands me the top one.

MISSING PERSON is written in large red letters across the top, above the photo we gave the police, the one of Grace on her sixteenth birthday, blowing out the candles on her cake. She's staring directly into the camera and the look in her eyes, so happy and carefree, claws at my heart. *Grace Appleton* it says underneath. *Ten thousand euros reward for information leading directly to her safe return.*

'What do you think?' asks Chris, hovering over me. 'Have I spelt everything right?'

Despite his size, his physical strength and his outward confidence, Chris is sometimes surprisingly insecure. Especially about stuff like this. He wasn't academic at school and even though he's been successful in adult life, setting up his own very lucrative business from scratch, with more practical intelligence than any man I know, that feeling of inadequacy has stayed with him.

'They're good,' I nod. 'But do you think a reward's such a good idea? Won't it result in lots of false leads? People who're just after the money?'

Chris looks annoyed. 'Maybe,' he shrugs. 'But just maybe one of those leads will help us to find Grace, had you thought about that? It's too late to change it now, anyway. I've already printed off hundreds and the printer has run out of ink.'

'Ten thousand euros, though. Can we afford it?' I murmur. Ten thousand euros is a lot more than we have saved in the bank.

'We'll find a way,' Chris says grimly. 'Can you put a price on our daughter's life?'

'No, of course not.' It goes without saying that I would do anything, pay any amount of money to find Grace, but I don't know how we can offer more money than we actually have.

'Well then,' says Chris, as if the matter is settled. 'Come on, Jack. Let's go.' And he picks up the posters and his keys and heads for the door.

As Chris opens the door Lola comes bounding up, thinking that it's time for her walk, and I'm suddenly reminded of the doll she found earlier. I guess it must still be out in the garden where I dropped it.

'Wait, before you go, I want to show you something,' I say, opening the French windows and stepping outside into the afternoon heat. The doll is still lying there in amongst the dried-up leaves and broken clothes pegs like the victim of some kind of natural disaster.

'Grace's doll,' Chris exclaims as I bring it inside and place it on the breakfast bar. The doll slumps there, staring at us blankly with its one eye. 'Jesus. What happened to it?'

I shiver. 'I don't know. I thought you might?'

He shrugs. 'Lola?'

'No, look, those aren't teeth marks. It's been cut with a knife or scissors. Anyway, since when have you known Lola to chew anything up?'

'Jack?'

'Do you know anything about this?' I turn to Jack, who frowns and shakes his head. 'Tell me the truth. Did you do this?'

He curls his lip sulkily. 'No, of course not. Why would I? I'm not some kind of psycho.'

I sigh and pick up the doll. I know it's not Jack. It's not the kind of thing he would do.

I stare into the doll's empty eye socket and it sends a shiver down my spine. When did I last see it? I'm sure it was recently. It always sits on top of the wardrobe in Grace's room. Was it there yesterday? I can't remember. But I can't shake the feeling that this is a warning of some kind – that there's someone out there who wishes us ill.

I watch out of the window as Chris and Jack head down the road towards the village, Jack's tousled ginger head nearly reaching Chris's broad shoulders. I think how similar they are, how much I love them both and how strange it is that that fact doesn't give me much comfort. You'd have thought it would make it easier, having a second child, wouldn't you? You'd have thought I could be grateful that at least I still have Jack, even if I may have lost Grace. But love's not like that, is it? It's not quantifiable. It doesn't divide neatly in half if you have two children or into thirds if you have three. Instead, love is infinite for each child and the loss of any child causes infinite pain.

Looking down at the doll in my hands, I feel a wave of despair washing over me. I let out a howl of anguish and rage and hurl it across the room. It lands in the corner and stares at me with its one eye until I can't stand it anymore. I can't have that thing in the house with me. I just can't. Snatching it up, I rush outside and shove it into the bin. I'm just pulling the bag out to take to the collection point when a police car pulls up outside and three officers get out – Dino and Eleni and one other man. Their faces are grim and purposeful, and seeing them, another wave of fear grips my heart. With an effort of will I replace the lid on the bin, wipe my eyes and force myself to walk to the front of the house.

'What's happened?' I blurt as I open the gate.

Dino takes off his sunglasses and gazes at me gravely. 'Is your husband at home, Mrs Joanna?' he asks.

'No. He's just popped into the village. Why?'

They've found Grace, I think. *They've found her dead and they want to tell me and Chris together*. I lean on the gate, trying to breathe. *Just tell me, please*, I think. *Tell me and get it over with*.

To be fair to Dino, he looks a little embarrassed as he waves the warrant under my nose. 'Er . . . Mrs Joanna. We need to search your house.'

They haven't found her. She's not dead. Relief floods through me and my legs buckle under me. I hold myself up by clinging onto the gatepost as the police officers sweep past me through the front door and into the living room. But the relief I feel is followed swiftly by confusion and annoyance. *Why the hell are they here? They should be out searching the streets, not looking in the one place we know Grace certainly isn't.*

'What are you doing?' I ask, following them inside. 'Grace isn't here.'

Dino shrugs and looks at the floor. 'Can you take us to her bedroom, please?'

I lead them upstairs, heavy boots tramping after me on the stairs, and I watch helpless as gloved hands go quickly and efficiently to work, picking through Grace's life, rifling through drawers and papers, exposing her, dissecting her. They are so quick I don't have time to protest. I don't have time to hide her dirty knickers still balled up in a corner. I don't have time to explain why I've left that apple core to rot on her desk. There's no dignity for the missing or for their families, it seems.

'We'll have to take her laptop,' says Eleni, unplugging it, coiling up the lead and placing it in a large plastic bag. 'Do you know her password?'

'No, sorry. I wish I did.'

'Never mind,' she smiles. 'We'll find a way.'

Once they've finished in Grace's room, the police officers spread out and search the rest of the house. They peer into cupboards, climb up to the attic, even tap on the walls. God knows what they're looking for. Do they think we've murdered Grace and hidden her in the walls? The idea would be laughable if it wasn't so tragic.

It makes me feel sick watching this farce and I can't keep an eye on all of them at once anyway, so I go downstairs to the kitchen and begin to prepare something for tea, turning up the radio loud, trying to block them out of my mind – to pretend they're not in my house. But Dino follows me downstairs and perches on a stool, watching me thoughtfully as I whisk eggs in a bowl.

'You didn't tell us your husband has a criminal record,' he says loudly over Queen's 'Bohemian Rhapsody'.

I put the whisk down and stare at him in surprise. Then I turn down the radio. That was so long ago, before I even met Chris. I'm amazed he even knows about it.

'I didn't think it was relevant,' I say. 'You can't think that he has anything to do with Grace's disappearance? He adores Grace.'

'No, I'm sure he hasn't,' Dino says soothingly. He wanders over to the window and casts a speculative eye over the garden. 'But we have to explore all the options.'

So that's why this search is so thorough, I realise with a shock. They suspect Chris.

'Grievous bodily harm,' murmurs Dino, tapping his fingers on the windowsill. 'In February 2002.'

'It was an accident,' I say. 'A misunderstanding. I'm sure he can explain it when he gets back, if you give him the chance.'

But I don't get to hear Chris's explanation because when he and Jack return from the village Dino pulls Chris to one side and I bundle Jack away into the kitchen. Jack doesn't know about his father's past and I certainly don't want him finding out like this. So I close the door firmly, turn up the radio and dollop out eggs and beans onto our plates.

'Aren't we going to wait for Dad?' asks Jack, pushing his food around with a fork. 'Why is the policeman talking to him?'

'He just wants to know a bit more about Grace, that's all – to help them in their search.'

'What did they say?' I ask Chris after the police have gone and Jack is safely tucked up in bed.

Chris winces and rubs his face. 'They wanted to know about Nathan Brown – what happened in the pub that night. I knew that would come back and bite me one day.' His face is red and a vein pulses in his head. He stares at the floor tiles angrily. 'They think I've done something to Grace. It's just ridiculous. You know I would never hurt her, don't you?'

'Of course,' I say, and I kiss the soft stubble on his head.

But the idea is out there now. It's been spoken and can't be unspoken. When we finally get to bed, I lie awake for a long time staring at Chris's broad back, wondering. But I know Chris and it's impossible to believe he could ever hurt Grace. As if to prove that to myself I curl my arm around him and press my body against his skin, damp with sweat. He smells of the earth. He smells of home. He makes me feel safe. He always has.

Chapter 12

2004

Thank God Grace is already asleep when the power goes out. She's terrified of the dark and won't go to sleep without the light on. I bought her a night lamp a few months ago, in an attempt to get her gradually used to sleeping in the dark, but all that's happened is that now she insists on having both the lamp *and* the main light on.

I'm enjoying a few minutes of hard-earned peace, watching an old DVD of *Dr Zhivago*. I've just got to the bit after Dr Zhivago is released from the partisan army and has returned to Yuryatin, where he's reunited with his lover Lara. It's my favourite bit of the whole film and it's just typical of my luck that the electricity has decided to fail at this exact moment.

With a sigh I stand up, feel my way to the window and open the curtains. The lights are still on in the house opposite and the street lamp too. So, it's not a general power cut, just my house.

I fumble for my phone, which I've left on the coffee table, use its light to find the fuse box in the hallway and try flicking a few switches. But nothing happens, so I ring my landlord. If I call an electrician myself, I know he'll refuse to pay – he's such a tight old git. But even he has to admit that this is an emergency and he agrees to send someone as soon as possible.

I light some candles and sit around watching the shadows flicker on the wall and listening to the sounds of the night, trying not to scare myself. In the blackness it's hard to stop my mind from straying to dark places. Dave was always full of ghost stories when we were kids. When he wasn't drunk or high, he would tell us how his Irish mother heard a banshee just before his grandmother died and how a poltergeist invaded their home when he was a teenager. Not that I believe in ghosts. Not really. Dave has always been full of bullshit.

It's only because I'm alone that my mind is wandering like this. If I had someone to talk to, things would be different. A wave of self-pity and loneliness washes over me as I pick up my phone and scroll through the numbers. *Who can I call at this time of night?* I don't know anyone well enough. I'm just wondering if it would be appropriate to ring Anya, a woman I met at toddler group a couple of weeks ago, when a sound carried on the air makes my finger freeze. The high-pitched cry of a baby.

It's only Grace, I think, trying to laugh at the way it makes me shudder. But it doesn't sound like Grace and I can't shake the thought that the cry is thin, more like a baby's grizzle than the cry of a sturdy three-year-old.

'Superstitious nonsense,' I mumble out loud and I fumble my way up the stairs to Grace's room. But by the time I get there, the crying has stopped. The beam of the torch swings around the room, illuminating the damp patch on the wall and the thin blue curtains, and lands on Grace, asleep in her bed, her little mouth open, breathing softly. A strand of dark hair sticking to her flushed cheek.

Did she cry out in her sleep or did I imagine it? Whatever it was, the crying's stopped now. But my legs are still shaking, and I'm so wired that I nearly jump out of my skin when there's a loud knock at the door downstairs.

A large shadow looms behind the glass. I guess it's the electrician, though it could be an axe murderer for all I know. But I don't really have a choice. It's already getting cold now the radiators are off. It's either let him in or freeze to death.

'Hiya, mate,' he says, shaking my hand as I open the door. 'I'm Chris. You got a problem with your electrics?' I can't really see his face in the darkness but his voice, deep with an Essex twang, immediately inspires confidence and I feel myself slowly relaxing. 'Can you show me where your fuse box is?' he asks.

I show him the box in the hallway. And then the one upstairs.

'The fuse has blown,' he says, and he takes out a tool box and begins rummaging around. I leave him to it and head downstairs. But after just a couple of minutes there's a noise and the lights come on. Then he comes down the stairs, whistling. In the light he's younger than I imagined, mid to late twenties, thickset and freckled with very short sandy hair. He stops halfway down when he sees me and gives me that look men sometimes give – the one that means they think you're fit. I pay no attention. He's not really my type.

'There's a leak in your roof,' he says, heading to the door. 'It's making the electricity short out. I can fix it for you temporarily but if you don't get your roof seen to, it'll happen again.'

'I know. I told the landlord, but he hasn't done anything.'

'Don't you worry,' he says as he steps out into the cold night air. 'I'll have a word with him.'

The next day Chris pulls up outside my house in a blue van with *Bright Sparks* painted on the side in electric yellow letters and a lightning bolt underneath. He's beaming from ear to ear as I open the door.

'I've come to fix your roof,' he says.

'I thought you were an electrician.'

'Jack of all trades, that's me.'

He looks down at Grace, who's clinging shyly to my leg. 'Hello, sweetheart.' And he smiles at me. 'Well, ain't she a cutie? What's her name?'

'Grace.'

'Pretty name. Where's your daddy then, Grace? He at work?'

Grace twists her body, sucks her finger and looks at me. She's not used to visitors. 'I don't have a daddy,' she whispers shyly.

'We're not together anymore,' I say quickly. It sounds less slutty that way.

Chris doesn't look shocked. He looks pleased in fact. 'Well, I have a lot of respect for single mothers,' he says. 'My mum was a single mother. Brought us up on her own, she did, worked two jobs. It's tough doing everything by yourself, I know.'

'It's not always easy,' I agree. I think it's the first time anyone's ever said that to me, and I feel so grateful I could almost cry.

Chris comes back the next day and the day after that to fix something else. He keeps finding new things to repair around the house. We chat a lot while he's working, and I find that he's surprisingly easy to talk to. During one of our conversations he tells me how he used to be in the army stationed in Cyprus.

'That's funny, I lived in Cyprus too and I must have been there about the same time as you.'

'It's like the universe wanted us to meet,' he says. And he moves a little closer, giving me that look. When he moves in for a kiss, I don't try to stop him.

It's only much later, after we're married, that he tells me about his conviction. We're on our honeymoon, staying in a B and B in Devon. The heating has only just started working, it's freezing cold and we're huddled together under the duvet, trying to keep warm.

'It was just after I came out of the army,' he says, his voice muffled in the darkness. 'It was a difficult time for me. I didn't know how to live in the outside world. I ended up drinking too much and one night I got into a fight with this bloke. Nathan Brown – right wanker he was, trying to chat up my bird. I pushed him off a wall. How was I supposed to know the wall was way higher on one side than on the other?'

'Oh my God, was he okay?'

'He cracked his skull and broke his arm, but he was all right in the end.'

I am silent. Chris turns my face towards his and looks searchingly into my eyes.

'Do you hate me now?'

'No.' I pull him towards me and kiss him on the lips. 'It's in the past, isn't it?'

After all, who am I to judge?

Wednesday, 20th September 2017

Chapter 13

Grace is crying in the back of the car.

'Shh,' I say, turning and stroking her cheek. 'Don't worry, Gracie.'

But something is very wrong. The car is moving. It shouldn't be moving, not like this. It's swaying and rocking like a boat, and when I look out of the window I see black water rising, threatening to swallow us up. We're in the lake, I realise, and I'm paralysed by terror as thick greenish water starts pouring in through the cracks. We're sinking and I'm struggling with the straps of Gracie's car seat, trying to get her out. But they're jammed, and no matter how hard I try, I can't unclip them. Water is filling the car, sloshing around. It keeps getting higher and higher until it reaches Grace's toes, then her waist, then her neck. And I'm crying and screaming but no sound comes out of my mouth. Then we're both underwater, unable to breathe. We're going to drown. I make a last desperate attempt to wrestle Grace free. I can't let her down. She expects me to save her. She needs me to save her.

When I wake up, I'm choking as if I really can't breathe and I lie on the bed coughing and gasping.

'You okay?' Chris mumbles next to me, still half asleep.

'No,' I say. Tears are streaming down my cheeks, soaking into the pillow. I know I'm not okay, but for a moment I can't remember why. Then it comes to me. Grace is gone. My daughter is missing.

The only thing keeping me sane is the hope. The tiny kernel of hope that she'll have come back in the night and be there lying in her bed. It's that hope that propels me out of bed and across the landing to her room. But she's not there, of course. Her bed is unslept in, the apple core in the bin turning brown. It smells sweet and sickly. The smell of Grace is already fading, overpowered by rotting fruit.

Chris has gone back to sleep when I go back to our room to get dressed. I slump on the bed with my trousers round my ankles, suddenly lacking the will to pull them up, tears streaming down my face. *How can he go back to sleep? Doesn't he care at all?*

But maybe it's for the best, I reflect after a while. If he was awake, he might insist on taking Jack to school with me. There's something that I need to do this morning, and I need to do it alone.

As quietly as possible, I check in the drawer in my bedside table, take out my passport and slip it into my handbag. Then I make Jack breakfast and sandwiches for his packed lunch and drive him to school.

'I might ask Angelo's mum to pick you up today. Would that be okay?' I say casually as we stop on the drive-through ramp.

'Sure,' Jack shrugs listlessly. He would normally be excited about a play date with Angelo but since Grace has gone missing, he seems to have lost enthusiasm for everything. 'See you later, Mum,' he says, slamming the car door shut.

I watch him plod in through the school gate, weighed down by his Guardians of the Galaxy bag. I watch until he's safely inside his classroom, then I check my phone and I look inside my bag. My passport is still in there. I haven't got any Turkish liras in my purse, but it doesn't matter; I'm sure if I need to pay for anything, they'll accept euros. I sit in the car thinking and trying to build up my courage until the hooting from behind becomes deafening and I drive off a little and park in a layby. Then I take out my phone and call Angelo's mother, Stella.

She speaks nineteen to the dozen as usual, not stopping to pause for breath. 'Jo, how are you? I heard about Grace. Are you okay? Stupid question. Of course you're not okay. You must be devastated . . . You know, if there's anything I can do . . .'

'Actually,' I say, when I can get a word in, 'I wanted to ask a favour.'

'Of course, of course. Anything. I would have rung you earlier but—'

'Could you pick up Jack from school today if I'm not there on time?'

There's a short pause. I picture her pretty face frowning, looking at her watch and wondering if she can fit it all in between her yoga lesson and her PTA meeting.

'Of course,' she says. 'That's no problem at all. Angelo would love to have him. He can stay for a sleepover if you want.'

I consider this. It would probably be good for Jack to escape from the toxic atmosphere of grief and anger in our house but the thought of not seeing him for a whole night terrifies me.

'Um, I don't know . . . he doesn't have his pyjamas or—'

'It's okay, he can borrow some. We've got a spare toothbrush. You don't need to worry about anything.'

'Thank you, but I'd rather he slept at home.'

'Sure, sure. I understand. I'll drop him back about seven this evening, okay? Don't you worry about a thing.'

Thank God for Stella, I think as I drive back through town. I've spent the past few months trying to ward off her friendship – her well-meant attempts to get me involved in the life of the school. But I must admit that I'm grateful to her now.

I drive on, as if I'm heading towards home. But instead of taking the turning under the bridge to the village, I turn off onto the motorway, towards the village of Pyla and the crossing to Northern Cyprus. The land is empty here in the buffer zone. There's nothing but scrubland, a few empty houses and unmanned UN guard posts. No one can agree about who the land belongs to. In fact, no one can agree who any of the land in Cyprus belongs to. The Greek Cypriots want the land they lost in 1974 returned to them and all the Turkish soldiers and settlers on the island to leave. But some of the Turkish settlers were born on Cyprus. It's their home now – so where would they go? Both sides keep talking about reunification, about healing the wounds of the past, but sometimes old wounds run too deep, I guess. And the past here is still very much alive, unforgotten and unforgiven.

It makes me think of the distance between me and Grace that has grown since she has become a teenager. Our very own no man's land, with Grace on one side and me on the other. If I'm brutally honest with myself, the truth is, our relationship was falling apart long before Tom ever appeared on the scene. I suppose it's a necessary part of growing up. When kids are young, they think their parents are perfect and they absorb your opinions as if they're gospel. But as they grow up, they swing to the opposite extreme. It's as if when they find out that you are fallible, they can't forgive you for tricking them into believing in you and they start to think everything you do and say is wrong.

People say that a mother's love is unconditional. But I don't think that's completely true. Love remains, of course, like a stubborn rock in a fast-flowing river, but it gets worn down by constant neglect; and there have been times, recently, I have to admit, when I haven't much liked my daughter. But right now, all that is forgotten – with Grace in danger, my love is as fierce and urgent as it ever was.

There's just one car ahead of me when I reach the border crossing. I park and hand my passport to a bored-looking Turkish official in a booth. She flicks through it, sipping her iced coffee in a plastic cup and tapping long, manicured nails on her keyboard. She hands my passport back without a word. She doesn't seem like the most helpful person in the world, but I show her the photo of Grace on my phone anyway.

'Have you seen this girl?' I ask.

It's a long shot, I know. Grace almost certainly wouldn't have come this way. She can't drive for a start. She would more likely have crossed by foot in Nicosia at Ledra Street and then got a bus or taxi to Kyrenia. That is, if I'm right about where she went on Sunday. But I must be right. Where else would she have gone? To my knowledge, there's no one else she knows in the North. She can only have come here to find her father.

The border guard glances at the photo.

'Sorry,' she says, shaking her head. 'Pretty girl.'

I climb back in the car and I drive through the villages, slightly poorer and shabbier in the North than in the South – the result of long-established sanctions. Building work has gone crazy on this side of the border and there are concrete buildings sprouting up everywhere alongside the old crumbling pre-war Greek houses, which they can't knock down in case one day there's a settlement and their Greek owners reclaim them.

How did Grace know where to find Hakan? I wonder as I head out onto the empty highway. I didn't tell her where he lived. But, of course, it was all there, in his book. His semi-autobiographical novel *If Life Gives You Lemons*. He left quite a bit out and changed a lot, but he didn't bother to change the name of the hotel. There can't be too many places called Paradise Beach Bungalows in Kyrenia.

Did I make a mistake, showing her Hakan's book? Did it create expectations that couldn't be met? All I can say is that at the time it felt like the right thing to do.

She was about ten years old when I told her, and she had just started asking lots of questions about her 'real' dad.

'What does he look like?' she asked, one day after school. In answer I went to the bookcase and took down the book, hidden from Chris behind the others. Chris knew all about Hakan, of course. But as far as he was concerned, Hakan was in the past – long forgotten. He wouldn't have understood why I needed to buy his book and he might have been hurt if he knew how well thumbed it was – how naturally the book fell open at the photo in the middle of Hakan.

'There. That's him. That's your father,' I said, tapping the picture on the back cover, looking older, but still handsome, along with some blurb about his life.

Hakan Guney was born in the East End in 1963, the son of Turkish Cypriot parents. He graduated from the London School of Economics and worked for a while as a lawyer before giving it all up to start up a hotel in Northern Cyprus. This book is about his experiences. He now lives in Kyrenia, Cyprus, with his wife, Helen, and their two children.

Grace stared at me in disbelief for a second, then snatched the book from me. She read the book in one evening then replaced it on the bookshelf the next morning without a word.

'He doesn't mention you or me at all,' she said over breakfast.

'No, I know.' Trust me, I scoured the book for hints, anything to suggest that I was on his mind when he wrote it, but there was nothing, just a single reference to Five Finger Mountain and no mention of a picnic near the old ruined monastery.

'Well, he left a lot out,' I said. 'I suppose he didn't want to upset his family — his other family, I mean.'

After that, Grace seemed to forget all about Hakan. And over the next five years I could count on one hand the number of times she mentioned him.

But then, about nine months ago, shortly after we arrived in Cyprus, we were sitting at Dhekelia beach on sun loungers, watching the sun set over the power station and talking about books in general, when she said out of the blue, 'Do you think he still lives in the same place?'

'Who?' I said, even though I could guess who she was talking about.

'My father. I mean, Hakan Guney.'

'As far as I know,' I said, curling my legs up, hugging them to my chest and staring out at the horizon. 'I could try and arrange a meeting if you like,' I said. 'We could meet in secret. His wife need never know.'

Grace sighed and turned over onto her front, pulling down her bikini bottoms over a red, raw patch where she'd forgotten to put sun cream. 'What would be the point?' she said. 'He plainly has no interest in meeting me. He's had fifteen years to get in touch if he wanted.'

I was surprised by the bitterness in her voice. Though I

shouldn't have been. I suppose it was inevitable that she should feel rejected. Just one more thing for me to feel guilty about.

'I'm sure he wanted to meet you,' I lied. 'But I suppose he was worried about his family finding out he'd had an affair.'

She propped her head up in her hands and squinted at me. 'I don't care,' she said. 'As far as I'm concerned, Chris is my dad and always will be. I don't need any other.'

'It was just an idea.'

'Well, it's an idea I'm not interested in,' she said firmly. And at the time I was sure she meant it.

So why the sudden change of heart now?

It's only when I'm halfway to Kyrenia that I remember Chris. I need to ring and tell him where I am, in case he gets back home before me and wonders where I am. He'll be worried about Jack too. I stop in a layby and take out my phone, but I've forgotten that our mobiles don't work in the North because Greek phone companies and Turkish companies won't make contracts with each other. *Damn it*, I think.

I carry on driving and I'm soon at the straight, flat road cutting through nothing but stubbly yellow grass and billboards advertising everything from casinos to universities. After about half an hour the road starts climbing through green forested hills and then I catch sight of Five Finger Mountain.

Chapter 14

2000

'Why's it called Five Finger Mountain?'

It's an idyllic day in December. Not too hot, not too cold. Fluffy white clouds are floating above our heads in the bright blue sky. We're lying on the grass. After the recent rain the hillside is newly green and the sound of goats' bells drifts from the valley below. There's nothing and nobody about, no traffic noise, just me and Hakan. It's easy to imagine we're the only people in the world.

Hakan turns so he's lying on his front with his chin resting on his hands, giving me a smile that makes my heart swell. 'There's a legend about a giant,' he frowns, as if trying to remember. 'He was running away from another giant, I think. And when he crossed the sea to Cyprus, he put his hand out and grabbed the mountain and made that imprint like five fingers, see?'

'Why was he running away from the other giant?' I ask, snapping off a blade of grass and twining it around my fingers.

'I don't know,' he shrugs. 'Does it matter? Maybe it was a female giant and the other giant was trying to have his wicked way with her.' He rolls over and pulls me down on top of him, giggling. And then he kisses my lips and slowly unzips my dress.

I can't be a hundred per cent sure, of course, but I like to think that that was when Grace was conceived. There, on that mountain, in the bright winter sunshine under the blue dome of the Cyprus sky.

Chapter 15

2007

My car struggles up the steep mountain range until I reach the top. When I get there, I can see the untidy sprawl of Kyrenia spread out below and the blue sea glittering on the horizon.

It's almost unrecognisable. So much has changed in the past sixteen years that I find it difficult to navigate through the tangled, snarled-up streets. But eventually, I make my way to the coast road, past the Turkish army barracks and the Lemar supermarket. Amazingly, the block of concrete shops is still here, half built, still unfinished, no nearer completion than when I was here seventeen years ago. And the sign still remains too, a little faded now. 'Paradise Beach Bungalows' written in large blue letters, with a silhouette of a palm tree and a setting sun underneath. I turn in off the main road and drive down the smaller road towards the sea and then turn again into a dirt track shadowed by jacaranda trees.

And then, suddenly, here I am. I park in the small gravelled area and look about. It catches in my heart. It's all so familiar, as if I were here only yesterday. Nothing has changed. The old cat feeding station is still here even, and a large ginger tomcat is reclining on the steps.

Chapter 16

2000

I wake up, thinking I'm still at home, but the bed is in the wrong place and there's something scrabbling around on the ceiling. I turn on the bedside lamp and see that the culprit is a gecko clinging to the wall, frozen in the light, its little beady eye watching me suspiciously. *You're not in Kansas anymore, Dorothy.*

I climb out of bed and open the heavy wooden shutters, letting sunlight flood in. Through a curtain of pink flowers, I can see a small square of sparkling blue sea. I breathe the salty air into my lungs and think, *This is it. I've done it. I'm finally in Cyprus and I'm free. There are two thousand miles between me and Mum and Dave and all their crap.*

Once I've dressed, I head over to the main building, where reception and the restaurant are, and I find Helen trying to get Adam to put his shoes and socks on. 'Joanna, welcome,' she says abstractedly, as Adam slips out of her grasp and runs away, chuckling to himself like a loon.

Helen chases after him and scoops him up in her arms, where he wriggles and screams. 'Did you sleep all right?' she asks.

'Like a baby.'

And she laughs but it's not really a happy laugh, more of a hysterical laugh, like someone on the edge of a nervous breakdown.

'You wouldn't say "like a baby" if you knew how Adam sleeps,' she says darkly. 'I don't think I've slept properly in weeks.'

Now I think about it, she does look exhausted. There are dark circles under her eyes, her hair isn't brushed and there are splodges of yoghurt on her top. She still looks beautiful, but she seems very different from the graceful, slightly aloof woman I met in London. This woman seems like she might be about to lose the plot. I should know. I've seen all the signs of mental breakdown before.

'Would you like me to take him for a while?' I say. I haven't had my breakfast yet but there's no harm in making a good first impression.

'Well . . .' Helen hesitates. She looks like she can't believe her luck. 'Okay, if you're sure, that would be great. I've got some errands to run in town.'

And before I can change my mind, she picks up Adam and plonks him in my arms. 'All his stuff is in this bag. Suncream, sunhat, snacks, nappies . . . Please make sure he wears a sunhat if you go out. Hakan is in reception if you need anything and you've got my phone number, haven't you?'

111

And so, just like that, I end up looking after Adam all morning. It's not exactly how I envisaged my first day in Cyprus. I thought I'd have some time to adjust before I started working, maybe spend the day at the beach, get a bit of a tan. But I'll do that anyway and I don't really mind Adam tagging along with me. I smother him with suncream and we go exploring hand in hand around the hotel grounds. He doesn't seem fazed by being left alone with someone he barely knows, and after some initial shyness, chatters away happily, showing me all his favourite spots – the jetty, the fish pond and a hidey hole under a mimosa bush.

Eventually, we find a small private beach for hotel guests, which is nearly empty. There's just one young German couple sunning themselves at the far end and so I claim a sunbed and sit under the shade of an umbrella watching Adam paddling in the shallow water. But I don't get to sit still for long. I soon find out that there's no relaxation to be had with a three-year-old at the beach. Adam needs constant entertainment and I find myself building a sandcastle and then digging a moat around it. I try to build a bridge over the moat, but it keeps crumbling. And then Adam decides to jump on the castle and destroy it. He's not as sweet as I remembered and he's beginning to get on my nerves, especially when he keeps taking his hat off and throwing it on the sand. In the end he gets so mad with me forcing him to wear it, he takes it off and flings it into the water. So then of course it's too wet and sandy for him to wear. So, I give up and leave it on the sunbed to dry.

It's about twelve o'clock and I'm thinking of heading back inside for some lunch and to see if Adam will go down for a nap when I see Helen walking across the sand towards me. As she gets closer, she breaks into a sprint.

'Joanna!' she shouts. There's an urgency in her voice which makes me think something terrible has happened – someone has died or at the very least badly injured themselves. Automatically, I look over towards Adam. Has he somehow waded into the water and got himself out of his depth? But no, he's still there playing happily in the shallow water, right as rain.

'Where's his hat? Why hasn't he got his hat on?' Helen puffs when she reaches the sunbed. She looks red-faced and furious.

'Oh, well, he kept—'

'I told you, you have to keep his hat on.'

'I'm sorry,' I say. I explain about the sand and the water but she's not really listening. She scoops up Adam and whisks him away as if I've put him in some kind of grave danger. And I'm left to clear up all his spades and other paraphernalia.

She's still going on about the sunhat when we sit down for a late lunch under the vines on the veranda.

'You really must make sure Adam keeps his hat on at all times, Joanna,' she says, eyeing me as if she's already regretting their choice of nanny. 'The sun in Cyprus is really strong.'

'It's okay. There's no harm done,' says Hakan, patting her hand. 'Calm down, Helen, Joanna won't want to stay with us if you keep on at her like this.' He gives me a conspiratorial wink and I feel myself relaxing a little. At least he seems friendly. I'm already beginning to think that Helen could well be a nightmare to work for.

Later that evening, Adam is tucked up in bed, all the hotel guests have gone to bed or are out and I'm sitting on the veranda chatting to one of the waiters, whose name is Yusuf, and drinking raki, when we hear raised voices coming from upstairs.

I can't hear anything they say, apart from a few swear words. There are several muffled thuds and then Helen's voice, loud and shrill, carries from the bedroom window.

'That's because you never fucking listen to a word I say!' she screams.

Hakan's voice in reply is low and indistinct.

Yusuf and I exchange embarrassed smiles.

'I hate you!' Helen shrieks again.

Hakan's reply is drowned out by a sort of crashing noise and Helen comes storming down the stairs. She doesn't look at me or Yusuf, just sweeps past us out of the restaurant. After she's gone Yusuf raises his eyebrows. 'She's a crazy lady,' he says, and I giggle. Then there's the sound of a car engine starting and driving off.

Hakan comes downstairs a few minutes later, looking weary. His shirt is half untucked, and his black hair is tousled.

'Did you see Helen?' he asks us.

Yusuf shrugs. 'She took the car. I think she must've gone into town.'

Hakan gives a big sigh. 'Well, I need a drink,' he says. 'How about you?' He pours himself a scotch and one for me and Yusuf too. 'I'm sorry about that,' he says, looking from Yusuf to me.

And I shrug. What am I supposed to say? 'Will she be okay?'

Hakan nods. 'Yeah, she'll be fine.' He takes a swig of whisky and smiles at me ruefully.

'I'm sorry, Joanna. You must have a terrible impression of us. It's not always like this, honestly.'

I flush a little, embarrassed. 'It's all right, I'm used to it. My mum and stepdad fight all the time.'

Hakan chuckles, then looks over his shoulder. 'There's someone at the bar. Would you mind, Yusuf?'

Yusuf stands up. 'See you later,' he smiles at me.

There's a short silence after Yusuf leaves, during which I look down awkwardly at my drink. 'Well, I suppose I should go to bed,' I say, making to stand up.

'Wait. Stay. Finish your drink,' Hakan says, placing a hand on my arm. 'How are you settling in? I mean, apart from the drama tonight.'

'Okay. Adam is a lovely boy.'

'You're not homesick at all?'

I laugh shortly. 'You wouldn't ask that if you knew my family.'

'Oh?' Hakan gives me a quizzical look. And somehow, I'm not sure how, because I don't normally spill my guts like this, especially to people I've just met, I find myself telling him everything: all about Dave – his drug addiction and his violent temper, the way he makes me feel uncomfortable in my own home. And then I tell him about my mum's depression – the way I've always had to look after her as if she was the child and I was the mother; how I've never really had a proper childhood. It all bubbles out of me like sewage from a blocked drain and Hakan listens quietly. He doesn't say anything. He just listens. I'm not used to people listening to me like this, as if every word I say carries weight and importance, and it feels liberating, like I'm rising to the surface of the sea and I can finally breathe. When I'm finished, he says, 'No wonder you're so mature. You've been through a lot, Joanna.'

And I feel warm heat rising in my cheeks because the way he's looking at me makes me tingle all over. It's like he's seeing me for real for the first time.

Chapter 17

2017

Sod's law.

Of course it would be Helen on reception. Who else? She's busy checking in a large German family and I have the chance to watch her unobserved. I have to admit that she's aged well. She's a little gaunter maybe and her hair is threaded with grey. But she still has her Grace Kelly figure and her skin is hardly lined.

A young boy shows the German family to their bungalow and Helen looks over and does a double take. Then her eyes narrow and her cheeks flush a little.

'Joanna?' she says. 'Is that really you?'

I nod and smile.

'Of course, Hakan told me you were on the island, but I didn't think . . .'

Didn't think I would have the nerve to turn up here? I complete her sentence silently. Out loud I say, 'I'm sorry. I wouldn't have come if it wasn't important.'

She gives me a short assessing stare. Then she nods abruptly.

'Come and sit and have a drink,' she says. 'Mehmet,' she calls to a young man standing nearby. 'Can you just watch reception for a minute? This is Joanna, an old . . . She used to work here.'

She leads me out to the veranda, and we sit under the trailing vines and look down at the sea glinting between their green leaves.

'What would you like? Coffee, tea?' She orders us coffee without waiting for my answer and sits back, unsmiling.

'You left so suddenly, without a word,' she says. 'We wondered what had happened to you. We were worried.'

Is she kidding me? Is it really possible she doesn't know? No, of course she knows. I knew that as soon as I saw her expression – the brief glitter of hatred in her eyes, quickly veiled. But, typical Helen, she wants to pretend everything's rosy. *Well, if that's what she wants, I'm happy to play along.*

'My mother was ill and—' I begin.

'Adam will be sorry he missed you,' she interrupts. 'He's at university in Southampton. All grown up now, studying engineering.'

'He always did love making things with Lego,' I smile.

'Look . . .' She fiddles with her phone and shows me a photo. It's a young man standing under a lemon tree, grinning confidently at the camera. I suck in my breath. He looks so much like a younger version of Hakan.

'Wow,' I say. 'What a handsome young man.'

'Yes.' She frowns again. 'He takes after his father.'

'And you. I can see quite a lot of you in him,' I add hastily.

'So, you're living in Cyprus now?' she says. She pauses just for a fraction of a second. 'Hakan told me your daughter visited the other day. I wasn't here but apparently they had quite a good chat.'

'That's right,' I say carefully. 'Actually, that's what I came about.'

'Oh?' She seems apprehensive. There's a hard look in her eyes and in that moment, I think she's afraid of what I might say. She needn't worry, though. I'm not about to confront her with unpleasant truths from the past. None of that matters now. All that matters right now is Grace.

'She's missing. She's been missing for three days now,' I blurt. As I speak my voice wobbles and I swallow back tears, feeling annoyed with myself. Why the sudden tears now? I don't want to break down here, not in front of Helen of all people.

Helen stares at me incredulously. 'What?'

'I dropped her off at school on Monday morning and she wasn't there when I went to pick her up,' I explain. I've said this so often now it's become almost rote, as if it's a line I've learnt for a play.

'Oh my God,' she says. 'That's terrible, Joanna. And you don't have any idea where she is?'

'No. Actually, that's why I wanted to speak to Hakan – to ask him if she said anything to him, anything that could give us a clue as to what's happened to her.'

'Oh, I see.' Her eyes narrow and she looks at her watch. 'Well, Hakan's not here. He's gone into town on business, but he should be back soon.'

'He didn't tell you anything, did he? Like, was there anything odd about her behaviour, anything she said to him?'

She shakes her head and her eyes slide away from mine. 'No, he just told me she'd been to visit, that's all. Nothing else.' She runs her finger around the rim of the coffee cup. 'Have you been to the police?'

'Yes.'

'And?'

'Nothing so far. They found out she'd crossed to the North on Sunday. That's why I'm here. I assumed she'd come here. She doesn't know anyone here apart from you and Hakan.'

'She didn't tell you she was coming?'

'No,' I admit. 'We haven't been getting along very well lately.'

I see her take this in and the faint look of satisfaction in her eyes. All was not perfect in my world, even before Grace disappeared, and she can't help taking some pleasure from that. I can't really blame her, I suppose.

She shakes her head. 'Hakan didn't say anything . . . just that . . .' She looks past me over my shoulder. 'Ah, speak of the devil,' she says lightly.

I look round and see Hakan walking towards us through reception. He must be at least fifty-two by now, I calculate. His hair is grey, his face tanned and more deeply lined than it was, but he's still a good-looking man and the sight of him takes me back seventeen years to the day I first met him. I've imagined this moment so many times over the years and I'm not sure what I was expecting. Love, desire, anger? But, in fact, I feel almost nothing. There's no room inside me right now for any emotion other than fear. Fear that I'm going to lose Grace. Fear that I've already lost her.

He starts when he sees me and stands there for a moment frozen with shock.

'Joanna!' he blusters, overly hearty, to cover up the shock. 'Well, well, well. Joanna Ewens as I live and breathe.' Then he comes over and kisses me lightly on the cheek. I sense rather than see Helen watching us.

'Joanna Appleton now,' I say primly. There's no harm in bringing my husband into this.

'Oh, yes, yes, of course, you're married now.' He sits down next to Helen and puts his arm around her, smiling awkwardly. Then he clears his throat. 'I met your daughter, Grace, the other day. She's a charming girl. You must be very proud.'

'She's missing,' Helen announces abruptly, shrugging off his arm.

This information takes a couple of seconds to sink in. Hakan stares at her open-mouthed. 'What?' he says. I watch him carefully and I'm fairly sure his shock is genuine.

'Joanna has come here to see if you can help find her,' Helen says. 'Well, I'll leave you two to it. I have to get back to reception.' She stands up and stalks away stiffly. I look at her go, her rigid back, the way she tucks her hair behind her ears. *She knows*, I think.

'Grace has gone missing?' Hakan says, once Helen is out of earshot.

I lower my voice. 'I'm sorry, I wouldn't have come here, I

121

know it's awkward, but I'm desperate. We haven't seen her since Monday morning. The day after she spoke to you.'

He absorbs this, tugging at his earlobe, an old familiar gesture that makes me catch my breath.

'You must be worried sick,' he says, stretching out his hand across the table. I ignore it. Worried doesn't even get near to expressing the way I feel.

'I was wondering if she said anything to you? I mean, she didn't say she was planning to run away, did she? Did she mention that we had argued?'

He frowns and shakes his head. 'No,' he says, then leans in close and whispers, 'Obviously you know the reason she came here. I think she was curious more than anything. She wanted to know if it was true, if I was her father.'

'And . . . ?' I hold my breath. 'What did you say?'

'I told her the truth, of course. I think she thought I would try to deny it. But why would I? She's my daughter. My beautiful daughter.' He gazes at me and tears well up in his dark, soulful eyes. 'Do you think there's been a day when I haven't thought of her and longed to see her?'

I breathe out, anger twisting in my gut. I'm not fooled by his crocodile tears. Not anymore. 'Does Helen know?' I ask icily.

'No.' He considers. 'At least, I don't think so. She might have guessed.'

I nod. 'She's not stupid. She can do the maths.'

Hakan sighs and rubs his head in his hands.

'Joanna . . . I'm sorry . . . It must have been hard for you.

I let you down, I let her down . . . I've messed up so much in my life.'

'Yes. You have,' I say bluntly. *None of this would have happened if he had acted differently*, I think, *if he'd lived up to his responsibilities*. For a moment I contemplate this alternate life where Grace grew up as Hakan's daughter, where we were one happy family. But of course, if that had happened, then Jack wouldn't exist, and I can't wish for that.

'It doesn't matter now,' I say out loud. 'What matters is finding Grace.'

'Yes, of course.' He nods eagerly. 'Is there anything I can do? I'll do whatever I can. You know, I have contacts in the police here.'

Same old Hakan – always with the contacts, always networking.

'Thank you. But she's not here in the North. The Greek police are certain. She came back the same day and her passport hasn't been used since.' I try not to think about how easy it would be to smuggle her out of the country. Border control checks are hardly thorough. It would be easy to get her past the border and onto mainland Turkey. But there's no point thinking that way. I need to believe she's still on the island and that she's safe.

'But I don't understand, why are you here then?' Hakan asks.

'I thought she might have said something to you – something that might give us an idea where she's gone. Was there anything she was worried about? Did she mention her boyfriend at all?'

Hakan clicks the bones in his fingers. 'Ah, yes, she did seem troubled. I got the impression it was connected to her boyfriend. She told me you don't exactly approve . . .'

'Yes, well. He's too old for her for a start.' As I say this, I stare at him directly and at least he has the grace to look away.

'Oh, I thought he'd been in some kind of trouble with the law.'

'Not to my knowledge.' I frown. 'What makes you say that?'

Hakan looks vague. 'I thought that was why you disapproved of him.'

'Did Grace say that?'

'No, not in so many words.' He hesitates. 'She did ask me a weird question, though.'

'What?'

'She asked whether if you knew about a crime and didn't report it, did that make you guilty too?'

A gecko scuttles over the wall and the trees shiver in a tiny breeze. Despite the heat I feel suddenly cold.

'And what did you say?' I ask slowly.

Hakan shrugs. 'I said it would depend on the crime.'

I lean forward. 'She didn't say what the crime was?'

'No, but I got the impression it was serious.' He frowns at the tablecloth. 'Oh my God, maybe she threatened him with the police, and he tried to shut her up . . .' He breaks off, realising what he's just said. 'I'm sorry.'

'It's okay,' I say. 'I have to consider all possibilities. But I know she's alive . . . I know it in my heart.'

'Yes, of course she is.' He places his hand over mine. His eyes are big with compassion. I've seen that look before. I know now it means nothing. I snatch my hand away and look out at the sea.

'What else did you and Grace talk about?' I ask.

Hakan folds his arms. 'Lots of things. We talked about my book and her love of music, how she must have got that from my family. My mother was a singer, you know. Did I ever tell you?'

I shake my head, though I did know because I read about it in his book, but I don't want him to have the satisfaction of knowing that.

'She told me about her brother and her father too,' he says carefully. 'Your husband.'

'She told you about Chris?' I ask, holding my breath, thinking of the police's suspicions. 'What did she say?'

'Just that he was a good father to her. That she had a happy childhood.'

Of course. I exhale slowly.

'That she *had* a happy childhood?'

'Well, I suppose she thinks she's not a child anymore.'

He's probably right. But her use of the past tense nags at me. It's as if she was already separating herself from us.

'What else did she say?' I ask.

'Not much. But I told her that I loved her, that I'd always loved her.'

I must have snorted or made some kind of disbelieving sound because he says, 'She didn't believe me either. But it's true.' He chews his nail thoughtfully then he stands up. 'Come with me, Jo. I want to show you something.'

I follow him inside and upstairs to their apartment above reception. The living room is pretty much as it was seventeen years ago. There's the same wine-coloured sofa and the same pictures of Paradise Beach Bungalows in various stages of development. There are some new photos on the mantlepiece of Adam and a girl, who I guess is his younger sister, but otherwise not much has changed, and I have a strange feeling, somewhere between nostalgia and regret, as I look around at this place that made such an impact on my life.

'Wait here,' Hakan says, and disappears into the bedroom. While I'm waiting for him, I pick up one of the photos of Adam. It was taken when he must've been about eight. He's lying on his front, his chin cupped in his hands, grinning cheekily at the camera, and his sister is straddled on his back laughing manically. It's a lovely, natural photo. *They had a happy childhood*, I think with a pang. Of course they did. Although Hakan has his faults he would have been a good father. I'm sure of that.

'Here it is.' Hakan reappears a few minutes later carrying a small wooden box.

'Guess what's inside,' he says, placing it in my hands. As he does, his hands linger a little too long over mine and I draw them away sharply. *Jesus. Does he seriously think I would be interested in rekindling old passions after all this time, after all that's happened?*

'I don't know,' I say, stepping back and looking at the intricate gold inlay on the lid of the box.

I run my hands over the smooth surface, feeling suddenly afraid of what I might find inside.

'I've kept it for sixteen years,' he says. 'I keep it hidden under the floorboards.'

I open the box cautiously. It's full of papers. On top is a letter. I pull it out and recognise my own handwriting, neater in those days. I can barely remember writing it.

Dear Hakan,

How are you?

I thought you ought to know that Grace Olivia Ewens was born on 28th of May 2001, one month ago. She weighed 7 pounds and 2 ounces, and she cries a lot! I hope you like the photo. I wish you could see her for yourself and hold her. She is the sweetest baby and I think she looks a lot like you. I miss you so much. All I want to do is hold you in my arms and kiss you all over.

All my love,

Your Jojo

I cringe at my eighteen-year-old self and Hakan's pet name for me. What had I hoped to achieve by sending that letter? Did I think he would realise the error of his ways and immediately jump on a plane to England? I was so naive back then.

Underneath the letter, there's a photo Hakan took of me sitting on a sunbed at Varosha beach, the empty apartment blocks towering behind me. He's taken me by surprise, and I

127

look startled. I'm wearing a blue bikini and I look so young, not much older than Grace is now. Under that, another photo of me looking sulky at the top of Hilarion Castle. I lift it out and inhale sharply as if I've been stabbed in the heart. Because at the bottom of the box is another photo, of Grace as a baby. She's lying on her front pushing her head up and smiling at the camera. It's a smile only a baby can give, so completely unself-conscious, heartbreaking in its innocence and joy. On the back I have written, *Baby Grace, June 2001.*

The photo trembles in my hand.

'You showed these to Grace?' I ask.

'Yes. I wanted her to know that I loved her and that there hasn't been a day all these years when I haven't thought about her. Even though I never met her, I loved her.' He gazes at me with what passes for sincerity. 'I know that sounds crazy but it's true.'

He almost has me believing him. He always was so convincing. I remember his head on the pillow next to mine, the way he stroked my cheek so tenderly and said, 'I love you,' over and over. And I believed him then. Maybe he did mean it at the time but in the end, it meant nothing.

'You'd better put that back before Helen sees it,' I say coldly.

I watch him disappear into the bedroom. *He's a liar*, I think. *And he's the most dangerous kind of liar, the kind that believes his own lies.* And just for a moment I wonder, *What if Grace had threatened to tell Helen?* I know he would do anything to protect his family. What might he have done to silence her?

Chapter 18

2000

We take to staying up late drinking on the veranda, me, Helen and Hakan, and the waiters, Yusuf and Emre. Sometimes there are guests there and Hakan entertains them with card tricks or funny stories about his dad. Other times it's just me and Hakan. Helen is usually the first to go to bed. The pregnancy is making her tired and sick. Yusuf and Emre usually leave not long after. And then it's just Hakan and me, and we talk away into the early hours about anything and everything.

During one of those evenings I learn that Hakan comes from a big family of all sisters and that the oldest sister still isn't speaking to him because he married Helen.

'They wanted me to marry a nice Turkish Cypriot girl, but my mum and dad have come around since Adam was born, so I don't know why she still has to be such a bitch about it.'

'How did you and Helen meet?' I ask. They seem like such a

mismatched couple to me. Hakan is so easy-going and sociable and Helen's so uptight.

'We met at university. She was an art student,' he grins. 'She had pink hair at the time. She was always the life and soul of the party in those days.'

I say nothing. I'm trying to picture this alternative version of Helen. The Helen I know is anything but fun.

Hakan stares broodingly into his beer. It's as if he's read my mind because he says, 'She's had a tough time lately. Her brother died, and she didn't really want to move to Cyprus. She misses her family. She suffered really badly from postnatal depression after Adam was born, and her mother helped her a lot with him.' He sighs. 'I try to help her, but it's not always easy.'

'I understand,' I nod. I know all too well what it's like living with mental illness. 'I told you about my mum, didn't I?' I say. 'She's bipolar. One minute she's high, the next in the depths of despair. And then there's my stepdad. He doesn't exactly help.'

Hakan leans forward over the table. His eyes are big and com-passionate.

'You told me he was violent. Has he ever hurt you?' he asks.

'Not physically, no. It was always my mum that got the brunt of it.' Strictly speaking, it's not entirely true. Dave has grabbed me by the arm so tightly it's left bruises before and once, during an argument, he threw a bottle of beer at me, but thankfully missed. I think about the twins, who I've left in that dysfunctional household, and feel a twinge of guilt, immediately followed by anger. It's Mum's fault, not mine. She should have left him years ago. 'I kept telling her to leave him, but she wouldn't. She thinks she loves him.'

'It's no wonder you wanted to get away from home,' Hakan says, and he takes my hand in his and looks at me with his big, Omar Sharif eyes. Suddenly I'm conscious of a kind of electricity passing between us. It's just for a second, but so much is communicated in that second that it feels more like an hour. Heat rises in my cheeks and I slide my hand away.

'I'd better go to bed,' I murmur. 'Adam will be up at five in the morning.' I look at my watch and laugh to cover my confusion. 'In about three and a half hours, to be precise.'

After that evening everything is different. I'm awkward and shy around Hakan, and sometimes I catch him looking at me with a mixture of amusement and something else that I can't quite read, but it makes my heart beat faster and my breath catch in my throat. I tell myself it's just a harmless crush, that I'll get over it. There's no way he's really interested in me. Not like that. He's way too old for me anyway.

Then one day, about three weeks into my time in Cyprus, I have a day off. Helen's sister is staying with us for a week and Helen and her sister have gone out for the day with Adam and Adam's cousins. It's a Sunday morning and I decide to have an early morning swim in the sea. I'm heading down the path to the jetty when I see Hakan coming towards me in the opposite direction. He's been swimming already. His hair is wet, and the sunlight catches in his eyes. I stare at him, bemused by how beautiful he looks.

'Hi, Joanna. What are you doing up so early?' He smiles and looks at me with his head on one side, like he's never seen anything as sweet as me, like I'm a puppy or a kitten.

'I just thought I'd go for a swim,' I stammer.

I'm not sure what I say next. I'm babbling, just saying anything so he won't notice the redness in my cheeks. Then, suddenly, without warning, he stoops and kisses me. It's a brief kiss on the lips. So brief, I almost think I must have imagined it. Then he steps back, gives me a searching look and smiles like he's satisfied.

'Well, see you later,' he says breezily, and he walks away whistling, up the path under an arch of bougainvillea.

I walk on towards the beach feeling dazed and dizzy with happiness. *Don't get ahead of yourself*, I tell myself. *It didn't mean anything. There was nothing sexual in it. He thinks of me as a child, that's all.*

But late at night, I find myself fantasising about him. In my mind he stops on the path and kisses me again, but this time he kisses me properly and he doesn't stop at just a kiss.

Chapter 19

2017

'Where the hell have you been? I've been worried sick. Where's Jack?'

Chris is at the gate when I pull up outside the house. He looks awful. His eyes are bloodshot and there's several days' growth of stubble on his chin. I feel a twinge of guilt. I've been so wrapped up in my own fear and grief that I've ignored his. Grace is his daughter too, after all, even if they're not related by blood.

'I'm sorry,' I say as I follow him into the house. 'It's okay, Jack's at Angelo's. Stella's dropping him back in about an hour. I tried to ring you, but I forgot that my phone doesn't work in the North.'

'You crossed the border?' Chris frowns. 'What were you doing there?' As he speaks, he stumbles a little and grabs my arm to steady himself and I notice his breath reeks of booze.

'You've been drinking,' I say. I don't mean it to, but it comes out as an accusation.

'So? I have to do something, or I'll go crazy.'

Guilt morphs into frustration and anger. I need Chris to be strong and solid like he normally is; instead, he seems to be crumbling in front of me. 'How exactly is that going to help?' I snap, flinging my handbag down on the sofa. 'You should be out there looking for her, not getting pissed and feeling sorry for yourself. What have you been doing? Have you heard from Dino?'

He shakes his head. 'No, nothing.'

'Well, what the fuck are they playing at?' I stomp into the kitchen and pour myself a glass of water.

'You didn't answer my question,' says Chris. I'm scrabbling around trying to find something to eat for dinner. We must carry on with some semblance of normality for Jack's sake. He'll be home soon, when Stella drops him off, and I must have something to feed him. But there's nothing in the fridge and next to nothing in the freezer.

'Jesus. You could have at least done some shopping,' I say, exasperated. 'What have you been doing all day?'

'I've been dealing with the press. They've been phoning constantly and there was a TV van parked outside all day. It felt like a siege.' Chris stares at me, bristling with hostility. 'Anyway, you're still not answering my question. Why did you go to the Turkish side?'

'I wanted to talk to Hakan.' I pull a packet of frozen burgers out of the freezer and an almost empty packet of peas. 'I guessed that she must've been to see him.'

Chris sits down at the kitchen table with a sigh. 'And had she?'

134

'Yes.'

'Why didn't you tell me you were going?'

'I don't know. I didn't think. Sorry.' The truth is, Chris would have insisted on coming with me and I wanted to see Hakan alone.

Chris goes to the cupboard and fetches himself another beer. 'I don't understand. Why now? Why does she suddenly want to meet him now? We've been here for months.'

'I don't know. But I . . . I thought he might be able to shed light on her state of mind.'

'And . . . ?'

I switch on the oven, trying to decide how much to tell him.

'According to Hakan, Grace was worried. She told him she was thinking of going to the police. She was concerned that someone she knew had committed a crime. Someone she loved. Hakan had the impression it was Tom.'

Chris puts down his beer can and gawps at me.

'He said that? And you believed him?'

I shrug. 'Why would he lie about something like that?'

Chris buries his head in his hands, rubbing his eyes with his knuckles. 'Do you think she meant Tom?'

'I suppose so. Who else?'

Chris stands up and paces the room. 'What kind of a crime was she talking about?'

'I don't know, she didn't say.'

'Shit. Fuck. Christ.' Chris kicks the fridge. 'You warned me from the beginning that boy was bad news. I should have listened.'

I nod. 'You weren't to know,' I say. I feel sick to my stomach.

Chris stares at the floor, rubbing his head, deep in thought.

'What if he knew she was thinking of going to the police?' he says suddenly. 'He could have . . .' His voice tails off. I know where he's going with this and neither of us wants to go there. He bangs his fist into his palm and looks at me, eyes blazing. 'The bastard. If he's harmed a hair on her head, I'll kill him.'

Chris does look as if he could kill someone right now. His eyes have a wild, crazed look and his muscular body is quivering with anger.

'We don't know anything for sure,' I say, trying to calm him down. 'All this is just speculation.'

'Yeah? Well, I'll get the little shit to tell us what was going on.' He goes to the hallway, picks up his car keys from the hook where they're hanging and stumbles towards the door.

I push my way past him and block his exit. 'You can't drive. You're drunk.'

'Okay,' he slurs, handing me the keys. 'You drive then. We'll both go.'

'No. Listen, you need to stop and think. We have no proof it was Tom she was talking about, and even if we did, what good would it do to confront him? He's not going to tell us the truth, is he?'

Chris stares at me wildly and, for a moment, there is such anger in his eyes I think he's going to push me out of the way or hit me, but instead he just sighs and slumps down on the sofa.

He buries his face in his hands and when he looks up his eyes are glistening with tears. 'You're right, Jo. I can't deal with this by myself. We need to tell the police what you just told me.' He takes his phone out of his pocket and begins fumbling with the keypad.

'I'll speak to them,' I say decisively, snatching the phone from him. Chris is unlikely to make much sense the state he's in.

Dino answers on the second ring.

'Mrs Joanna,' he says. 'I was just about to call you. Um, I have some news.'

He sounds pleased with himself and for a second hope leaps in my heart.

'You've found Grace?'

Dino clears his throat. 'No, but we've been looking into that young man you told us about, Thomas Mitchinson.'

'Yes, about him—' I start. But Dino interrupts before I have the chance to finish.

'We talked to him, and we also interviewed several of his neighbours. The woman who lives in the apartment directly below his had some very interesting things to say. Apparently, she heard a loud argument on Saturday night.'

I try to remember Saturday night. When Grace arrived home, she was in a foul mood, but I'd assumed that was because she was still angry with me over the row we'd had earlier.

'What exactly did she hear?' I ask.

'She doesn't speak much English and wasn't sure what was said, just that there was a lot of shouting and banging.'

'Banging?' I say, unease twisting in my gut.

'Yes, that's what she said,' Dino says quietly. 'And that's not all. She said that she saw Grace outside his apartment on Sunday evening.'

'Sunday evening? Are you sure?'

'Yes.'

'He told me the last time he saw her was on Saturday,' I say. 'He was quite definite about it.'

'Yes, that's what he told us too . . .'

'So, he lied?'

'Yes, it looks like it,' Dino says cautiously. 'The question is, why?'

Why did he lie? The question reverberates in my head as Stella drops Jack back home and the three of us sit round the table, eating our dinner in silence. It's still dominating my thoughts as I take Lola for a walk up the hill behind our house after tea. We always go the same way, up the steep, dry, scrubby path to the picnic site. Lola likes sniffing round the rubbish left over from people's barbecues and I like the view over Larnaca.

When we reach the top, the sun is already setting, bleeding red into the sea. From up here I can see a long way, the bay flanked by the Dhekelia power station at one end and the cranes in Larnaca harbour at the other. Up here the sea looks like it's been painted with thick oil paint and I can see the Troodos Mountains, blue-grey in the distance. There's a clear view of all of Oroklini and Larnaca. And it kills me to think that maybe Grace is down there somewhere amongst that maze of streets and buildings; that if only I had better vision, maybe I could zoom in on her.

'Where are you, Grace?' I say out loud. 'Please come back. Please forgive me.'

Thursday, 21st September 2017

Chapter 20

I'm underwater. I can't see much in front of me. Just rays of dirty green sunlight . . . The surface is a long way away and I'm trying to find something I've lost but I don't know what it is, so I just swim forwards, pushing through the thick, murky water. Suddenly, out of the corner of my eye, I see something – a dark shape drifting towards me. As the shape gets closer, I realise it's a woman. No, not a woman, a girl, a teenage girl. Closer still and I can see her face, eyes wide open, staring, her dark hair floating upwards like weeds sprouting from her head.

'Grace!' I scream. But the sound doesn't come out. I've lost my voice.

I grasp her by the hand and try to pull her up to the surface, but everything is in slow motion, apart from the weeds which grow up quickly and twine their way around her legs like octopus tentacles. They slither their way around her body and drag her downwards. I try to hold on but I'm being dragged with her. Deeper and deeper . . .

I'm woken abruptly by the sound of the phone ringing right next to my bed. I fumble for it and hold it to my ear.

'Hello?' I say croakily.

It's my mother.

'Joanna?' she says at the other end. 'Oh my God, how are you, my poor baby?'

'Hello, Mum.' I rub my eyes, still blurry from sleep, still shaken from that awful dream. 'I'm not too good actually. I don't know whether you know . . .'

'I heard,' she says. 'It's all over the news. I can't believe it. Why didn't you tell me? It was a terrible way to find out. Our little Grace. Have you had any news?' There's a sort of choking sound and then a silence and I realise that she's sobbing.

Great. This is precisely why I didn't tell her about Grace being missing in the first place. I knew that she would react in the way she always does to any problem – by falling apart.

'Nothing yet. But the police have some good leads,' I say cheerily, slipping into the role I always take with Mum: the strong, optimistic one.

'I can't bear to think of anything happening to that sweet little girl,' she says and there's more snuffling. 'Can you ask Dave to call me? He hasn't been in contact and I'm all on my own here.'

Dave is hardly likely to help, I think. In my experience, there isn't any problem he can't make worse. Out loud I say, 'What do you mean, ask Dave to call you? Isn't he with you?'

Mum stops crying for a moment. 'No, haven't you seen him? He flew out to Cyprus last week. There were some cheap flights and one of his friends had a spare ticket. I wanted to come too but you know how I am with aeroplanes.'

I do. Amongst my mother's many neuroses is a fear of flying, and travelling in general, which means that even when she's been well, she's never been further than Scotland in her life.

'He said he was going to visit you,' she adds. 'I don't under-stand.'

'I didn't even know he was in the country. But I'll get him to call you when I see him, I promise.'

'Thank you, baby. Because I don't think I can deal with this on my own. Grace going missing has just knocked me for six.'

'I'll let you know if we hear anything,' I say curtly as I hang up. I can't believe Mum is making this about *herself*.

I look at the clock on my phone. It's nine o'clock. I've been asleep for ten hours and Grace has been missing for three days, one hour and thirty minutes. My stomach curls with guilt. How could I have slept so long when every minute could be crucial. It's weird, I reflect, climbing out of bed, that Dave hasn't been in contact, but then I guess he's probably drunk or in a heroin-induced coma somewhere. Well, I certainly am in no rush to see him but why did he come here in the first place?

I have a shower and get dressed, still thinking about Dave, and then I head downstairs, checking Grace's room on the way, just in case by some miracle she's back home.

Chris is in the living room on his phone, scrolling through Facebook.

'Did you know Dave was in Cyprus?' I ask, and he looks up

143

at me distracted. 'No,' he says. 'Though come to think of it, I might have had a couple of missed calls. What's he doing here?'

Good question, I think. The more I think about it, the more I get a bad feeling. Wherever Dave is, trouble follows, and I wouldn't be at all surprised if he had something to do with Grace's disappearance in some way. Would he hurt Grace? I don't think so. What would his motive be? Though I'm pretty sure Dave is capable of anything if there was some advantage for him.

I'm about to try to call him to find out what the hell he's up to, but Chris grabs my arm.

'Read this, Jo! It's just fucking unbelievable.'

'What is it?'

'Just read it.' He passes me his phone and I look at his Face-book feed. Someone has posted a newspaper article from the *Cyprus Daily* – the local English paper. There's a large photo of Grace we gave to the police. Underneath is the headline:

LARNACA TEENAGER MISSING

I force myself to read the article.

> *Concerns are growing over the safety of a young Eng-*
> *lish girl who went missing in Larnaca earlier this week.*
> *Grace Appleton, a sixteen-year-old pupil at the*
> *Mediterranean Academy, was last seen at seven thirty*
> *on Monday morning when her mother dropped her off*
> *at school.*

I break off and look at Chris. 'I don't see the problem. It's good, isn't it? It's got to help. The more people who know, the more chance we have of finding her.' For once Grace's beauty is turning into an advantage because I doubt the newspapers would have made this into such a big story; I doubt it would be a news story in England at all if it wasn't for the fact that Grace is such a photogenic young girl. The press love stuff like that, don't they? Pretty British girl goes missing abroad.

'Read on,' says Chris grimly.

> Teachers and pupils say she did not turn up to lessons and concern is growing that something may have happened to Grace. Classmates describe Grace as popular, bright and a generally happy pupil, but stated that lately she's been having problems in her home life. She lives with her brother, mother and stepfather.
>
> If anyone has any information regarding Grace's whereabouts, please contact the police on this number. All phone calls will be dealt with confidentially.

I look up from the screen. 'I still don't see the problem.'

'Read the comments.'

So, I scroll down through the remarks people have posted. There are hundreds of them, mostly expressing concern and sympathy.

This is soo sad, says Dora Charalambous. Her profile picture is a Yorkshire terrier and she's added three crying-face emojis.

145

We're praying for her safe return, says someone called Michelle Martin.

Our thoughts are with the family. And so on.

Someone says they've seen someone resembling Grace riding a bike on the seafront road, someone else has seen her in Ayia Napa and one person even says they've seen her in New York.

'Read this one.' Chris taps a comment about halfway down.

It's from George R and his profile picture is an image of forked lightning.

I wouldn't be surprised if the stepfather has killed her, he's written. *I've heard he had a criminal record.*

I heard she was scared of him. Just look at this photo of him. Now that's a thug if ever I saw one, someone else has added. *Why haven't the police arrested him?*

'Oh,' I say.

'You see what I mean?' says Chris.

I snap the laptop shut. 'Ignore it,' I say decisively. 'It's just stupid people gossiping because they've got nothing better to do. They're morons. They don't know what they're talking about.'

Chris stands up and paces the room. Agitation emanates from him. 'How do they know about my criminal record, though?'

'I don't know.' I shake my head. I'm as puzzled as he is.

'And what's this shit about Grace being afraid of me?' he says. 'She's not afraid of me, is she, Jo?'

'Of course not.' The idea is crazy. Chris loves Grace and Grace loves him. Grace is his little princess. Always has been. Chris has been spared most of Grace's teenaged vitriol. She knows she can wrap him around her little finger and so long as she gets her way, she's as sweet as pie. No, it's always been me that's borne the brunt of Grace's moods because it's always been me that's been the one trying to impose rules and guidelines.

'How do they know about my criminal record?' Chris repeats, staring at me wildly. 'They must have got that from the police.'

'You don't know that.'

'Yes, I do. Who else could it be? They're the only people who could know.' He picks up a cushion and punches it. 'I'm going to kill that fucking detective.'

'Calm down,' I say, standing behind him and wrapping my arms around him. 'Why would it be Dino who told them? It could have been anybody on the police force.'

'I don't know,' Chris says darkly. 'But I wouldn't be surprised if it was him. There's something I don't like about the guy.'

I shrug. Dino seems all right to me. A little smug at times maybe. And perhaps not the best detective in the world. Eleni, now she would be a better person to lead the case. She really gives the impression she knows what she's doing.

'Speak of the devil,' I add a couple of seconds later as my phone rings on the coffee table and Dino's name flashes up.

I snatch it up before Chris has a chance to get to it.

'Hello?' I say as calmly as possible.

Chris tries to grab the phone. 'Give it to me. I want to have a word with that piece of shit.'

I dodge away out of his reach. The last thing we need is Chris flying off the handle at the police. 'Let me deal with this,' I hiss.

147

'Ah, Mrs Joanna. How are you?' Dino sounds ridiculously buoyant and happy on the other end of the line.

Stupid question. My daughter's missing. How am I supposed to be? Out loud I say, 'As well as can be expected.'

'Well, Mrs Joanna, we've found something I think you need to see.'

'What is it?' I ask, holding my breath.

'I think you'd better come to the station and take a look for yourself.'

'Just do me a favour, will you?' I say to Chris, as we're driving into town. 'Don't mention the newspaper article. We don't know it was Dino who told them. We don't want to piss him off. We need his help.'

'Yeah, 'cos he's been doing such a great job so far,' Chris snorts sarcastically.

'Please,' I say. 'We have to focus on Grace.'

His shoulders slump over the wheel. 'Okay, but I really want to punch him in his smug face.'

I sigh. 'I know. Me too. But that's not going to do anybody any good, is it?'

There's been an accident on the Dhekelia road, a motorbike overturned at the roundabout, and while Chris crawls through the traffic, I take my phone out of my pocket and try to ring Dave's number, but there's no answer. So, I try to ring Mum again to find out the name of the hotel he's staying in, but she's not answering her phone either. *So much for being worried about*

Grace, I think bitterly. If she was truly as worried as she made out, she would answer my calls immediately.

The police station is in an old colonial building near the seafront. It's made of sandstone with blue painted shutters, dwarfed by the high-rises that have sprouted up around it. The police officer on duty is watching TV. He heaves himself up reluctantly and opens the door when we ring the bell.

We ask for Detective Markides and are shown across a dusty courtyard to a small dingy office in a low building at the back where Dino's sitting at his desk on the phone, talking loudly in Greek. There's a half-drunk frappe and a framed photo of his family on his desk. Three happy, rowdy-looking girls and a plump, pretty wife all squashed together on a sofa. *They look like a happy family*, I think wistfully.

He smiles expansively when he sees us and covers the mouthpiece. 'Mr Chris, Mrs Joanna. Please take a seat. I'll be with you in just one minute.'

Some more shouting and arm waving. I don't know what he's saying but I catch the Greek word for money and hospital.

'My wife,' he says when he's finished, as if that explains the shouting. 'She has some problems with my mother-in-law. That woman drives me crazy.' He rolls his eyes and grins at us. 'Would you like a drink?'

Chris shakes his head, his mouth in a tight line, a vein bulging in his neck. He's still fuming about the newspaper article. But at least he's controlling himself for now.

I clasp his hand and squeeze it to show that I appreciate his reticence. 'Just water, please,' I say to Dino.

Dino pours a plastic cup of water from the water cooler and sits at the desk, elbows resting on the table. I wipe the sweat from my hands. It's hot and stuffy in this room. The ceiling fan stirs the air but doesn't really cool it and I'm feeling faint. The relentless anxiety of the past few days is catching up with me.

'You said you had something to show us?' Chris says impatiently.

Dino beams. 'Ah, yes. We found something that could be very important.' He rummages in a filing cabinet, pulls out a clear plastic bag and hands it to me with a triumphant flourish.

'We found this in Tom Mitchinson's apartment. We believe it's a letter from Grace.'

'From Grace?' I exclaim, holding the bag like it might suddenly explode. A mix of emotions flare up inside me – hope, fear, confusion. 'When did she send it?' I ask, starting to open it.

'Please, don't touch it. We haven't checked it for fingerprints yet. But I've made you a copy. Look.' Dino slides a piece of paper towards us across the desk.

'Was there a postmark on the envelope? When was it posted?' I ask eagerly. This could be a real breakthrough. If we know where she posted it, it'll help us find where she is.

Dino holds up his hands. 'Slow down, Mrs Joanna. I'm afraid it doesn't have a postmark. It was in Mr Mitchinson's mailbox. Hand delivered. And I'm afraid we don't know exactly how long it's been there.' He taps the paper. 'But I think you will be interested in what she has to say.'

My hand trembles as I take the paper. I'm scared of what I'm about to read. Scared and hopeful at the same time.

'First of all, can you confirm that it's your daughter's handwriting?' Dino asks.

'Yes, it's definitely from Grace.' The writing is messy, messier than usual, as if she's written it in a hurry or without anything to rest on. But it's Grace's. There's no doubt about that. The funny way the y's loop, the way her d's curl over is unmistakeable. But the contents are a different matter. What she's written doesn't sound like Grace at all.

> *Dear Tom,*
> *I'm sorry but I can't see you anymore. I'm not the person you think I am. There are some things . . .*

Here there's something illegible, crossed out.

> *This has nothing to do with you. You're a great person and I know you'll find someone else, someone who'll give you the love you deserve. I'm going away soon. Please don't try to contact me.*
> *Grace*

Where she's signed her name, she's pressed so hard she's almost gouged through the paper.

I read the letter through again to make sure I haven't misunderstood. 'Wow,' I say at last, shocked. I'm not sure what I was expecting but it wasn't this.

'Let me see,' Chris says. I pass him the letter and he reads it silently.

'I don't understand,' he frowns, turning to me when he's finished. 'Did you know anything about this, Jo? Did you know she broke it off with Tom?'

I shake my head helplessly. 'I had no idea.' As far as I know, Grace is still madly in love with Tom. We had a big argument about her seeing him only last Saturday. How could her emotions have changed so quickly?

'This letter is a good thing,' Dino is saying. He picks it up again and reads aloud, '*I'm going away soon*. Along with the missing sleeping bag and clothes she took, it strongly suggests that she planned her disappearance. She wasn't abducted. It means there's a good chance she's alive and well.'

He's right, of course. We should be relieved, and I *am* relieved. But there are so many questions swirling around in the back of my mind that any relief I feel is tempered by a nagging anxiety.

'Why not tell Tom face to face?' I ask. 'It doesn't seem like Grace somehow. She's not a coward.'

Chris agrees. 'Yeah, it's weird. And even if she wasn't going to tell him face to face, why not just message him? I don't think Grace has ever written a letter before in her life. Do kids these days even know what a letter is?'

Dino chuckles gently. 'Good point,' he says. 'My guess is

that she's got rid of her phone or she's not using it because she doesn't want to be traced. If she was still using her phone, we would have been able to find her by now.'

'Why didn't Tom tell us about this before?' I ask, looking from Chris to Dino.

Dino taps his finger on his desk. 'He claims that he didn't check his mailbox so he hadn't read the letter.'

I think about this. It's plausible, I suppose. The post in our village comes rarely – about once a week. I often forget to look inside. But I still feel that there's something not right about that letter.

'I wouldn't believe a word that little shit says,' fumes Chris, narrowing his eyes. 'Why don't you tell the detective what Hakan told you?' he adds, turning to me.

I roll my eyes and bite back annoyance. I hadn't decided yet whether or not to share what Hakan had told me with the police, but now it seems I have no choice. Dino is looking at me, waiting expectantly.

'Grace told a friend that someone had committed a crime,' I say. 'Do you know anything about that?'

'No.' Dino leans forward. 'She said that? Do you know what the crime was?'

I shake my head. 'No. Just that it was serious. Do you think she could have been talking about Tom?'

Dino jots something down on a piece of paper. 'Maybe. It's certainly very interesting. We'll look into it.' He chews his pen. His eyes stray to Chris thoughtfully. 'Tom doesn't have a criminal record, though. We checked.'

I glance anxiously at Chris. The mention of a criminal record will set him off for sure, I think. But, to do him credit, he manages to control himself, speaking quietly, his anger, for the moment, simmering away below the surface.

'Yeah, well, that's the whole point, isn't it? Just because someone doesn't have a criminal record, doesn't mean they can't commit a crime and just because they do, doesn't mean they're going to commit another. By the way, someone leaked some information about me to the press . . .'

'Oh?' Dino looks confused.

'Yes, well, that doesn't matter now,' I say hurriedly. 'Can we keep this copy?' I ask Dino, picking up the letter and standing up. I know from experience that I need to get Chris out of here before he works himself up into a rage. 'Thank you for all you're doing to help find Grace.' I flash a smile at Dino and wave the paper. 'This is great work.'

He smiles back, looking gratified. 'I'll be in touch,' he says. 'I feel sure that we are going to find her very soon.'

Chris and I step out into the bright midday sunshine and the heat wraps itself around us. We walk along in silence for a while, each lost in our own thoughts. My head is swimming. The road is clogged with traffic and traffic fumes and it feels hard to breathe.

'It's a motive,' says Chris suddenly, stopping outside a cheap boutique. His face is drenched in sweat. He looks like he's about to pass out.

'What?' I don't have the strength to help Chris right now.

Right now, we're like two people drowning with only each other to cling on to. Feeling faint myself, I lean against the window steadying myself, staring blankly at the lacy black lingerie in the window.

'The letter gives Tom a motive,' Chris says slowly. 'I know he said he hadn't read it, but what if he lied about that? If he had read it, imagine how he must have felt. He would've been fuming. It would explain the fight he had with Grace on Saturday night.' He wipes his face with a tissue and stares at me. 'God, if he's hurt her' – his voice rumbles with anger – 'I swear I'll kill him.'

'She was fine on Sunday,' I remind him. I put my hand to my head. I'm getting another headache. 'And we don't know when the letter was written.'

'Even so, we should speak to him.'

'You said we should leave the investigating to the police.'

'Yeah, well, I changed my mind,' Chris says grimly. 'That guy couldn't organise a piss-up in a brewery.'

Chapter 21

We find Tom down at the marina tethering his boat. He's in his wetsuit, peeled to the waist. Sleek wet hair clings to his neck and his blue eyes catch the sun. He looks healthy and vibrant. *He shouldn't look so good*, I think resentfully. *He should be broken like us*. But here he is carrying on with life like nothing's happened and there's no outward sign of the trauma that he should be feeling. He doesn't care about Grace. Not really. Not the way I do. How can he? He's only known her a couple of years whereas I've loved her all her life.

'Hey,' he says, straightening up and shielding his eyes from the sun. 'Mrs Appleton . . . Mr Appleton.'

He shakes our hands and Chris eyes him up like a boxer before a fight. 'We need to talk,' says Chris. 'Have you got time for a coffee?' His tone is deceptively polite. Anyone else would be fooled. But I know him too well. I know the way he bottles up his anger, compressing it into a tighter and tighter space until it explodes.

Who would win in a fight between Tom and Chris? I wonder. Tom has the advantage of youth, but Chris is heavier, thicker set. My money's on Chris. I picture him punching Tom in the face and realise that I wouldn't mind seeing that.

'Sure,' Tom says evenly. He tucks his wet hair behind his ear. 'I'll just get changed.'

He disappears into the bowels of the boat and Chris and I wait, watching the cats that congregate on the jetty sunning themselves and looking at the sailing boats, their rigging clinking in the wind.

A few minutes later Tom reappears wearing shorts and a faded green T-shirt that says *Insert logo here*. His hair is tied up in a knot and his phone is shoved into his pocket, earphones poking out the top.

'Is there any news about Grace?' he asks as we walk along the beachfront to Fini's Bar.

'In a way, yes,' says Chris grimly. 'The police found a letter in your apartment . . . But you know about that.' We both look across at Tom to watch his reaction to this news.

'Oh that.' Tom winces. He looks suddenly sad and lost like a little boy. And for a second, just a second, I almost feel sorry for him. I know all too well what it's like to bask in the sunshine of Grace's love and affection and then to suddenly have that love withdrawn.

When we reach Fini's Bar we sit at a table looking out at the sea. Chris orders beer for himself and Tom and a Coke for me. There's a heavy silence as we sip our drinks. We're all lost in our own thoughts. Chris glares out at the sea, then turns suddenly on Tom.

'Why did you lie?' he says. His voice is quiet but full of menace. Not for the first time I'm glad that Chris is my husband. Chris is a good person to have on your side. I wouldn't like to have him as an enemy.

'What?' Tom's hands flutter nervously. He looks frightened. Not surprising, I suppose, under the circumstances. It doesn't necessarily mean he has anything to hide.

'You told Jo and the police that you last saw Grace on Saturday night, but your neighbour says she was at your flat on Sunday evening.' Chris's hands clench, his expression grim. I put my hand on his knee to remind him to tone it down. Tom doesn't have to talk to us if he doesn't want to. We don't want to scare him away.

Tom puts his glass down. His hand is trembling slightly, but he looks at us defiantly. 'My neighbour must have made a mistake because I was out on Sunday. All day. I took a party of tourists out on the boat and then I went to my friend's flat-warming in Nicosia. I asked Grace if she wanted to come but she said no.' Frank blue eyes hold mine and I look away.

'And your friend can confirm that, can he?' Chris leans forward, resting his elbows on the table.

'Yes, of course . . . I've got his number.' Tom fumbles nervously with his phone, scrolls through and scribbles down a name and number on a napkin. 'His name's Nick. Call him if you like.'

'Oh, I will, don't you worry.' Chris gives a nasty grin and slots the napkin into his back pocket. He takes a sip of beer. 'What time did you get back from the party?' he asks.

'I stayed over. I didn't want to drink and drive. I didn't get back until midday on Monday.' Tom looks over at me. 'I'd only just got back when you came around looking for Grace.'

Chris raises a sceptical eyebrow. 'So how come your neighbour saw Grace at your flat on Sunday evening?'

Tom opens his mouth to answer and then closes it again as Chris bulldozes on.

'It looks pretty suspicious, you've got to admit. You said you invited her to go with you to your friend's house, so she must have known you were out.'

Tom stares at him sullenly. 'Are you accusing me of something?' he says, standing up and pushing his chair back. 'Because I don't have to listen to this.'

'No, please stay,' I say, giving Chris a warning look. 'We're not accusing you of anything. Of course we're not. We're just trying to understand what's happened, that's all. We're all on the same side here. We all want to know what's happened to Grace, don't we?'

He hesitates, clenches his fists tightly into a ball, then, to my relief, sits down again with a sigh.

'Yes,' he says reluctantly. 'Look, I don't know why Grace was at my house on Sunday night. Maybe she forgot that I said I was going out. How should I know? Maybe that was when she put that letter in my post box.'

'Why didn't you tell me that Grace had finished with you?' I ask gently.

Tom flinches, and a mixture of hurt and anger shows on his face. 'That's because I didn't know when I last spoke to you,' he says. 'It was the police who found the letter. I don't check my post box all that often. The post doesn't get delivered very frequently so there's no point.'

'Do you know why she called things off?'

He shrugs and looks away, but not before I see that his eyes have filled with tears. I wait for him to compose himself. When he turns back, he seems more in control. 'I don't understand it at all,' he says. 'I thought everything was fine between us . . . I mean, we had an argument on Saturday night, but I thought that was all sorted.'

'Yes, the police told us that you had a fight,' I say carefully.

His eyes narrow warily. 'Well, I wouldn't describe it as a fight exactly, more of a disagreement.'

'It must have been a pretty loud disagreement if the people in the flat below could hear you,' Chris says, and I kick his leg under the table. Tom bristles but, to my relief, stays sitting. Tom and Chris stare at each other. Tom scared but defiant. Chris angry as hell and barely controlling it.

'Yeah, well, it wasn't a physical fight if that's what you're hinting at,' Tom says.

'What did you disagree about?' I ask, stressing the word disagree.

Tom stares out at the horizon, not answering. *Is he buying time to think*, I wonder, *or battling difficult emotions?* He squeezes his bottom lip between his thumb and his forefinger. The gesture reminds me strangely of Grace and I feel a sharp stab of longing in my chest.

'It's complicated,' he says at last. 'I was going back to the UK and Grace wanted to go with me. But I didn't think it was a good idea for her to take so much time off school. I said that she'd have to ask you.'

'That's big of you,' Chris says sarcastically.

Tom ignores him and continues, looking at me. 'She was really angry about it. She said that if I really loved her, I would want her to be with me no matter what.'

I can easily imagine that. Grace can be fierce and dogged when she sets her mind on something. More than once throughout her childhood we've given in to her just for a quiet life. It must have taken some strength of personality on Tom's part to refuse her. But perhaps he didn't want her with him, after all. Perhaps he'd grown tired of her.

'Were you returning to England permanently?' I sit back, chewing a nail thoughtfully.

'No, but it would have been for a while. My mother, she received some bad news recently and she needs me at home. She's on her own now.' A shadow flits across his face. 'I don't know whether you know, but my stepdad passed away last year.'

'Grace did mention it. I'm sorry.'

'It's brought it all back, all the grief she felt when we lost my sister . . .' He tightens his fists. 'And then my dad.'

Chris is battling conflicting emotions. I can see in his easy-to-read face the way he's squashing any sympathy he feels for Tom.

'Why aren't you in the UK now then? If your mother needs you there?'

161

There's a flash of anger in those pretty blue eyes. 'The police won't let me go,' Tom says. 'They think I had something to do with Grace disappearing.' He looks at us both square in the eyes. 'But I didn't. I would never hurt Grace, I swear. I love her.'

'I don't buy it,' says Chris as we head back to the car park. 'It makes no sense at all. Why would she be begging him to let her go with him to England one day and breaking it off the next? You don't fall in and out of love in one day.'

Don't you? I certainly didn't fall in love with Chris in one day. That was a slow burner. But Grace's father was a whole different story.

Chapter 22

2000

I think about him constantly. When I wake up, he's in my head. And when I play with Adam, I look for signs of him in Adam's broad cheekbones, the soft, shy looks he gives and the sudden bursts of laughter that shake his whole body. When Adam cries because he's scared of the dark, I wonder if Hakan's afraid of the dark too and, when I comfort him, I imagine I'm comforting Hakan.

It's just a crush, I tell myself. *The kiss didn't mean anything. It was the kind of kiss you might give a child. Nothing has happened.* But at night I find myself going over and over it in my head, unpicking the moment. Freeze-framing it. The meeting on the path, the sunlight trapped in his eyes, the feel of his dry lips brushing against mine. In my fantasies he doesn't stop, but he kisses me again like a lover, cupping my chin with his hand, and we melt into each other's arms.

I've had sex only once, with a boy in my class called Darren. It was nothing like the romantic experience I'd imagined it would be. He spent a long time fumbling with the condom and when he finally shoved himself into me it was painful and over within seconds. But the lovemaking with Hakan in my head is nothing like that. In my head, he tells me he's never desired a woman like he desires me. He kisses my neck, then my shoulders and our clothes evaporate by magic. I know it's just a fantasy and the reality, if it ever happened, would probably be nothing like that. But there's no harm in dreaming, is there? Thinking isn't the same as doing. Nothing will ever happen anyway. He's married to Helen. He would never be seriously interested in a girl like me when he has a woman like Helen.

I look in the mirror every morning and find a lot of faults. My face is too square, and my thighs are too chunky. I'm crazy to think someone like Hakan would ever look twice at me. And yet he does. Secretly, when he thinks no one's watching.

He's looking at me now, as I stand on the beach cupping the tiny turtle in my hands, and his look takes my breath away. He's looking at me fascinated, as if I'm something rare or as if he's just solved a difficult equation. I blush and look away at Adam, who's hopping up and down in excitement.

'Can I hold it? Can I?' he says.

I look at the volunteer, a round-faced girl about my age, maybe a couple of years older. She nods, and I show Adam how to cup his hands. 'You must hold it firmly but not too tightly. You don't want to hurt it.'

'This little guy is a green turtle,' says the volunteer, whose name is Amber. 'We think that green turtles live on average eighty years – though it's difficult to estimate exactly how long they live . . .' She goes on to spout a series of facts about turtles. I am only half listening. Most of my mind is focused on Hakan. He's not looking at me now but at Amber, a half-smile on his lips, but I can tell that he's aware of me – the same way I'm aware of him.

Amber lifts a cloth off a bucket full of baby turtles clambering over each other and the small group of tourists gathers around.

'Only one per cent of these little guys will survive to sexual maturity,' she says, 'which is why it's so vitally important that a large number of hatchlings make it to the sea.'

We all turn off our torches so the turtles won't be confused by the lights and then we're each given a baby turtle and we place them on the sand near to the sea. Adam hops up and down excitedly as the baby turtles stumble along the beach. A couple veer off course and we steer them back in the right direction. Adam holds on to his, refusing to let go.

'I want to keep it,' he says. 'Can't I keep it?'

'Sorry, son, you can't,' says Hakan, gently unfurling Adam's little hand. 'He won't be happy. He wants to be in the sea with his brothers and sisters.'

It's pitch-black as we make our way back to the car and Adam falls asleep as soon as his head hits the car seat.

We drive back in silence along an unlit dirt road, a few sparse trees lit up like ghosts in the headlights. We're in the middle of nowhere here and it feels like we're all alone at the end of the world. All I can hear is the sound of the car engine and Adam snoring softly in the back. I allow myself the fantasy that we're a family, Hakan, Adam and me, and that Helen doesn't exist.

'It was good of you to come with us,' says Hakan, interrupting my thoughts as we bump over ruts in the ground.

'I wanted to come.'

'Seriously, though, you should be out having fun.' Hakan stares straight ahead at the road. 'You should have a boyfriend . . .' There's a silence. 'Aren't there any boys you like?'

'Not really.' *Not boys*, I think. And I'm glad it's dark because he can't see my face, which is hot.

'What about Yusuf? That boy has a crush on you for sure.'

I laugh. Yusuf is a year younger than me and has an infantile sense of humour. I've never even thought of him in that way. 'I don't think so,' I say.

'Oh, I'm pretty sure he does,' Hakan says, still staring straight ahead. 'I can't say I blame him . . . Poor boy. Are you going to break his heart?'

My face is burning now. 'I'm sure he's just a friend. Anyway, I'm not interested in him. He's just a boy.'

Hakan is silent for a minute. 'Well, you should get out more with people your own age.'

'But I like hanging out with you . . . and Adam.'

'Really?'

'Yes.'

He stops in the middle of the road and kills the engine. Then he gives this big shuddering sigh and puts his hand on my knee. He gazes into my eyes. 'Truth is, Joanna, I can't stop thinking about you.'

'Oh.' I'm staring back at him. I can't look away. My chest is rising and falling, my breath coming in ragged gasps.

'I've been fighting it all this time but there's something about you, Jo . . .' He reaches out and strokes my cheek. And the next thing I know, we're kissing. I can feel the bristles on his chin and his lips are soft and taste of cigarettes. Kissing him, I feel like there's a hunger in me I hadn't even known was there. I feel like I want to melt into him, lose myself in him.

In the end it's him who pulls away first. 'Oh God,' he groans, putting his head in his hands. 'I'm sorry, Jo. I shouldn't have done that.'

'I wanted you to. I want you to . . .' But he shakes his head vehemently and starts up the engine, driving fast, jolting over the bumpy track like if he drives fast enough, he can escape from this thing that's possessed us.

Later, when I'm in bed, there's a knock on my door. When I open it, Hakan is standing in the doorway swaying. He's been drinking. I can smell the raki on his breath and his eyes are unfocused and full of lust.

'Joanna . . . I . . .' he says.

And I throw myself into his arms.

Friday, 22nd September 2017

Chapter 23

I should have protected her. I should have kept her safe. I've failed in the first and most important duty of a mother. I've failed spectacularly, and the thought torments me.

I'm tortured by memories: Grace as a toddler falling and grazing her knee, me kissing it better. Grace crying because some girl in her class had been mean to her and me storming to the head teacher's office to complain. Her problems were so easy to fix in those days. When I close my eyes, I see Grace's first smile and the magical purity of it. I remember that moment so clearly and I remember thinking, '*I will always protect you. I never want you to be hurt. I never want you to feel any pain or sorrow, not ever.*'

I'm clinging on to my sanity by a thread. On Thursday I wake in the middle of the night, after a couple of hours of shredded sleep, my heart pounding. It's still pitch-black outside. The windows are wide open, letting in the cool night air, and Chris is lying next to me snoring away. *How can he sleep so peacefully with Grace missing?* I think. *How can we both be lying here doing nothing?*

There's a pain and a rage in my chest that is too big to contain in one small body. I can't just lie here. I must do something. So, I climb out of bed, creep past Jack's bedroom and down the stairs. In the living room I pace up and down, tugging at my hair. Thinking, thinking. *Where is she? Where is she?*

What if she's somewhere nearby, ill or injured? We have searched the area close to our house already but what if we missed something? I stare out at the empty house across the road. Its black windows seem to be trying to communicate something to me. Half the houses in our estate are empty. The gardens are overgrown, the swimming pools empty. I remember Grace's fascination with that house, the way she always wanted to go inside and explore, and I'm seized by the sudden conviction that she could be there, right under our noses – hiding in plain sight.

Within seconds I've shoved on my flip-flops, grabbed a torch and am out of the front door. I haven't bothered dressing and I suppose I must look like a crazy woman, wandering around in just my nightshirt in the middle of the night, but who cares? It's dark and there's no one about anyway. I cross the street and push my way in through the gate, up the overgrown path, treading gingerly through the long, dry grass.

The door is ajar, and I push it open and walk in. The house smells musty and the empty rooms are surprisingly cold. I shiver and swing the torch around, illuminating bare white walls with electric wires poking out. The house has obviously never been occupied.

'Grace,' I call out, my voice echoing in the empty room.

But of course, there's no answer. Someone has been here, though. There are cigarette butts and empty Coke cans crushed up in one corner. *Local kids probably*, I think. Anyway, Grace isn't here.

After I leave the house, I wander the streets aimlessly for a while, looking in gardens, under hedges and even in skips – though what I expect to find in a skip I'm not sure. Until at last I return home exhausted and climb the stairs to Grace's room. I curl up in her bed, inhaling her scent and clutching her pillow tightly. And I burst into tears, sobbing hopelessly, my tears soaking into the soft cotton.

Eventually I fall asleep thinking of a time we went to Skye on a family holiday. Grace must have been around seven at the time and Jack was just two. It was a beautiful sunny day and Grace and I held hands and paddled in water that was surprisingly warm for Scotland, while all around us seaweed popped as it dried in the sunshine. I think of the feeling of her sticky little hand in mine and realise that it was one of the few moments in my life when I was purely, simply happy.

I'm woken by the sound of the doorbell ringing downstairs and for a split second I'm confused, caught between the real world and the world of sleep. For a moment, I exist in a world where Grace is still with us – a world in which our family is complete. Then reality comes crashing back.

The bell rings again, rudely, insistently, and I crawl out of bed and look out of the window, but there's no car outside, not even Chris's van. *Where is he? Why doesn't he answer the door?* I look at the clock on the bedside table. It's ten o'clock. *Jesus!* Guilt twists in my belly. How have I slept so long? Next to the clock I notice a hastily scrawled note. 'Jo – have taken Jack to school. Didn't want to wake you. You were out for the count! Chris'. But Jack starts school at seven thirty. Chris should be back by now. He must have gone to work again. Biting back my annoyance, I pull on a T-shirt and a pair of shorts, stumble downstairs and open the door.

I can't be awake. I must be having a nightmare. Because Dave's standing there on the doorstep, like a malign ghost from the past. His hair is grizzled, and his cheeks are thin, but he's still got that same antagonistic smile on his face. The one that makes me want to slap him.

'Dave,' I sigh. 'What are you doing here?'

'Joanna.' He sways slightly and grabs the doorjamb to steady himself. I roll my eyes. 'Well, that's a nice greeting for your old dad, I must say.'

You were never my dad.

'Aren't you going to invite me in then?'

I stand back reluctantly, and he steps inside, filling the room with his life-sapping presence. I feel myself shrinking back to the scared, insecure little girl that I was when I lived with him. *I'm an adult now*, I remind myself. *This is my house.*

'Mum told me you were in Cyprus,' I say.

'Yeah. I tried calling you,' he says, 'but you never answer your bloody phone.'

'I've been a bit busy,' I say coldly. 'I don't have a lot of time to talk. I don't know whether you heard, but Grace has gone missing.'

'Yes, I heard about Grace,' he says. 'That's why I'm here. I thought I might be able to help.'

I don't believe it, not for a second. No way. Dave has never helped anyone in his life. He never does anything unless there's something in it for him. *What's he after this time?*

'You know you ran away yourself once, do you remember?' he smiles. 'You were about five at the time. You packed a back-pack full of biscuits, crisps and a bottle of Coke and set off one morning. You didn't get very far, as I recall, just down the end of the road, before one of the neighbours brought you back.'

I don't answer. The way Dave tells it, it was an amusing little escapade, the quaint antics of a five-year-old. But what he seems to have forgotten is that just before I tried to run away, he and Mum had had a huge fight and he'd smashed her head against the fridge door. The truth was that my five-year-old attempt at escape was a cry for help.

'Well, you've got a nice place here, I must say.' Dave plonks himself down on the sofa and looks around. 'Your husband's doing all right for himself, isn't he?'

I make a mental note to clean the cushions later.

'Not too bad,' I answer cautiously.

'You got a drink for me, sweetheart? I've got a bit of a thirst on.'

I look pointedly at my watch.

175

'Look, I really need to get out. I'm meeting the police soon,' I lie. 'They want to talk to me about Grace . . .'

But Dave doesn't take the hint. He shows no sign of moving, just sits there, staring at me thoughtfully. 'Actually, I saw her the other day.'

'Who? Grace?' I ask, startled.

He grins, enjoying my shock. 'Yeah. I came around about a week ago. But you and Chris weren't in.'

It's possible, I suppose. Chris and Jack and I had gone to a PTA barbecue afternoon at the school last Friday. Grace, sulky teenager style, had refused to come.

'Grace was nice enough to entertain me. Didn't she tell you?'

I think back. When we got home from the barbecue Grace was shut in her room and didn't come out all evening. It wasn't particularly unusual these days and I hadn't thought anything of it.

'She didn't,' I say. *Why not?* I wonder. Sure, we haven't been talking much lately, but even so, I would have thought the arrival of her step-grandad in the country might have been something she would've considered worth mentioning.

Dave pulls a packet of fags from his bag and lights a cigarette. 'Hope you don't mind?'

I shrug. 'Would it make a difference if I did?' *Of course I mind*, I think furiously. I mind him being here in this room with me. I mind his existence on this planet.

'Oh, don't be like that Joanna.' He sucks on his cigarette and blows out a cloud of smoke. Then he sits back with one arm resting on the back of the sofa and his feet on the coffee table as if he owns the place.

'Well, it's good to see you again, Jo. I must say, you're looking very well.' His eyes linger on me a moment then run around the room, settling on a photo of Grace and Jack. It's a photo at a film museum we went to once. They're standing back to back, brandishing light sabres and framed by life-size models of C3PO and R2D2.

'It was really good to see little Gracie too. I haven't seen her for such a long time.' He chuckles. 'Not so little anymore, is she? She's grown into quite a young woman now.'

I eye him warily. There's something salacious about the way he says that. It reminds me of the way he made me feel so uncomfortable when I was a teenager – the way he would look at me and comment on my changing body or try and strike up conversations about boys and periods. I've kept him at arm's length from Grace and Jack for most of their lives for good reason.

'Yeah, we had quite a good chat, me and Gracie,' he says, running his tongue over his lips. 'She was in the pool when I arrived. She was wearing a nice little blue bikini, if I recall correctly.'

'Oh?' I grip the armrest, digging my nails into the soft fabric.

'You know, it's funny. But I almost didn't recognise her. The last time I saw her without clothes was when she was a baby. It must've been when she was about three months. You were changing her nappy. I came around to fetch my DVD player, do you remember?' He laughs. 'You always were a thieving little

177

toerag. Couldn't stand it when somebody had something you didn't.'

I can't breathe. The air in the room has suddenly become toxic. What's he getting at? He's trying to make a point and I'm afraid that I know what it is. I knew there was something. There always is with Dave.

'It made me think, I can tell you . . .' he continues, standing up and sitting next to me on the sofa. He pats me on the shoulder with a bony hand and I flinch. The stench of alcohol on his hot breath makes me want to vomit.

I shift away. 'Think about what?' I say stiffly.

'Does she know?' He leans close and whispers in my ear.

I shift away to the other end of the sofa. My heart is beating really fast, but my voice is calm. 'Does she know what?' I hear myself saying.

He taps his fingers on his knees. Dirty fingernails beating out a rhythm, like a battle drum. 'The truth about her mother – about all the naughty things you've done.'

'I've no idea what you mean. You're high again, aren't you?' My voice is cold, like ice. I'm frozen to the spot.

'Oh, I think you do, Joanna,' he grins.

'What is it you want from me, Dave?' I hear myself saying.

He raises his eyebrows, all innocence. 'I don't want anything. I'm just trying to help, that's all. I've always thought honesty's the best policy'.'

Since when? I think. Since he told mum he'd spent all her money on a private operation for his back, when really he'd frittered it all away on drugs and gambling. Or since he had an affair with some woman right under Mum's nose?

I hate him so much I could strangle him with my bare hands. 'What did you say to Grace?' I ask through gritted teeth. 'What did you do?'

He shrugs. 'Nothing. Honest.'

His eyes slide away from mine. It's hard to tell when Dave's lying. So much of what he says is a lie. I'm not sure that he even knows when he's lying himself.

'Is it money you want? Is that it?'

'Of course not.' He taps ash out onto the plate I've provided as an ashtray. 'Though I am a bit short, now you mention it. And I need to settle my hotel bill and pay for the flight home.'

Of course it's money. I should have guessed. He's bled my mother dry, now he's come for me and Chris.

'How much do you want?' I sigh.

He grins, yellow fangs bared – the stray dog that got the bone. 'A couple of thousand should tide me over.'

'A couple of thousand! Don't be ridiculous,' I say. 'We haven't got that kind of cash spare, even if I wanted to give it to you.'

'That's not what I heard. I heard that husband of yours was doing all right. And it certainly looks like he is.' He waves his hand around at our spacious living room. 'You can afford this fancy place with a swimming pool.'

'It's not ours. It's rented.' I stand up and take my purse out of my handbag. There are a couple of fifty-euro notes in there. I take them out and shove them into his bony hands.

'There, that should cover your air fare home,' I say. 'I suggest you get a flight home as soon as possible. Oh, and Mum asked me to get you to ring her. This whole thing with Grace has sent her into a nosedive.'

'Thanks, Jo,' he grins, curling his fist around the money and shoving it in his back pocket. To my intense relief, he stands up to go. 'Do you think you could give me a lift back into town?' he says at the door. 'I walked here, and it nearly killed me in this heat, what with my back.'

'All right,' I agree. Anything to get him out of my living room and out of my life.

As we drive into Larnaca along the coast road, Dave sits in the passenger seat humming away to himself.

'I see why you like it here, sunshine all year round,' he says, staring out at the blue sea glittering in the sun.

'Yes, well, apart from losing my daughter it's just great,' I say bitterly.

'Grace'll turn up when she's good and ready.'

I can't escape the suspicion that Dave is involved in all this somehow. 'Did she say anything to you, when you spoke?' I ask. 'Anything strange? Was she upset?'

Dave taps his fingers on the dashboard and stares out as we pass the old oil refinery. 'She was stressed about her exam results, said you were angry with her for doing badly.'

'I wasn't angry,' I say. But I can't deny it has the ring of truth to it. One of the things we argued about over the summer was

Grace's GCSE results. I felt she hadn't revised enough because she'd been spending all her time with Tom and I hadn't been able to stop myself letting her know how disappointed I was. But why tell Dave about that of all people? She knows how much I despise him.

'Yeah, well, she thought you were angry. She said she felt she was never good enough for you, whatever she did. I know how she feels. You always were a bit of a princess, weren't you? Thought you was too good for me and your old mum, that's for sure.'

I don't have to listen to his bullshit. I turn up the radio to drown out the sound of his voice. But as I drive, I think, *Is it true? Did I make Grace feel inadequate?* I didn't mean to. I just wanted her to be the best she could be – not fuck up her life the way I had.

When we get into town, I squeeze into a parking space on the seafront not far from Dave's hotel.

'Use that money I gave you to get a flight home,' I say. 'You're not welcome here and if I find out that you've got anything to do with Grace's disappearance, I'll . . .' I think of a phrase Chris uses sometimes. 'I'll string you up by the balls.'

Dave stares at me through narrow eyes. 'You know, Jo, I don't think the money is enough, not for all the trouble I've been through. But I'm not in a rush. I'll give you a few days to think about it,' he says, climbing out of the car.

I don't answer. There's nothing to say. The past is coming back. I can feel its dark tentacles stretching, worming their way into my life – into my family – and I'm powerless to stop it.

Chapter 24

2000

It's getting cold. The evenings are the worst, when you're sitting still. The houses here are not designed for the winter. There's no central heating or proper insulation and the chill sea wind rattles through the hut while I sit wrapped in a duvet watching TV. Sometimes I rent a DVD from the video shop. Sometimes Hakan joins me and we huddle together. I like the old classics: *Gone with the Wind*, *Mildred Pierce* and my favourite, *The Sound of Music*. I love the bit where Captain Von Trapp is singing 'Edel-weiss' at the competition in front of all the Nazi guards and he can't sing because he's overcome with emotion and then Maria steps in to help him. I want to be like that for Hakan. I want to be the person who supports him and fills his life with song, because Helen isn't, that's for sure. She just drags him down.

Thank God she's in England at the moment, having her baby. She doesn't trust the doctors here, she says, and she wants to be sure that they'll speak in English to her if something goes wrong. That's fine with me. It means that Hakan and I get to spend the next two weeks together uninterrupted. He still has to be careful about what the staff see but he trusts most of them to be discreet. Sometimes I even stay in the house in his bed. A couple of times I stay the whole night.

We wake up, limbs tangled, skin on skin, so close that I'm not sure where he ends and I begin. The birds are singing outside the window and a shaft of light pools on the skin of his back. I stroke his cheek, my hand catching on his stubble, and he opens his eyes. I've never seen it before, that moment of first consciousness. It's like he's being born again, and his eyes are brown, full of amber light and love.

'I love you, Jojo,' he whispers, cradling my face in his hands. We're so close I can see the pores in his skin, the small lines around his eyes and the threads of grey in his hair. There's a part of his earlobe that's strangely deformed. I rub it with my finger and then I turn my head away because tears are filling my eyes and I feel silly.

'Why are you crying?' he asks, holding my head in his hands, and I can't answer. I'm crying because I've never felt so safe or so loved, but I can't say that out loud.

'I love you too . . . maybe . . .' I say, laughing, and he crushes me close. He kisses my neck, then my shoulder, then even my armpit, which makes me giggle, and he tickles me, which makes me giggle more, and he rolls on tops of me and I feel the weight of him.

'You're my girl,' he says, pinning back my arms and gazing into my eyes. 'Say you're my girl.'

'I'm your girl,' I say, and he kisses me. But just then there's a hammering on the door and someone tries to turn the handle.

'Daddy?' Adam calls out from the other side. Thank God Hakan remembered to lock it last night.

'Shit.' Hakan scrambles up. 'Get in the bathroom,' he hisses. 'Just a minute, Adam. I'm coming.'

I scoop up my clothes and rush into the en-suite. In the bedroom I can hear Adam snivelling.

'Daddy, I had a bad dream. Where's Mummy? I want Mummy.'

'It's all right, son. It was just a dream. Mummy's not here. She's gone to the UK, remember?'

'But I heard her.'

'You must have imagined it, son. Now, why don't you go back to bed, there's a good boy.'

On the tiled floor, I dress quickly, shivering with the cold. Suddenly I feel like I'm making a terrible mistake.

Chapter 25

2017

I watch Dave shuffle along the street, taking in the stooping shoulders, the shambling walk. God, how I hate him. I hate everything about him. I even hate the way he moves. I grip the wheel with shaking fingers, breathe in deeply and exhale slowly, trying to calm myself. *He doesn't know anything. He has no power over you*, I tell myself. *You've escaped from that life, from the mess of your past. You're a different person now.*

At home I stack the dishwasher and mop the tiled floors, trying to exorcise my demons. I don't know if it's my imagination or not, but I can still smell Dave in the air. That distinctive blend of the roll-ups he smokes, and his BO seems to have permeated the house, as if he's an animal that's marked the place with his scent. I spray air freshener liberally around the living room and open all the windows wide, but the stench still lingers. *I'll never escape him*, I think grimly.

It can't be a coincidence, I tell myself, as I put the cushions outside in the garden to air. Dave turns up in the country and then shortly afterwards Grace goes missing. *Could he have had something to do with her disappearance? Could he have hurt her? Killed her even?* I shiver at the thought. But realistically, I know it's not likely. I wouldn't put anything past Dave, but he has no real reason to hurt Grace that I can think of. No, whatever's happened to Grace, the answer is somehow connected with that letter. I just know it. *What happened between her and Tom? Why did she break up with him so suddenly?*

I go to my handbag and take out the copy of the letter Dino gave us. Then I sit at the kitchen table and read it again, tracing my fingers over the writing as if I could divine Grace's thoughts by imitating the movements she made as she wrote.

I need to talk to Maria, I decide. She'll know what happened between them. If Grace has confided in anyone, it'll have been her. Relieved not to be obsessing over Dave and to have a plan of action at least, I take out my phone and ring her number.

'Maria, it's Jo. I need to speak to you,' I say when she answers.

'Er, I'm at school, Jo.' She sounds a bit breathless, like she's walking somewhere. There's the sound of children screeching and laughing in the background. 'I'm late for my next lesson.'

'Can I come and see you at your house, after school?'

'Of course. Any time.'

'I'll come at about two thirty this afternoon, okay?'

'Okay, gotta go now,' she says and rings off before I can say anything else.

I'm just trying to decide what to do next when Lola scratches

186

at the door and I realise I haven't fed her yet. I let her in and scratch behind her ears. And I'm just spooning out her food when my phone rings. It's Chris.

'Jo—' he begins.

'Where are you?' I interrupt. 'Don't tell me you've gone to work again. I need you at home. Dave's been here stirring up trouble like he always does and—'

'No, I'm not at work. I'm at the police station,' Chris says.

'What? Why didn't you wait for me?'

There's a sigh on the other end of the phone. 'I didn't have a choice. They've brought me in for questioning. They picked me up outside the school and wouldn't take no for an answer.'

'What? Why?' I say, shocked. I picture them handcuffing him in front of all the kids and parents at drop-off. *In front of Jack.* I shut my eyes and shudder.

'Why don't you just come down to the station?' he says wearily. 'I'll explain when you get here.'

About twenty minutes later, I'm in the reception at the police station. I demand to see my husband but instead I'm shown to an interview room by a lethargic-looking officer. The room is bare apart from a desk and a couple of chairs with a large mirror covering one wall. Dino and Eleni are sitting at the desk, not smiling.

'Where's Chris? What the hell's going on? I don't . . .' I begin. But my voice tails off as I fully take in the formality of the situation and the expression on their faces. The explosive rant that I'm about to deliver dies on my lips.

'Sit down, please, Mrs Joanna,' Dino says gravely, pulling up a seat for me.

I stay stubbornly standing, clutching the back of the chair. 'Where is he? Is he okay?'

'He's okay. He's here, in the police station. You can speak to him in a while. But first I must ask you some questions. Please . . .' He gestures for me to sit. 'Do you mind if I record the conversation?'

I perch reluctantly on the edge of the chair. 'Go on then. But please make it quick,' I say, glancing at my watch. 'I don't want to be late to pick up my son from school.'

Dino pushes a button on the recording device and looks at his watch. 'Okay, the date is the twenty-second of September and the time is twelve thirty. Present are myself, Detective Constandinos Markides, Constable Eleni Michalis and Mrs Joanna Appleton.' He clears his throat.

'Mrs Joanna, do you know where your husband was on Monday morning – the day Grace went missing?'

So, that's why Chris has been detained. They're still pursuing the ludicrous idea that he had something to do with Grace's disappearance. I feel a wave of helpless anger. They should be out finding her, not wasting time harassing Chris.

'Of course I know where he was,' I snap. 'He was at work.'

'No, he wasn't,' Dino answers calmly. 'We checked with the manager of Lambros Developments' – he looks down at some papers on his desk – 'Mr Markos Lambros. He says he fired your husband from the project two weeks ago.'

188

It takes me a minute to understand what's just been said.

'Two weeks ago?' I repeat blankly. 'That's impossible.' My mind is whirling, stirring up memories, trying to make sense of this new information. *It can't be true, can it? But then again, why would Dino lie?* I think back, trying to remember any signs that I may have missed. It's true Chris returned from work in a foul mood one evening a couple of weeks ago, saying he'd had a row with Markos. But that wasn't that unusual, and he certainly hadn't mentioned anything about being fired.

'It must be a mistake,' I murmur weakly.

Dino taps his fingers on the desk and gives me a sympathetic look. 'So, you didn't know?'

'No.'

How could I have? Chris went off in his van every morning for the two weeks before Grace disappeared, just like normal. He came back at about six o'clock every evening, like he always did. He even talked in detail about his day. Was *that all lies? And where was he going all that time if he wasn't going to work?*

Dino leans forward, clasping his hands together. 'That's not all,' he says gently. 'We have a witness who says they saw his van parked outside the school on Monday morning.'

I stare at him, stunned. 'What? Who?'

He shrugs. 'I'm afraid I can't tell you that.'

One of the busybody parents concocting stories to make themselves seem important, I think indignantly. 'Well, they must have made a mistake,' I say out loud.

Dino is looking at me strangely, almost as if he feels sorry for me, and I feel a twinge of disquiet.

'I don't think it was a mistake,' he says. 'As you know, it's quite a distinctive van.'

I can't argue with that. Chris brought his old van from England, the one with the lightning bolt painted along the side. It's difficult to miss, even for someone like me who hasn't the slightest interest in cars. So not a mistake then, but a malicious rumour?

There's an awkward silence as Dino shuffles some papers. 'I'm sorry but there's another question I must ask you. It's not a comfortable question to ask, but I must ask it all the same.'

'Okay,' I nod. It can't get much worse than it already is, I suppose.

'Has your husband ever been physically violent towards you or your daughter or given you cause to feel afraid?'

I stare at him for a moment then shake my head emphatically. 'Never.'

Dino gives me a searching look. 'Are you sure about that? Take your time. Think carefully.'

There's no denying that Chris has a temper. There was a time early on in our relationship when he punched a hole in the door during an argument after a night in the pub, but he's never laid a finger on me or either of the children and I've certainly never been afraid of him.

'I'm absolutely sure,' I say, meeting Dino's eyes directly.

Eleni, who has been silent up until now, leans forward and says, 'You said before that Grace said to a friend that someone she knew had committed a crime. We assumed it was Tom, but do you think she could have meant your husband?'

I shake my head. 'No, Grace didn't know about Chris's criminal record.'

Dino and Eleni exchange a glance. Then Dino clears his throat. 'We didn't exactly mean that. Do you have any reason to believe your husband may have been abusing your daughter? Sexually?'

My mouth falls open. The idea is completely insane, of course, and I would laugh if I didn't feel like the whole world was suddenly lurching like a boat in rough waters. I grip the chair, holding on tight, and shut my eyes, battling a wave of nausea.

'You can't be serious,' I manage.

'I'm afraid we're very serious, Mrs Joanna.' Dino purses his lips. 'Some allegations have been made.'

'By who?'

'Your daughter never claimed that he did anything inappropriate to her or that he made unwanted advances?'

'No!' I dredge my mind. Have I missed something? But no. Grace loves Chris. I have never for one single moment suspected that he was anything but a loving father to her.

'You never saw anything that made you uneasy? Anything between them?'

'No!' I picture Chris tapping Grace on the bum with a fly swat or embarrassing her in front of her friends by tickling her. It was inappropriate behaviour maybe. But I'm sure there was nothing sinister about it. It's just that he still thinks of her as a little girl and hasn't realised how quickly she's growing up.

'Look, I don't know who's made these allegations,' I say. 'Maybe it's someone who has a grudge against Chris for some reason. All I can say is that it's completely untrue.'

'Can you think of someone who might have a grudge against him?'

'Not really,' I admit. 'But he has a bit of a temper and he sometimes gets people's backs up because he doesn't mince his words.'

'Mince his words?' Dino looks confused.

'I mean, he says it like it is.'

Dino nods. 'I see. I'm still working on my English.'

I don't answer. If he's fishing for a compliment, I'm not really in the mood to oblige.

'You may be right,' he says at last with a sigh. 'We get all kinds of false information during an investigation but when these allegations are made, it's our duty to follow them up. I'm just doing my job, I hope you understand that.'

I do understand, of course, but right now I'm too angry and agitated to admit it. 'Is he under arrest?' I ask.

'No, he's not under arrest. We just wanted to ask him a few questions, that's all.'

I breathe a sigh of relief. If he's not under arrest, they can't have any solid evidence or real suspicion that he's guilty.

'Good. So, then he can come home with me,' I say. 'Can I see him now?'

Dino looks at Eleni, who nods, and he turns off the recording device. 'I don't see why not.'

192

'Mrs Appleton, are you sure you know your husband as well as you think you do?' Eleni says as I head to the door.

I stare at her defiantly, my hand on the door handle. 'Well enough to know that he's a good man. How well do you know *your* husband?'

She shrugs and smiles faintly. 'Sometimes we believe what we want to believe because anything else is too painful,' she says gently. 'Are you sure that's not the case with you?'

Chris is waiting in the reception area of the police station. He's rocking backwards and forwards in his chair, the legs thumping on the floor, a grim expression on his face.

'Jo, thank God,' he says when he sees me. 'Let's get out of this loony bin.' He gives the officer at the desk a filthy look and sweeps outside into the stifling hot air.

We walk in silence to my car, which is parked outside the post office. Eleni's last words to me are still reverberating in my head. Have I been kidding myself? Is it possible that this man walking next to me is a stranger?

'There's no point in going home now,' I say once we reach the car. 'We might as well pick up Jack. Where's your van?'

'I had to leave it outside the school,' he sighs heavily.

'I suppose you know why they brought me in?' he says as we drive off slowly, caught up in the one-way system through the town centre.

'Dino told me. I . . .'

'You know that it's a lie, don't you?' He stares straight ahead as we crawl through the backed-up traffic.

'Yes, of course,' I say with more conviction than I feel right now. 'I know you would never hurt Grace. But Dino said you lost your job, is that true?'

'I wasn't fired. I quit,' he mutters darkly. 'You have no idea what an arrogant twat Markos is.'

I absorb this in silence. I look across at his profile, the blunt freckled nose, the laughter lines around his eyes. I thought I knew him inside out, but clearly I was wrong. I try to ignore a nagging sense of unease. If he's managed to hide this from me, what else could he have been hiding? We draw near the school, where the traffic is even more chaotic with all the parents picking up kids. There are cars blocking the road, refusing to move, and other cars hooting wildly at them. I manage to squeeze into a tiny space between two parked cars and I kill the engine.

'I don't mind you quitting,' I say quietly. 'It's the lies I mind.'

He sighs deeply. 'I know, I'm sorry.'

'I mean, what have you been doing all this time? You've been going out every morning in your van as if you were still working.'

'Looking for a job mainly. Also, just driving around. Sometimes I go swimming in the sea.'

'Why didn't you just tell me?' *Okay, I might have been angry at first,* I think. *But I would've understood.* I thought we were a team, me and Chris – that we worked through our problems together.

194

'I didn't want you to worry. I thought I'd find more work really quickly and you'd never have to know.'

Under normal circumstances I would be angry that he'd lied to me but right now is not a normal circumstance. I've been feeling so much fear, anger and suspicion for so long I really don't have the energy to feel anything.

'Where did you go on Monday morning?' I ask wearily.

Chris sighs. 'Not you too, Jo! Dino's got into your head, hasn't he?'

'No, of course not. I just want to know where you were, that's all. It's to our advantage. If you can prove where you were all morning, then the police will have to stop hassling you and can concentrate on finding Grace.'

Chris frowns and drums his fingers on the dashboard. 'That's the problem. I can't prove where I was. I drove to Kiti and went swimming by the lighthouse. There were a few tourists around, but I doubt they would remember me even if they were still in the country.'

'The police said that someone saw your van outside the school,' I say carefully, watching him to see his reaction. He flinches slightly but his answer comes smoothly enough.

'Yes, I did park there for a while. I went to get a sandwich at the Tuck Inn to take with me to the beach.'

'What time was that?'

'About nine thirty.'

'You didn't see Grace outside the school?'

'Don't you think I would have said something if I had?'

195

It's difficult to know what to believe . . . The Chris I know would never hurt Grace – not in a million years. But then again, the Chris I know wouldn't have lied to me about losing his job and I know all too well that it's possible to keep secrets from your spouse.

There's the sound of the school bell and children begin surging out of the gates.

I ignore the tight knot in my gut and focus on the here and now – on what needs to be done. It's the only way I can handle this situation. If I start suspecting Chris, I think I'll go mad.

'I said I'd meet Maria at two thirty', I find myself saying. 'Can you take Jack home?'

'Okay', Chris says, starting to get out of the car. But at that moment we see Olga crossing the road, breezing past, blonde hair bouncing like she's in a shampoo advert.

'Oh God,' he groans, climbing back in the car and ducking. 'She was there this morning. I'm sorry, Jo, but I can't face her or any of them. They all saw me leaving with the police. They all think I'm guilty.'

'Okay, don't worry,' I say. 'You go get your van and drive up to the pick-up point. I'll get Jack and bring him to you.'

If I go into school alone, it'll cause less of a stir than if Chris comes with me, I think. But it turns out I'm wrong about that, because the moment I get to the playground I'm surrounded by a group of mums who don't usually give me the time of day, all wearing the kind of expressions I imagine they usually reserve for cancer patients or newly bereaved widows.

'Jo, how are you? I've been meaning to call.' Sad face.

'We're all so worried about you.' Concerned face.

'It must be awful for you.' Pouty face, unable to express emotion because of too much botox.

'The police were here this morning,' Olga says, placing a hand on my arm. 'Is there any news?'

'Not yet but they're hopeful. They have some leads.'

They all look at me, willing me to say more. They've definitely heard about Chris, I realise. Not surprising given the way gossip spreads amongst the expat community in this place.

I'm relieved when Stella arrives. At least I feel she's genuinely on my side. 'Oh, Jo,' she says, folding me in her arms and promptly bursting into tears.

'Thank you for taking Jack the other day,' I say, pushing her away gently. If she cries any more, it'll make me cry and I don't want to break down here, not in front of all these vultures.

'It was absolutely no problem. Are you okay? Do you want me to take him again?'

'No, it's okay, thank you.'

I bat away more questions and expressions of concern until at last Jack appears trailing down the stairs, his shoelaces undone as usual, dragging his jacket on the floor.

'Where's Dad?' he asks anxiously as I whisk him out of the playground. 'The police were here this morning . . .'

Oh God. What does he know? What has he heard?

'Your dad's fine, don't worry,' I say with false cheeriness. 'He's waiting for you in the van. You can see for yourself. He's going to drive you home. I have someone I need to see.'

Jack hangs back. 'Can't I come with you? I don't want to go with Dad.'

'Why not?' I stop abruptly, staring at him.

He looks at the ground. 'I don't know. Kids in my class . . . they've been saying things.'

I give a deep, shuddering sigh and rest my arm around his shoulder. 'We have to stick together, Jack. Now more than ever. We can't let a few malicious people get to us.'

Jack nods and wipes his nose. 'What does malicious mean?'

'Never mind. Just go and get in the van. I'll see you at home, okay?'

'Okay.' I watch him as he crosses at the zebra crossing. I watch him shuffling along, his head bent as if he's carrying the weight of the world on his shoulders, and I feel a sudden wave of anger at whoever's done this to him, whoever's done this to our family.

Chapter 26

Maria's house is near to the highway – a huge flashy mansion, gleaming white, with Greek statues lining the stairs up to the front door. I've been here many times to drop off or pick up Grace, but I've never been inside, and I'm awestruck by the grandeur of the place as a Filipino maid answers the door and shows me through to the back garden. Maria is sitting on the swing seat, her legs folded under her with a sleek black cat curled up in her lap.

'Beautiful cat,' I say, stroking it. The cat stares back at me with suspicious yellow eyes and leaps off, stalking away, its tail twitching.

'He's a naughty boy. Got a mind of his own.' Maria rubs her fingers together, trying to call him back, but the cat curls up a short distance away and stares at us balefully. 'You know it was Grace who gave him to me,' she says. 'She found him when he was just a little kitten.'

I'm not surprised. 'That sounds like Grace,' I say.

It must have been one of the kittens she brought home last November. She found them abandoned by the roadside. There were five of them in a cardboard box, mewing incessantly and clambering all over each other.

'We're not keeping them,' Chris said as soon as he came home from work. 'What about Lola? She'll eat them alive.'

'But look at them, Daddy.' Grace only uses the word 'Daddy' when she's after something. She was giving him the full works, pouting and even putting on a baby voice. 'They're so cute. Please . . . Please let's keep them.'

Usually Grace can wrap Chris around her little finger but on this occasion, he was adamant. 'They can't stay,' he said. 'No way.'

'Well, what am I supposed to do with them?' Grace's eyes filled with angry tears. 'I can't just leave them. They'll die. The cats' homes are all full. I rang them. There's no space anywhere and if you give them to the authorities, they just kill them.' She sighed dramatically. 'I suppose I could drown them. Is that what you want?'

Chris shrugged his broad shoulders. 'Maybe it's for the best. There are too many stray cats on the island anyway.'

'How can you be so heartless? Mum, tell him . . .'

'Why don't you just put them back where you found them?' I suggested weakly. 'Maybe the mother will come back. Maybe she's looking for them right now.'

'There's no point,' Chris said. 'The mother will reject them now they have your smell on them. You do more harm than good picking up these strays.'

'You're evil and I hate you,' Grace shouted, storming up the stairs.

I was just glad that for once it was Chris who was at the receiving end of her wrath instead of me.

'Grace is always picking up strays,' I say to Maria, watching the cat delicately licking its paws.

'Yes,' Maria agrees. 'She's so kind-hearted – such a beautiful soul. I love her so much.' Tears spill out of her eyes. I look away, across at the empty plot of land, the dry grass, the pale blue swimming pool wobbling like jelly in a tiny breeze.

Grace is many things, I think, *so many contradictory things*. Kind, cruel, headstrong, sometimes brave, sometimes timid. It's impossible to sum up a person with a few adjectives when you really know them inside out like I know Grace.

'She really cares about you too,' I say out loud.

Maria nods and sniffs. 'Have you heard anything from her?'

I shake my head. 'I'm afraid not. But the police have found something important. That's why I'm here in fact. I thought maybe you could help explain it.'

Maria wipes her eyes and her nose and stares at me.

I take the copy of the letter out of my handbag. 'The police found this in Tom's flat.'

I watch Maria's expression carefully as she reads it, but I register nothing but surprise and confusion. 'I don't understand. She split up with Tom?' she says at last, after reading it through twice.

'It looks like it, doesn't it?'

The sun is beating down on me, an angry, unforgiving sun, and I shift my chair a little so that I'm further in the shade. I take the letter from Maria and read aloud. '*I'm sorry but I can't see you anymore*. Did she tell you they were having problems?' I ask.

She hesitates just for a second. 'No . . . I had no idea,' she says and then more firmly, 'No. As far as I know, she was really in love with him. She said they were soulmates. She even talked about marrying him one day.' She flushes. 'I mean, I know you don't like him . . . but she thought that you and her dad would come around eventually.'

'It wasn't a matter of disliking him,' I say defensively. 'He's too old for her, that's all.' I fold up the letter and put it back in my handbag. 'Were they having any arguments recently? Can you think of any reason why she might have wanted to break things off with him?'

'No.' She hesitates, then more emphatically, 'No.'

'Are you sure?'

'Yes.'

Again, I'm left with the impression that she's holding something back.

'Maria, I know there's something you're not telling me.'

Her eyes widen, and she picks up a sequined cushion and hugs it to her chest.

I make my voice as gentle and persuasive as possible. 'You need to tell me everything you know. You won't get into any trouble, I promise you, and it could be so important. It could help us find Grace.'

'It won't help.'

'It might.'

'I promised,' she whispers, tears welling up in her eyes. 'I promised her I wouldn't tell anyone.'

I lean across to grip her hand tightly. I'm on to something. I can sense her wavering and I need to lay it on thick. 'Please, Maria. If you care about Grace at all, you need to tell me, whatever it is. It could be a matter of life and death.'

She's crying properly now, tears running down her cheeks. 'I'm sorry,' she gulps, taking a tissue out of her pocket and blowing her nose. 'It's just that I miss her so much. Of course I care about her. I love her, but I don't think betraying her confidence will help. I don't think it has anything to do with her disappearance.'

'But you don't know that for sure,' I persist. 'Every little thing could be important. What is it, Maria? What were they arguing about?'

'They weren't arguing. I don't think he even knew . . .'

A chill enters my heart and I shiver despite the heat.

'Knew what, Maria? What didn't he know?' My voice is a stone dropping into a deep, empty well because suddenly I know what's coming. And I know in my bones that the thing I've always feared has happened.

Maria's voice is not much more than a whisper. 'She was pregnant.'

Maria is crying again. I stare at the swimming pool blankly, watching a beetle drowning in the water. A red dragonfly perches on the edge of the pool, its wings twitching. I thought we'd found sanctuary here, a place where we could keep Grace safe. It turns out I was wrong.

'I'm sorry,' she's saying, sniffling into a tissue. 'I should have told you before, but she made me promise . . .'

'When?' I manage. 'When did she tell you?'

'About three weeks ago,' she says. 'She asked me if I knew anyone who could, you know' – she lowers her voice – 'get rid of it.'

Just three weeks ago. Just three weeks but it feels like a lifetime. Were there any signs I missed? Why wasn't I paying more attention? But I'm sure there were none of the usual clues. She didn't throw up in the toilet or complain of feeling nauseous. She locked herself in her room a lot, but I'd put that down to normal teenaged moodiness.

'And did you? Did you know a doctor? Is it even legal here?'

Maria blows her nose. 'Officially no, not usually. But you know Cyprus. In Cyprus rules are made to be broken.'

There's a long silence. 'Are you angry with me?' she asks.

'No, I'm not angry with you. It was brave of you to tell me. You did the right thing.' I reach out and pat her hand. My own hand is shaking, I realise. I need to hold it together, but it's difficult to do that when I feel that the whole world is shattering around me. 'Can you give me the number of the doctor you recommended?'

She nods and scrolls through her phone.

'He's called Doctor Stavrides,' she says. 'My older sister had her baby with him. He's very good.'

'Have you told anyone else?' I ask as she shows me the number and I add it to my contacts.

'No, of course not.'

I believe her. Maria is the kind of person that exudes trust-worthiness and kindness. And I'm not surprised that Grace chose to confide in her, but I am gutted that she didn't feel she could talk to me about this momentous thing. Why didn't she feel she could come to me?

But of course, I know the answer to that. There's a gulf between us that, at least in part, I've created. I close my eyes, trying not to think about how alone and scared she must have been feeling. It's not too hard for me to imagine. I know that feeling all too well.

Chapter 27

2001

'Shit!' Hakan flings the hammer down on the ground and clutches his hand. 'Fucking useless piece of shit,' he exclaims. He's been trying to nail up a 'Customer Parking Only' sign outside the restaurant and he's hit himself with the hammer.

He glares at me, sucking his finger. 'Are you sure?'

'A hundred per cent. I took two tests and I've been to the doctor.'

'Shit, shit, shit,' he says. He pulls a tissue out of his pocket and wraps it around his finger.

'I thought you'd be pleased,' I say.

'Pleased? Are you fucking crazy?'

I'm trying not to cry. But I can feel tears pricking at the back of my eyes. I'm taken aback by his reaction. I'm not sure exactly what I expected, not unadulterated joy maybe, but certainly not this. He seems so hostile and his eyes are wild with fear and anger, like he's a trapped animal. Like I'm the one that's trapped him.

'But you're on the pill, right?' he says.

I shake my head slowly. 'No.'

'Oh my God, Jo.' He covers his face with his hands. 'Why the hell didn't you tell me?' His voice rises until he's almost shouting.

I look around anxiously. A family of tourists is walking up the path from the beach carrying buckets and spades. 'Shh,' I say. 'Someone will hear.'

'Well, why didn't you?' he asks more quietly.

This is so unfair. Angry tears burn at the back of my eyes. 'You didn't ask.'

He glares at me for a moment then he gives a big sigh. 'You're right, Jo. It's my fault too. I'm sorry. I should have known better. I should have been more careful.'

'What are we going to do?' I ask.

I don't want to hurt Helen, much as I dislike her. But their relationship has been on the rocks for a while now. She's not really happy with Hakan anyway. And surely it isn't good for Adam growing up with such a toxic relationship. In the long run it will be better for everyone if Hakan leaves her. Perhaps this will give us all the impetus we need to sort this mess out.

Hakan paces up and down, still clutching his hand.

'I know a good doctor,' he's saying. 'I can take you there. I could take you there tomorrow. I'll pay for everything, of course. You've no need to worry.'

I don't understand what he means. 'I already had my first check-up,' I say. 'The doctor said everything was fine.'

'For God's sake, I don't mean for a check-up. I mean . . . well, you must know what I mean . . .' He stares at me, willing me to get it.

It takes a few seconds for it to sink in and it's like a knife twisting in my heart. 'But I don't want to get rid of it,' I say. 'I thought . . . I thought . . .'

Hakan sits on the steps staring at the gravel. When he speaks his voice is gentle. 'But you can't keep it, Jojo. You must see that. How would we explain it to Helen? To Adam?'

'Maybe it'll be for the best. You don't make her happy, you said so yourself. Maybe if we leave, go back to England . . .'

'I can't leave Adam. I won't leave him,' he says, shaking his head. His mouth is set in a grim line. For a moment he looks like a stranger. I can't believe that this is the same man who only a few nights ago lay in bed with me and told me I was his girl – told me he loved me.

'No, well, we could stay here then,' I say. I sit next to him on the step, put my hand on his knee. 'We could stay in Kyrenia, maybe move out into a flat. I'll go wherever you want to go.'

Hakan holds my hand. He turns and looks at me directly. His eyes are like stones, beautiful brown stones.

'I can't leave Helen either. I'll never leave Helen.'

'You don't love her.'

'It's complicated. There are different kinds of love. I love you

208

both in different ways. But she's my wife, the mother of my children. I can't just abandon her.'

But you can abandon me.

I can hear the words, but they make no sense, as if he's speaking a foreign language. Nothing makes sense anymore. All I know is that he doesn't want me. He puts a hand on my shoulder and tries to draw me close to him.

'Don't touch me,' I say, pushing him away, and I run away towards the sea, stumbling over the paving stones, tears blurring my vision.

Sometimes I hate Helen and the baby she's carrying. Sometimes I imagine that they don't exist. I fantasise that I kill them. But it's just a fantasy, that's all. Thinking about something is not the same as doing it.

Saturday, 23rd September 2017

Chapter 28

It's Saturday morning – the earliest appointment I could wangle – and I'm sitting in the doctor's waiting room flicking through a magazine, trying to make sense of the Greek writing and looking blankly at the pictures of Greek celebrities that I've never heard of. I've come here alone, slipping out before Chris and Jack were awake. I see no reason to tell Chris what Maria told me yet. It would only worry him and, if Grace went ahead with an abortion, there may be no need for him to ever know.

There's a fish tank in the corner of the room. While I'm waiting, I watch the tiny striped tetra dart about a model of a shipwreck and angelfish hover, fluttering their fins. A largish grey fish stares back at me with blank, round eyes and I shiver. I've always hated fish. They remind me of Dave and his fish tank at home. An image flashes into my mind: Dave's fish writhing on the dirty green carpet, mouths gaping. Dave, his face red with fury, picking them up and flinging them at my mother.

'What did you do that for, you fucking bitch!' he shouted and I felt a cold, wet slap in the face as he missed my mother and hit me on the cheek. I remember how much I hated him in that moment. How much I still hate him.

'The doctor can see you now,' says the receptionist, interrupting my thoughts.

I banish Dave to the murky recesses of my mind where he belongs and head to the doctor's office.

Dr Stavrides is about sixty with grey hair, a friendly smile and twinkling brown eyes. On the wall he has certificates from UK universities and Greek icons. There's a sign that says 'Please do not confuse your Google search with my medical degree'. *So, he has a sense of humour, I think, if maybe a somewhat prickly one*. He fiddles fussily with some papers for a moment as I come in, then gestures for me to sit down.

'Do you speak English?' I ask in Greek, one of the few phrases I've learnt. In Cyprus the answer is almost always yes, but it seems only polite to ask.

He beams and says in fluent English, 'Of course. You know, I lived and worked in England for thirty-six years. And you? Whereabouts in England are you from?'

'From Gloucestershire, the Cotswolds.'

'Oh yes, a beautiful part of the world. I know it well. I've visited there many times. But I lived and practised in Birmingham.'

'Oh?' *I really didn't come here to have a chat*, I think, impatient to get to the point, but I realise that rushing him could be counterproductive. He's old school, and maybe if we establish a rapport,

214

he'll be more likely to help me, because I know he probably shouldn't give me the information I'm about to ask for.

'Yes,' he continues happily. 'My sons were born there and grew up there. Now one lives in Australia, one in England and one here in Cyprus. I have two grandchildren, you know.'

'Really? You don't look old enough.'

His beam widens. 'I'm sixty-two, would you believe?'

'No, I wouldn't.' I'm laying it on a bit thick perhaps, but hopefully it's working.

'Anyway, how can I help you?' he asks finally, leaning across his desk and clasping his hands together.

'It's about my daughter. I think she might have visited you . . . about two weeks ago. Her name is Grace Appleton.'

'Oh . . . ?' he frowns. 'Wait a minute.' He taps something into his computer and peers at the screen.

'Grace Appleton? No. I have no record of any Grace Appleton coming to my surgery. You know it's better if you—'

'She might have used another name. Look.' I take out my phone and show him a picture of Grace.

He puts his glasses on his head and squints at the screen.

'She does look familiar,' he says slowly. Then he smiles and slaps his thigh. 'Yes, that's it. I remember now. She did come to see me about two weeks ago.'

'About having an abortion?'

'Oh.' He frowns and shifts back in his seat. 'I'm not at liberty to divulge that kind of information, I'm afraid.'

'But I'm her mother,' I exclaim, frustrated. 'She's only sixteen.

I have a right to know.' I gaze at him pleadingly. 'All I want to know is did she go ahead and have the abortion? Please.'

He shifts uncomfortably in his chair then leans forward and lowers his voice. 'You know, strictly speaking abortion is not legal here in Cyprus. There are some doctors, I believe, that are willing to break the law, but I'm not one of them. I suggested she try a clinic that I know in Limassol. But I told your daughter that she would need her parents' consent before proceeding. Didn't she speak to you about it?'

I shake my head, trying not to imagine how Grace must have felt when he told her that. She must have been so frightened and desperate. *Oh Grace*, I think. *Why didn't you speak to me? We could have sorted this mess out together.*

'Thank you,' I say. 'Did she say anything else? Anything about the baby or the baby's father?'

He frowns. 'No, not that I remember. I assumed that the father was the young man she came with.'

My jaw drops open. 'She was with someone?' *Tom*, I think angrily. So, he's been lying to us. 'Was he English? With long, dark hair. Good-looking?'

Dr Stavrides shakes his head. 'No, he wasn't English. He was Greek. He had bushy hair' – he raises his hands over his head and pats imaginary hair to demonstrate how thick it was – 'and bad acne.'

Andreas, I think, shocked. But it makes no sense. Why would Grace have asked Andreas of all people to come with her to the doctor's?

216

Dr Stavrides polishes his glasses, puts them back on and gives me a direct stare from kindly brown eyes. 'I don't want to take a liberty, but I would suggest that you talk to your daughter, Mrs Appleton.'

I would give everything to be able to talk to Grace right now, I think as I leave the doctor's surgery and walk back to my car. I want so badly to comfort her and reassure her, to tell her I'm sorry – to beg her forgiveness. I want her to know that I don't blame her. If anything, I blame myself. If only I had been less intransigent, if only I'd been more flexible about the whole Tom thing, maybe she wouldn't have got into this mess.

Tears are blurring my vision as I cross the road and I don't see the car. It screeches to a halt in front of me, hooting madly.

The driver opens the window and shouts at me in Greek.

I ignore him and get into my car, banging the steering wheel in frustration. *She must have been feeling so alone*, I think. Did she think we wouldn't have done everything we could to help and support her? Did she trust us so little? Christ, she even trusted Andreas more than us. Andreas of all people. I wipe my nose and start up the engine, swerving out into the traffic and causing the driver behind to hoot at me again. *I need to talk to that young man*, I think, but first I want to see Chris to let him know what I've discovered.

Chapter 29

When I get back home the sound of laughter, rough, cackling laughter, comes from the garden and my heart sinks.

Dave, I think. *What's he doing here?* Dave and Chris are sitting out on the back veranda, drinking beers, laughing and chatting like old friends. Chris has that fatuous smile on his face that he gets when spending time with members of my family, and Dave is telling a story, tipping his chair back, waving his arms around wildly.

'Hello, Joanna,' he says, breaking off from his story as I slide open the patio door.

'I thought you were going back home, Dave?' I glare at him and he grins back at me. His skin is sunburnt, and his face is red with white rings around his eyes where his sunglasses have been.

'Thought I'd stay a bit longer, didn't I? It's a great place, Cyprus. You're really living the dream here, you are.' He puts his feet up on a chair and takes a slurp of beer.

'We've been talking about Tom,' says Chris. 'Also,' Dave adds, 'I remembered something about Grace. I thought you'd want to know.'

'What?' I say wearily. I sit down at the table opposite him, shielding my eyes from the sun. I don't for a second believe he really has anything to tell us about Grace. It's just a tactic — a way to get under my skin.

Dave puts his can of beer down. 'I saw her,' he says.

'When? Where? Why didn't you tell me yesterday?' I ask sharply. I would bet a lot of money that he's lying, but we can't afford to ignore any leads.

He pauses for dramatic effect, enjoying the attention. 'It was last night. I can't be a hundred per cent sure it was her but . . . It was at a club in Ayia Napa. She was dancing with some bloke. I tried to go and talk to her. But by the time I'd managed to get through the crowd she was gone.'

'Which club?'

'I think it was called Moon something . . . No, that's it, Castle Moon. It's a little place in the centre.'

'Who was she with?' asks Chris eagerly.

'Some bloke,' says Dave vaguely.

'Can you describe him?'

'Um, well, he was tall and dark. He looked Greek, you know.'

'So, basically almost anyone here,' I say acerbically.

Chris gets a notepad and starts writing stuff down. He's swallowing it all up hook, line and sinker. He doesn't know Dave like I do. I'm pretty sure Dave's just bullshitting. It's what he does.

'Can you tell us anything else? Like what was he wearing?' Chris asks, sucking the end of his pen.

'Uh, jeans and a T-shirt. I think the T-shirt might have been blue.'

'And what was Grace wearing?'

'Some kind of dress, if you could call it a dress. You know the kind of things young kids wear nowadays.' He grins at me. 'A slinky little number. Red with holes cut in the back and the front. Didn't leave much to the imagination, if you know what I mean.'

Now I know that he's lying. Grace doesn't have a dress like that, and she would never wear anything with a low back. She has a large birthmark under her right shoulder blade. She's very self-conscious about it. She almost always covers it up.

'There was something different about her, though,' he continues, staring at me. 'Can't quite put my finger on it.'

'Maybe that's because it wasn't her,' I say coldly.

Dave shrugs and takes a slug of beer. 'Yeah, maybe you're right. Maybe it wasn't.'

'Well, either it was her or it wasn't,' says Chris impatiently. 'I'd have thought you'd recognise your own granddaughter.'

'You'd have thought so, wouldn't you? I don't know, maybe I'm going a bit senile in my old age.' He sits back and gives me a slow, pointed stare.

'What are you still doing here, Dave?' I snap. 'I thought you were flying home a couple of days ago.'

'Would you believe it? I had my wallet stolen. My card and all my money was in it. I've got no money to get home even if I wanted to.'

No, I wouldn't believe it, I think.

'Didn't you book a return flight?' Chris asks.

'No, I didn't know when I was going back, you see.'

'Well, I expect we can loan you a couple of hundred quid.' Chris stands up and fetches his wallet. Then he shoves a few notes into Dave's hand. 'There you go, mate. That should cover your air fare. And there's another hundred to tide you over.'

'Thanks, son. I appreciate it.' Dave grins at me. 'You've got a keeper here, Joanna.'

Just get out of my fucking house, I scream in my head. Out loud I say calmly, 'Actually, Dave, there's something urgent I need to discuss with Chris. So, if you don't mind?' I stand up, hoping he'll take the hint.

'Well, okay.' Dave drains his beer and stands up. 'You don't want me around, I understand.'

'It's not that . . .' says Chris.

Yes, it is.

'I'd like to help if I can. I'm worried about her. She's my granddaughter after all.'

'Of course you are. You've already helped a lot,' says Chris, patting him on the back. 'We'll look into this Ayia Napa club.'

'I'll be in touch,' Dave whispers to me as he leaves.

I watch Dave through the window. I watch him walk towards the bus stop. Heading to the airport, hopefully. I imagine him sitting on a plane and I picture the plane plummeting to the ground. Who would miss him really?

Chapter 30

2001

I'm going home. There's nowhere else for me to go. The plane lands at Heathrow late in the evening and I get the bus back to Cirencester. It's dark and the streets are deserted when I arrive. There's not a single taxi in sight, so I walk the kilometre to our house in the dark, dragging my suitcase along the pavement.

Dave is at the door after I hammer on it for what seems like hours. He's dressed in silk boxers and that's all, his slug white chest covered in a smattering of hairs. He smells of aftershave, which is weird, as normally the only scent he wears is eau de cigarettes and booze.

'Jesus, Joanna. Do you know what time it is?' he says.

'Welcome home, Joanna. Good to see you,' I say sarcastically, dragging my suitcase past him into the living room.

The place is a tip. Ashtrays are overflowing, empty takeaway boxes and beer cans are scattered around, and there are some small bowls and spoons that make me guess he's been using again. The smell is overpowering and makes me feel nauseous. As soon as I'm through the door I retch and rush to the toilet.

'Christ,' says Dave, lighting a roll-up when I return to the living room. 'What have you been eating?' He gives me a shrewd look. 'Oh no. You're not pregnant, are you?'

I stare at him. Dave has an uncanny way of hitting the nail on the head sometimes.

'Oh my God,' he exclaims. 'You are, aren't you? That's all we need, another sprog in the family. Haven't you ever heard of birth control?'

'Where's Mum?' I ask coldly, lifting the cat and sitting on the sagging leather sofa. I didn't really expect to get much sympathy from Dave but maybe Mum will change the habit of a lifetime and miraculously morph into a proper parent now, in my hour of need.

'She's not well. She checked herself into the loony bin.'

My heart sinks. I want to talk to my mother. I need her more than ever now. I feel angry tears welling up in my eyes. *Why has she always been so useless? Why did she ever have children if she couldn't handle the responsibility?* But my anger is mixed with guilt too. Perhaps I should never have left her alone with Dave and his violent mood swings. If I'd been here to defend her, maybe she wouldn't have fallen apart again.

'And the twins?' I ask. Surely Dave isn't looking after them by himself? God forbid.

'They're in Wales, with their nana. I couldn't look after them.

Not with my back. It's been giving me a lot of grief lately.' He winces and arches his back to make his point. 'You really left us in the lurch, you know, when you went to Cyprus.'

I think about Dave's mother, Nana Carol. She's an evil witch of a woman whom I loathe, but the twins will probably be better off with her than with Dave. At least she can boil an egg and clean a toilet. Things that Dave seems incapable of doing.

I stand up and look at my watch. I've only been in the country five hours. Five minutes at home and already I want to kill him.

'Where are you going?' he asks.

'Well, I'm quite tired. I thought I might head to bed.'

'You can't stay here. Mandy won't like it.'

'Who's Mandy?'

As if in answer a small, stringy blonde woman wearing a long blue T-shirt and not a lot else appears at the door. There's a fag hanging out of her mouth and smudged make-up around her eyes. 'Who the fuck're you?' she says.

'This is Gemma's daughter, Joanna,' Dave explains. 'Is it okay if she stays just for one night? She's got nowhere else to go. She's gone and got herself up the duff.'

Mandy lights a cigarette and gives me a hard stare. 'I suppose it'll have to be, won't it?'

Even Dave can do better than Mandy, I think.

In the end I stay a week, sleeping in my old room, which Dave has turned into a storage room. I lie on my back squeezed between boxes, staring at the ceiling, and rub my still-flat belly. *At least I have this*, I think, *this new life growing inside me*. It's part of Hakan. It's a connection between us that can never be broken. When it's born, I think, Hakan will come to me. He won't be able to help himself. He'll be drawn to us, to his child. I imagine the reunion with tears rolling down my cheeks. Hakan at the airport, running towards me and lifting me up in his arms, swinging me around, kissing me on the lips.

'My girl, my Jojo,' he'll say. And everything will be okay.

Chapter 31

2017

'That was a bit harsh,' says Chris once Dave has gone.

'He deserves it.'

'I know he hasn't always been the best father to you, but he really seems to be making an effort lately. He flew all the way out here to see you and he's really trying to help with Grace.'

I think Chris identifies with Dave as a fellow stepfather. He's always making excuses for him. Like I say, he doesn't know Dave the way I do.

'You don't know the half of it,' I say.

'Do you think he really saw Grace in Ayia Napa?' Chris asks, clearing away the beer cans and stuffing them into the recycling.

'I seriously doubt it.'

'Why would he make that up, though?'

'Because it's what he does,' I say bitterly. 'He makes things up. He always has. He can't help himself.'

'We should check out this club in Ayia Napa, just in case.'

I sigh and nod. I'm almost certain it'll be a waste of time, but Chris is right. We can't afford to ignore any leads, no matter how dubious the source.

Chapter 32

2001

As soon as I can, I move out, away from Dave and Mandy and into my own place. I land a job at a retirement home, emptying commodes and wiping old people's wrinkly arses. It's not ideal. It's quite depressing in fact, but it pays the rent and I actually get quite attached to some of the residents. There's this old dear called Mary who I'm especially fond of. She has a record player in her room, and she likes it when I play her old jazz records. She enjoys watching me dance around her room. She says I'm a breath of fresh air – that I make her feel young again. But I don't always dance. Some songs I can't dance to, like her favourite song. Her favourite is 'Amazing Grace' and when I play it, tears well up in her eyes and she warbles along in a shaky voice, like she's an opera singer or something.

'I used to sing really well,' she tells me. 'I used to be a pretty little thing too, like you. There were so many men who wanted to court me. But then the war came . . .' And she stares with her faded blue eyes beyond me at something I can't see. 'But you don't want to know about all that,' she says after a while. 'Tell me what you've been up to . . .'

Sometimes I think Mary's pretty much my only real friend in the world.

The job in the old people's home is not my only job. At night I work in a pub and try to save some money because I know when the baby comes money's going to be tight. God knows I can't rely on Mum or Dave to help me out.

One day I take a bus to Cheltenham to visit Mum in the hospital. I buy some flowers before I go, yellow roses, which I think will cheer her up. When I get there, the nurse on duty tells me to wait. So, I sit in reception, staring at a black and white photograph of the hospital building in the old days, when it was a workhouse. I wait for what seems like hours, until the nurse comes back looking a little flustered and embarrassed.

'I'm afraid your mum isn't well enough to receive any visitors today,' she says gently. 'Would you like to leave a message?'

'Just tell her that her daughter's pregnant, if she gives a shit,' I say, standing up and storming out. Outside I rip up the flowers and fling them in the bin. Then I catch the bus back home fuming all the way.

At home I write a long, passionate letter to Hakan. I write pages and pages, pouring out my heart, telling him how much I miss him and, when I've finished, I put it in the post box at the end of my road. I wait for weeks for a reply, rushing to the door every time a letter drops onto the mat. But there's no letter, only bills and adverts.

I'm getting bigger every day now and soon it's obvious to everyone that I'm expecting. Tessie, my boss at the retirement home, isn't happy about the fact that she's going to have to find someone to replace me, but there's not a lot she can do about it. I start going to antenatal classes, but I feel so out of place amongst all the smug couples that I stop. And I go to the hospital for a couple of scans. On the first visit they tell me I'm expecting a girl and at the second they tell me everything is on track and that she should be coming any day now.

The pains start in the middle of the night. At first, they're like bad period pains, and I think this is going to be a walk in the park. What's all the fuss about? But after a while it gets worse. Much worse. Each contraction shakes my whole body as if I'm being electrocuted. I lose track of time and I throw up everywhere, little piles of sick all around the house. When I really can't stand it anymore, I ring the hospital. But my waters haven't broken yet and they say that my contractions are still too far apart for me to be in labour. 'Run a bath,' the woman on the other end of the phone says. 'It'll soothe the pain. And take a couple of paracetamol.' *Paracetamol! Is she crazy?* The woman I'm speaking to has clearly never experienced labour cramps.

But as I haven't really got anything else I can do, I fill the bath with warm water and immerse myself, watching my round belly float above the water. But it has little to no effect on the pain, so I clamber out again. And as I'm dressing, a wave of agony washes over me like nothing I've ever felt before. And soon I am on all fours, wailing like an animal. And it's all I can do to drag myself to the phone and ring for a taxi.

The taxi driver looks doubtful when he sees the state I'm in. 'You look like you're in labour, love,' he says. 'Don't you need an ambulance?'

'Could you just take me to the hospital, please,' I say through gritted teeth.

'Sure, sure . . . Come on then,' he says, shepherding me into the passenger seat.

On the drive to the hospital I concentrate on not throwing up on his new-looking leather upholstery. And it's a huge relief when we finally reach the maternity ward and they hook me up to a machine that measures the contractions. As the midwives bustle about, I watch the graph rise and fall, making a sort of etch-a-sketch of my pain, and I feel strangely soothed.

'Is there someone we can call?' asks a young, blonde midwife, coming in and checking my chart.

I shake my head impatiently. There's really no one to call. *Mum? No way. Dave? Ha!* The only person I want here is Hakan and he's two thousand miles away and doesn't really care, or else he would have replied to my letter. I shake my head and wipe a tear from my cheek. I don't think I've ever felt so alone.

The baby is finally born at six o'clock in the morning.

'A beautiful baby girl!' the midwife announces as she brings her to me and lies her against my chest, skin on skin. I gaze down at her, overwhelmed and amazed that I have created this tiny, perfect, wriggling creature.

'Do you know what you're going to call her?' asks the midwife as I sit up in bed eating white toast with margarine like I've never eaten before in my life.

'Grace,' I say. 'I'm calling her Grace.'

I think of Mary warbling along to the tune. *Amazing Grace, how sweet the sound that saved a wretch like me.*

Grace is an appropriate name, I think, because this little creature is the one who's going to save me.

Chapter 33

2017

Castle Moon is a seedy-looking club in the back streets of Ayia Napa. It's only six o'clock and it's obviously not open for business yet, but the black-painted door is ajar, so we walk on in. Inside it's dark and dingy. There's a strong smell of stale cigarettes and alcohol. Near the bar a cleaner is hoovering the stained carpets. At a round table a middle-aged man and a woman are sitting drinking espressos and smoking, hunched over a large blue file.

'*Ne? Boro na se voithiso?* Can I help you?' says the man, looking up suspiciously as we enter. He's portly, with a large beer belly and greasy black hair. He doesn't exactly look welcoming.

'Sorry to bother you, mate,' says Chris, 'but we're looking for our daughter. We were wondering if she'd been to your club.'

The man looks confused, so I speak more slowly. 'Grace Appleton. She's our daughter.' I take out my phone and show him the photo, tapping at the screen. 'Have you seen her? Someone said they saw her here last night.'

He takes the phone and peers at the picture of Grace. Then he hands it to the woman, who shakes her head and speaks rapidly in Greek.

'No, sorry. We don't see your daughter,' he says at last, handing me back the phone.

'What about your bar staff. Who was working last night?'

He calls to a young man who's just appeared behind the bar and he too comes over and examines the photo and after a moment shakes his head slowly. It seems as though no one at Castle Moon has ever laid eyes on Grace, though when I show them a photo of Dave, they recognise him instantly.

'He didn't pay his bar bill,' says the barman. 'We had to throw him out.'

'Well, that was a complete waste of time,' says Chris as we step outside. The sun has gone down and although it's not dark yet, there's a cool breeze wafting towards us as we head down towards the seafront where the car is parked.

'I knew it would be,' I say. 'I told you Dave was bullshitting.'

'But I don't understand.' Chris frowns as we stride along, winding our way through the tourists. 'Why would Dave make something like that up?'

'He can't bear it if he's not the centre of attention.'

Chris doesn't answer immediately. We've reached the car park and he leans on the railings and looks out at the sea. The sky is tinged with pink and a dusty yellow moon is hanging low. There are several large yachts moored in the marina. They have names like *Athena* and *Aphrodite* and *Galina*. *Funny how boats are almost always named after women*, I think vaguely, and the embryo of an idea stirs at the back of my mind, but before I have time to grasp it Chris interrupts my thoughts.

'It's nearly a whole week since Grace went missing and we're back to square one,' he says, eyes glistening with angry tears. 'We still have no idea where she is or why she's disappeared.'

'We're not exactly back to square one.' I take a deep breath. I've been dreading this moment, but Chris has a right to know.

'I need to tell you something, something I found out today, about Grace,' I say.

Chris stares at me. 'What?'

'She's pregnant.'

His eyes widen with shock and his breathing becomes ragged. For a moment I'm worried he might be about to have a heart attack. 'How do you . . . ?' he splutters.

'Maria told me. Grace found out a few weeks ago apparently. But she made Maria promise not to tell anyone.'

He clutches his chest. 'Is it Tom's?'

Why would Chris even consider that the baby wasn't Tom's? Unless . . . For a split second a horrible, unthinkable suspicion uncoils and slithers through my thoughts. What if Dino's source was right about Chris? *Impossible*, I think, consigning it to the deepest, darkest recesses of my mind.

'Well, I suppose it must be Tom's,' I say. 'Who else's?'

'I'm going to kill that piece of shit,' Chris growls. 'Do you think he knows?'

'I don't know.'

Chris fishes his phone out of his pocket. 'I can't stand this,' he says. 'I'm going to phone him and give him a piece of my mind.'

'Wait. There's something else I haven't told you yet,' I say, placing my hand over his. I swallow. There's no easy way of saying this. 'She went to see a doctor about having an abortion about a week before she went missing.'

He stares at me. 'And did she go ahead with it?'

'I don't think so. The doctor told her she would need our permission.'

'Oh God, oh God, oh God . . .' Chris clutches his head.

'That's not all,' I say. 'I spoke to the doctor this morning. He said she wasn't alone when she came to see him. She was with someone.'

'Tom?'

'No. From the description he gave I'm pretty sure it was Andreas.'

'Andreas? You mean, that kid in Grace's year, the one Maria told us about, the one she said was a junkie?'

I nod, chewing my nail and thinking of the meeting I had with the boy down by the seafront. He seemed so nervous, from the way he avoided my eyes to all his strange, nervous tics. I put it down to shyness, but perhaps it wasn't that at all. He knows more than he let on, that's for sure.

'I knew he was lying,' I say out loud.

Chris shakes his head. 'Jesus Christ, what has she got herself mixed up in?' he says, staring at me wildly. 'Do you think she's been taking drugs?'

An image of Grace lying overdosed somewhere in a pool of her own vomit crashes into my mind. I shiver, then shake my head firmly. 'I don't think so. I lived with a heroin addict for years, remember? I know the signs.'

Chris nods and breathes deeply, exhaling through his nose. 'Who knows what that little shit has done? If he's hurt Grace, I swear I'll—'

I look at my watch. 'We need to get back for Jack. Let's go and talk to him tomorrow,' I say. 'Find out what he knows.'

'Yes, but don't ring him first. We need to take him by surprise.'

It's not such a bad idea. 'Okay,' I say, taking my phone out of my pocket. Trying to stay calm, I tap in Maria's number.

'Hi, Maria, it's Joanna,' I say smoothly. 'Sorry to bother you but do you have Andreas Pavlou's address?'

'Do you think that's why she's run away?' Chris says as we drive back along the motorway towards Larnaca. 'Because she's pregnant?'

'I don't know. Maybe.' It's getting dark now and the headlights of the other cars are dazzling and distracting. I grip the wheel tightly, fighting a strange and disturbing urge to swerve the car into the oncoming traffic.

'She's just a baby herself,' Chris continues darkly. 'I can't get my head round the idea that she could have her own child.'

'I know.' I have rarely thought much about becoming a grandmother and never in my wildest nightmare did I imagine a scenario like this.

'It doesn't bear thinking about.' Chris drums his fingers on the dashboard. 'I mean, she can barely look after herself. Can you picture her as a mother?'

I can't. But then I suppose she's not much younger than I was.

Chapter 34

2001

Nobody told me it would be this hard. All she does is cry and cry. I don't get any respite. I hardly sleep. She wakes me up all through the night crying and demanding to be fed. Feeding her is so painful it makes *me* cry. My nipples are cracked and sore. My body is not my own anymore. It belongs to this tiny tyrant.

Despite it all, I love her. I love her so much it hurts. It's as if my heart is no longer inside me. As if she *is* my heart now and so it is out there in the world, unprotected and vulnerable. I worry about her night and day – that something might happen to her; that I'm not looking after her properly.

Maybe if Hakan was here, things would be different. I long for him so much – to feel his arms around me, to hear him whisper *Jojo* and tell me everything's okay.

I'm lonely too. I don't think I've ever been so lonely. Days go past when I don't speak to another adult human being. The girls from work paid a brief visit about a week ago and brought presents for Grace, but they're too busy with their own unencumbered lives to be bothered about mine. None of them have babies and I could tell that they couldn't wait to get out of my nappy-stinking house.

It will all be worth it when Hakan sees her, I tell myself. He's going to love her, I know. He'll take one look at her and realise what a mistake he's made, choosing Helen over me. With this in mind, I take a photo of Grace, in her nappy, lying on her front on her mat, and post it to him, along with a long letter detailing her weight and height, the way she can push her head and chest up now with her arms, the way she has his eyes and face shape. At the end of the letter I write, *I miss you and Grace misses you. She doesn't want to grow up without knowing her father.* I send another copy of the same photo to my mother too. I haven't completely given up on her and you never know, she might be able to shake off her depression long enough to take an interest in my life.

A couple of weeks later a short note from Hakan arrives.

Dear Jojo,

Sorry it's been so long. I hope you're okay and the baby is doing fine.

I'm coming to England next week to visit relatives. I'd like to see you and Grace if that's okay. I'll call you to arrange a time.

Love Hakan

Sunday, 24th September 2017

Chapter 35

'This must be it,' says Chris, parking outside a small semi-detached house next to a field of stubbly yellow corn. In the far distance, across the farmland, I can see part of the big salt lake and a section of the old Venetian aqueduct. Chris stares up at the house. 'It looks pretty run-down to me.'

Run-down is a bit of an understatement. The plaster is cracked and tiles are falling off the facade. The yard is full of junk too: there are bags of rubbish, an old sofa, a dismembered motorbike and a sailing boat under a tatty plastic tarpaulin. I think about what Maria told us about Andreas being a junkie and his brother being involved with the mafia, and I'm glad that we dropped Jack at Angelo's on the way here. At least I know he's safe.

'You wait here. Let me do the talking,' I say, opening the car door.

'Are you joking? No way, Jo. I'm coming with you,' Chris says firmly. 'This kid could be dangerous.'

I sigh. Chris will probably bulldoze in and spoil my strategy, which is to get Andreas to trust me and confide in me. Also, there are certain things I don't want Chris to know. Let's hope that Andreas doesn't know as much as I suspect he does. It's frustrating but I can tell from the expression on Chris's face that he's not going to back down this time.

'All right,' I nod, 'but leave the talking to me, okay?'

We pick our way up the path, through the rubbish. As we reach the door a cockroach scuttles under a dead pot plant and I shudder.

Chris rings the doorbell three times before Andreas answers.

'Hello?' he says vaguely, as if he doesn't recognise us. He looks as if he's high. The flushed skin and dry lips are a dead giveaway.

'We need to speak to you about Grace. Can we come in?' Chris says. 'I'm her dad.'

Something flickers behind his eyes as Andreas looks up slowly at Chris. 'I know who you are,' he says tersely, opening the door. I try to identify his expression. *Is it fear or guilt? No, I'm pretty sure it's hostility. Deep, intense hostility.* I guess he's heard the rumours about Chris being involved in Grace's disappearance. There's no smoke without fire. That's what people say, isn't it? And most of the time it's true, I think. But not in this case. That's what I believe. What I need to believe.

We follow him into a cramped, smelly living room. The place is chaotic, with dirty plates and glasses heaped on every available surface: the coffee table, the TV table and the floor. A video game, a first-person shooter, is on pause. And underneath the smell of BO and rotting food there's an acidic, vinegary smell that makes me certain that he's been taking drugs.

I look around the room. There's no sign that anyone else is home. 'Where's your brother? You said you lived with your brother,' I say.

He seems confused and drowsy.

'What?'

'Your brother, where is he?'

'Oh, Yiannis? He doesn't live here anymore. He's moved in with his fiancée.'

Chris and I exchange a look of relief. That makes things a lot easier.

I glance around at the room. There are pictures on the wall, old-fashioned prints of flowers and embroidered lace. They don't look like the kind of pictures a teenage boy and a young man would choose, so I'm guessing they've been left here from before their mother died. There are also a couple of photos. A picture of a woman who I'm guessing is his mother and an old photo of a hotel, a tall 1960s-style tower block with rounded balconies and *Grecian Bay Hotel* in large blue letters above the portico. 'Where's this?' I ask, taking the hotel picture from its hook and brushing off the dust.

Andreas takes the picture from me and hangs it back up. 'It's our family hotel in Famagusta, in no man's land. When the Turks invaded, my family had to flee. My grandparents lost everything. They left with just the clothes on their backs.'

I think briefly of all the people whose lives were changed

forever by the war and then I clear a space on the sofa and sit down.

'Andreas,' I say cautiously, 'we need you to explain something to us. Is that okay?'

'Sure,' he nods warily.

'I went to see Doctor Stavrides yesterday. Apparently, Grace went to see him a week or so before she disappeared. Do you know anything about that?'

His eyes widen. I watch his Adam's apple move up and down in his throat as he swallows.

He shakes his head.

'I think you do,' I say slowly, 'because, you see, Doctor Stavrides told us that she wasn't on her own. There was someone with her. And the person that was with her sounded very much like you.'

He doesn't answer immediately. He sits in the armchair tapping his thighs with his long, bony fingers.

'She made me promise not to tell anyone,' he says at last.

Chris leans forward. There's a muscle in his cheek flexing.

'Why did she tell you?'

Andreas shifts slightly, stares out of the window and then back at us. 'What?' he asks vaguely. *Drug-induced confusion or delaying tactics?* I wonder.

'Why did she tell you about the pregnancy?' Chris repeats more loudly.

'She trusted me, I suppose.'

'Are you the father of the baby?'

Andreas looks startled. Then he laughs a high-pitched nervous laugh. 'No, of course I'm not.'

'Who is the father then?' Chris asks.

Andreas gives him a sly look. 'I don't know. You tell me.'

You could cut the tension in the room with a knife. Andreas opens his mouth to speak. I have the feeling that he's about to tell us something important. But just then my phone rings, startling us all, and Chris and Andreas watch silently as I fish it out of my handbag. I glance at the screen, Dave's name flashing up, and scowl.

'Shit,' I say and stab the 'end call' icon. Trust Dave to call at such a critical moment and ruin everything.

'Who was that?' asks Chris.

'Dave.' I replace my phone in my handbag. 'We should have bought the ticket and escorted him onto the plane. That's the only way we'll ever get rid of him. Sorry about that,' I say to Andreas. 'You were about to tell us about Grace.'

'I was just going to say that—'

In my bag the phone rings again and I snatch it up angrily.

'Dave? What do you want?'

'Joanna, thank God,' he says. 'I've been calling and calling, trying to contact you.'

I bite back the expletive on the tip of my tongue. 'Listen, this is not a good time. Can I call you back?'

I can hear him breathing on the other end of the phone – and the irritating sucking sound he always makes when he runs his lips over his teeth. 'I've remembered something about Grace,' he says. 'About the night I saw her in the club. It could be important.'

'What?' I snap impatiently.

'I can't tell you over the phone. Why don't we meet somewhere? We could meet at the marina.'

'Dave, I'm kind of busy right now. I'll meet you later, okay?'

'When?'

I sigh. I very much doubt he has anything to tell me. 'Two o'clock at the marina,' I say abruptly and hang up.

'Dave again?' Chris raises his eyebrows. 'What did he want?'

'He says he remembered something else about the night he saw Grace. He's so full of bull.'

Chris sighs. 'Well, next time tell him not to come anywhere near me or I won't be held responsible for my actions. Time-wasting twat that he is.'

Andreas picks up a coaster and taps it against the coffee table, glancing from me to Chris.

'You were about to say . . . ?' I ask.

'Nothing.' He puts his hands on his knees and stares at us defiantly.

'Really?' Chris says sceptically.

'Yes, really.' Andreas flashes him another look. The look is full of deep hostility. *I didn't imagine it earlier*, I think. *He really hates Chris*.

'What would you say has happened to her, if you had to guess?' I try.

He shrugs. 'How should I know?'

I sigh. I don't think we're going to get anything more out of him. Maybe he's telling the truth. Maybe he really doesn't know anything. But I seriously doubt it. There's something suspicious about his manner. I could swear he's hiding something. I stand up and walk to the window. Looking out at the half-finished block of flats and the dry fields opposite, I remember what Dino said at our first meeting: *She's probably at a friend's house*. What if he was right?

'You don't mind if we just take a look around, do you?' I say to Andreas.

He looks alarmed. 'Um, well . . . I don't want—'

'She wasn't asking your permission,' says Chris grimly, standing up and looming over him. 'It's a good idea, Jo,' he nods at me. 'I'll have a look round down here. You do the bedrooms.'

'You're not the police,' Andreas protests. 'You can't just search my house.'

But I'm already halfway up the stairs. I can hear him behind me on his phone, speaking urgently in Greek. I hope to God that he's not calling his brother. If he is, we probably haven't got much time. I whizz around the bathroom. Not many hiding places there. Then I open a random door on the landing.

'You can't go in there.'

'Can't I, though?' I say. 'Watch me.'

I'm guessing this is Andreas's room because there's a school shirt scrunched up on the floor and school textbooks spread untidily over the desk. I look in the wardrobe, rifling through a bunch of nondescript T-shirts and jeans. Then I pull open drawers and I even duck under the bed, but find nothing but dust, a smelly T-shirt and a few balled-up tissues. Is it possible that Grace is hiding here, right under our noses? From the way Andreas is anxiously hovering I'm certain there's something here he doesn't want me to find. It's like a game of hot and cold. The more agitated he becomes, the closer I am to finding it.

When I look in the chest of drawers, I know I'm on to something because Andreas seems ready to explode with anxiety. And there, sure enough, shoved into the bottom drawer, I find bowls, spoons, tied-up condoms, syringes and a few fat plastic bags of white powder. I would have to cut the bags open to be certain, but it looks very much like the stuff Dave used to shoot up. I take the bags from the drawer and spread them out on the floor. I have no idea of the going rate, but I imagine he must have at least a few thousand pounds worth of heroin here. Anyway, it's way more than could be just for personal use.

'This stuff will kill you, you know,' I say, weighing one of the bags in my hand.

'Please . . .' he begs. 'Please don't . . .'

'It's all right. I don't really care.' I sit down on his unmade bed with a sigh. 'I'm not going to tell anybody. All I want is to find Grace.'

I feel deflated. I was so sure I would find something here that would lead me to her.

'Where is she, Andreas?' I ask wearily. 'I think you know.'

'No, I don't,' he says. He sits at his desk and stares back at me defiantly.

We're sitting there eyeballing each other, like a game of who blinks first, when there's the sound of a car pulling up outside and the car door slams, making us both jump. There's the sound of heavy footsteps on the path and then angry shouting in Greek. I can just hear Chris's voice in between the shouting, trying to sound conciliatory.

'All right, mate, calm down. I can explain.'

Andreas runs out of the room and after a couple of seconds I follow. But I freeze halfway down the stairs, because in the living room Chris is backed up against the wall and a large man is standing in the doorway, pointing a shotgun at him.

The man is tall like Andreas, over six foot, but unlike Andreas he's broad and muscular, easily as big as Chris. His hair is shaved, and he's dressed in camo. He has a hard, nonchalant expression on his face that makes me pretty sure he wouldn't think twice about pulling the trigger.

Andreas speaks to him rapidly in Greek, and the man, who I guess is his brother, answers. I catch a few words – *police, wanker* and then the name of the head of the mafia in Larnaca. At the sound of that name the hair lifts from my scalp and my throat tightens. Chris stares at me, terrified, and I stare back, frozen with fear.

'Does he speak English?' Chris asks Andreas and Andreas nods, wide-eyed. He seems almost as scared of his brother as we are.

'Look, we don't want any trouble,' Chris stammers. 'We just want to find our daughter.'

Yiannis sits down in the armchair, still pointing the gun casually at Chris. Then, slowly he swivels it, so it's aimed at me. My heart skips a beat and my knees buckle.

'Please,' I beg. 'Like he says, we just want our daughter.'

Slowly he turns so it's aimed at Chris again. His eyes are stone cold, his expression impassive.

'Do you know who I am?' he says at last and Chris shakes his head. He opens his mouth and then closes it again. He looks like a fish gasping for air. If it wasn't so terrifying, it would be comical. 'I have friends who can make your life very hard.'

'Listen, mate—'

'If you come near our house or my brother again,' he says slowly and deliberately, 'I will kill you. Do you understand?'

Chris swallows and nods. I feel my knees trembling. I'm rooted to the spot, unable to move.

'I'm sorry about your daughter,' he continues quietly. 'But my brother, he don't know where is she. So, leave him alone, all right?'

'All right,' Chris nods eagerly.

Yiannis sighs and places the gun on the floor next to him. 'Now go,' he says. 'And don't come back.'

We don't wait to be told twice.

Chapter 36

I sit in the car, breathing deeply, trying to stop the shaking that's taken over my whole body. Even Chris looks rattled. He stalls the engine as we start up, then takes the corner too quickly and the car skids and screeches as he stamps on the brakes.

'You okay?' he asks me once we're on the main road and he's sure we're not being followed.

'I think so. I've never had a gun pointed at me before.'

'Me neither,' he laughs grimly. 'That guy was scary. I think we're in over our heads, Jo.'

I stare out of the window at the betting shops and cash-for-gold places that sprung up everywhere in the wake of the economic crisis.

'Did you believe Andreas?' I ask. 'Do you believe that he doesn't know about Grace?'

Chris purses his lips and squints at the road. 'I don't know. We keep coming back to him, don't we? He was the last person to see her, and he was there at the doctor's with her. It can't be a coincidence.'

We drive past the front of Grace's school. It's Sunday and the school's closed but there must be an event on because there's a crowd of kids outside and, as we stop at the traffic lights, a group of teenage girls surge past, long brown hair flicking, shrieks of laughter. For a second, I think I see Grace amongst them and my heart flips but then the girl I thought was Grace turns her face and I see that it's not her, that she looks nothing like Grace, not really.

'Did you find anything downstairs?' I ask, ignoring the stab of pain in my chest.

'Not really, you?'

'No.' I decide not to mention the large stash of drugs I found in Andreas's bedside table. It'll only worry him, and it probably has nothing to do with Grace.

We pass the turning to the police station and Chris suddenly indicates. 'I hate to say it, but I think we should tell Dino about this,' he says.'

I know he's right. Andreas's brother is clearly a career criminal and, tough as Chris is, he's no match for someone like him. I doubt Dino will be much interested in what we have to say, seeing as he seems to have fixated on the idea that Chris is the guy he's looking for, but it's worth a try.

But as Chris is heading to the car park on the edge of town my phone rings.

It's Dave. Again.

'Where are you, Joanna?' he says, sounding aggrieved. 'I've been waiting half an hour.'

'Okay,' I sigh. 'I'm in town now. I'll be with you in a couple of minutes.' To Chris, I say, 'Can you drop me here. I forgot I said I'd meet Dave.'

Chris stops by the zebra crossing. 'Are you sure you want to bother? He's only going to waste your time again.'

'Yeah, I know, but I might as well hear what he has to say, just in case.'

Chris shrugs. 'Okay. Your call. I'll ring you when I'm finished.'

'No, it's all right,' I say. 'You don't have to bother. Don't wait for me. I'll get the bus back.'

There's just a single shred of cloud in the sky and a meagre breath of wind from the sea as I head towards the marina. A teenage boy is whizzing around on a skateboard, doing tricks, jumping up on the wall around the fountain. Families parade along the front, small children carrying balloons and mothers pushing prams. But this otherwise idyllic scene is somewhat spoiled by Dave, who is at the marina, sitting hunched on the sea wall, smoking a roll-up like some kind of malign goblin.

He glances up as I approach and grins. 'Well, you're a sight for sore eyes,' he says. 'You remind me of your mother when she was your age. She always was a good-looking woman. Mind you, she could never keep time either.'

'I thought you'd have left the country by now,' I reply tartly.

He shrugs and chucks his cigarette butt on the pavement, grinding it with his heel. 'Yeah, well, some tosser nicked all me money.'

'Oh really, again?' I raise my eyebrow.

'Yeah, really.' He looks aggrieved. 'I left it on the beach when I went for a swim and when I came back it was gone.'

'Look, Dave, I really don't have time for all your crap,' I snap. 'You said you had something to tell me about Grace. Why don't you just spit it out?'

'Have you got any money? I'm starving. I haven't had anything to eat all day.'

He's obviously still using. Where else is the money going? I feel like leaving him there. I'm tempted to push him off the wall into the water. It would be very satisfying to see his face as he tumbled backwards and to hear the splash as he hit the water. Instead I swallow my annoyance and say, 'All right then. Come with me.'

I take him to a cheap restaurant on the seafront near the old fort and watch him gobble down a plate of fish and chips like he hasn't eaten in days.

'Thanks for this, Joanna,' he says, draining the beer I've bought him. 'You're a good girl really. I always said you wasn't a selfish bitch.' *To whom?* I wonder. But at this point I'm really past caring.

'What did you remember about Grace?' I ask coldly. 'You said on the phone that you remembered something about Grace.'

He puts a forkful of fish in his mouth and chews. His lips smack together as he eats. The sound grates on my nerves and I want to scream, punch him or both. Instead I sit with my hands folded in my lap watching him, trying to hide my loathing. I'm pretty sure he hasn't remembered anything. This is all just a ruse to get me here so he can leech more money out of me.

'She was a beautiful baby, wasn't she, your Grace?' he says dreamily. 'Looked like a tiny little doll.'

'You're wasting my time,' I say, standing up.

'I saw her in Ayia Napa,' he blurts.

'You already told us that. We went and checked the club where you claimed you saw her. No one there had ever laid eyes on her. I don't believe she was ever there.'

He shrugs, looks vaguely out to sea. 'Maybe it was a different club. I can't remember. But I saw her all right. I didn't tell you that she spoke to me, did I?'

I dig my nails into my palms. He's lying, I'm sure, but I sit and listen to him anyway, to the bullshit spewing out of his mouth.

'I tried to persuade her to come home. I said, "Your mum and dad are looking for you, Grace, they're worried sick." But she didn't want to listen to me, did she? She was drunk or high on something. She shouted at me. Do you want to know what she said?'

'Not really,' I say.

But he leans forward anyway and whispers in my ear.

I walk along the seafront, my mind working overtime. After leaving Dave at his hotel my thoughts are churning and my body is full of nervous energy. I need to calm myself, so I go to the marina, head out along the jetty and lean on the railing, looking down at the sea. The water is green and restless, constantly moving, casting dancing ripples of light on the boats' hulls. The sight of the sea usually soothes me but right now I am too agitated to be comforted, and my thoughts are too confused. I know that Dave was lying about seeing Grace in Ayia Napa and what she said to him. There were too many details in his story that didn't add up. But they did speak last weekend, when he came to the house. I'm terrified that Grace knows the truth now, that he told Grace what he'd figured out or at least said enough for her to guess. Could that be why she's run away? Is *he* the reason I've lost her?

I take a deep shuddering breath and head to the bus stop. My feet feel heavy and it's an effort just putting one foot in front of the other. Everything feels as if it's slipping out of my control and I have no idea what to do about it.

When I finally get home there's no sign of Chris or Lola. Chris's van is parked outside, and the front gate has been left wide open. The gate is always closed in case Lola smells a cat or something to eat and decides to wander off so I'm guessing that Chris has taken her out for a walk. Good, it gives me time, the time I need to compose myself.

I unlock the door and kick off my flip-flops. Then I fling myself down on the sofa and close my eyes, trying to block out all the images crowding in my head. I need to focus on what really matters. And what really matters is Grace and Jack and Chris. *Whatever I do, I need to keep this family together*, I tell myself. Whatever I've done I've done to protect Chris and Grace . . . and Jack.

258

Jack!

Shit. It's five o'clock already and I said I'd pick him up from Angelo's at four. With all that's been going on I completely forgot. I rummage in my bag for my phone, expecting to find lots of missed calls from Stella. But my phone isn't there. Not in the front pocket and not in any of the other compartments. *That's weird. Where could it be?*

I sigh with annoyance and, ridiculously, feel tears springing up in my eyes. It's laughable to cry at this moment over something so trivial as a lost phone when there's so much else to cry about, but I suppose it feels like it's a symptom of something bigger – further proof that everything is slipping out of my control. *Calm down, Jo,* I say to myself. *It can't just disappear.* When did I last have it? When I was speaking to Dave on the phone in Chris's van. Please God, let me have left it there and not with Dave. No, I'm almost certain I didn't have it with me when I met Dave, I think, with a flood of relief.

I snatch Chris's keys from the pot on the hall table, head outside and open up the van. There's no sign of the phone on the seat or dashboard. So, I rummage in the side pockets and in the glove compartment. There's nothing but Chris's insurance details and a couple of CDs. Next, I look on the floor under the seats and find a pen and a chewing gum wrapper but no phone. There's only one other place it could be. I slide my hand down the back of the seats and to my intense relief I find it. But that's not all I find. There's something else lurking there, behind the seat. Something cold and metallic. Call it an instinct or a premonition, but I feel a chill as I pull it out and catch a glimmer of gold. Grace's necklace – the one Tom gave her for her sixteenth birthday, the one she was wearing on the morning she went missing. It takes me a couple of seconds to grasp the significance of finding it here, and then it hits me like a sledgehammer.

And my heart stops.

Chapter 37

2001

'Your daddy's coming,' I say as I change Grace's nappy.

She wriggles her chubby little legs and smiles at me. I know she's not supposed to be able to smile at this age, but I could swear she does – the little secret smile she saves just for me.

I laugh for pure joy and kiss her belly. The skin there is so smooth and smells so good.

'Your daddy's going to love you,' I coo. 'And I love you too.' It's true. I do love her. Love has snuck up on me and taken me by surprise. And it's a fierce love, a strong love, a kind I haven't felt before, perhaps stronger even than my love for Hakan.

I throw the nappy in the bin. I don't mind the smell at all. I don't mind anything at the moment. I'm so happy I could burst. Hakan is coming and he'll be here within a few days. I don't even mind that Grace's sleepsuit is soiled and I'm going to have to change it and that maybe it'll be stained. None of that matters because Hakan is coming. I'm so happy I'm humming a tune to myself as I tug her out of the suit, and then the doorbell rings.

It's Hakan already, I think, my heart leaping in my chest. Maybe he's come early to surprise me. Trembling with excitement, I rush to the door and fling it open.

It's not Hakan, of course. But it's Dave, slouching in the doorway, his hands thrust deep in his pockets like he's fiddling with his balls. 'Hi there, Joanna,' he says with a nasty smile.

'What are you doing here?' I ask, swallowing my disappointment. *It doesn't matter*, I tell myself. *Hakan will be here soon*. I can bear anything, knowing that. I can even bear Dave.

He stares at me. 'Well, since you ask, my DVD player's gone missing . . . amongst other things.' He peers round me into the living room. 'Yeah, I thought so. There it is. Blimey, you've got a nerve, haven't you?'

He pushes past me into the room and gives me a smile that isn't a smile. 'You really are a thieving little toerag, Joanna,' he says.

I breathe in deeply. I don't want to get into an argument right now. Not when I was having such a good day.

'You don't need it anyway. You've got two,' I point out.

'Yeah, well, the other one's broken, isn't it?' he says, heading over to the TV and unplugging the DVD player.

'I'm pretty sure it's Mum's but go ahead and take it if you must,' I say. I just want him out of here. I don't want him anywhere near Grace and I definitely don't want him to meet Hakan. Just his presence feels polluting.

But Dave is in no hurry to leave. He takes off his jacket, slings it over the arm of the sofa and plonks himself down. Then he looks down at Grace who's wriggling around on the floor in her nappy.

'So, this is Grace, is it?' he says. 'Pretty little thing, isn't she?' He frowns. 'She'll get cold like that. Why don't you put more clothes on her?'

'I was just changing her,' I mutter, irritated. 'Like you're the expert on looking after a baby all of a sudden.' *Dave is the last person in the world I need childcare tips from*, I think.

'Well, I know enough not to let them freeze to death,' he shrugs. He watches me balefully while I put on a fresh sleepsuit and do up the poppers.

'I need a slash,' he announces. 'Where's your toilet?'

'Through the kitchen.'

When he comes back, he's carrying a drill and a food mixer.

'I believe these are mine too,' he says.

I don't answer. What's the point? He's going to take them anyway, whatever I say.

Once Dave is gone, along with the DVD player, the drill, the food mixer and the smell of booze and fags, I rock Grace to sleep. Then I clean the whole flat from top to toe. I want the place to be spotless for when Hakan arrives. I change the sheets on the bed, and I put Grace in her pram and head out to the shopping centre. What Dave doesn't know is that while he was in the toilet, I extracted the wallet from his jacket and took out a few notes. He'd only waste it on booze or drugs. Isn't it better I spend it on clothes for Grace?

In town I stop at Mothercare to buy Gracie some sleepsuits and a new outfit: an adorable cream silk dress with embroidered flowers and a matching cardigan. When Hakan sees her in this he'll just have to fall in love. He won't be able to help himself. I pop into the shop next door and get some clothes for myself too: a slinky blue dress that shows off my curves, new jeans and a red off-the-shoulder top. I try them on in the changing room, touching the smooth skin on my neck and collarbone and remembering how it felt when Hakan kissed me there.

Back at home, I stand in front of the mirror, swishing round and trying to look sexy. I'll wear the jeans when Hakan comes, I decide. I don't want it to look like I've tried too hard. I examine my face from every angle to see which expression is most flattering, and I rehearse what I'll say and do when he arrives. What I want to do is throw myself into his arms and tell him how much I've missed him but that might be too intense. I don't want to scare him away.

'Did you have a good flight?' I say coolly to my reflection. *No, that's too boring.*

'Well, fancy meeting you here.' *Cringe.*

It's probably best to just play it by ear.

I don't get too long to think about it because Grace wakes up and starts crying. I'm feeding her in front of the telly watching *Fifteen to One*, shouting the answers at the screen, when the phone rings. I turn down the volume on the TV, count to five and pick it up.

'Hello,' I say trying to make my voice sound low and throaty, just in case it's him.

It is him.

'Er, Jo, hi. This is Hakan.' His voice, so familiar, cuts through me to my heart.

'Yes. Where are you? When are you coming? I could come and meet you at the airport if you like.' I pause for breath, trying not to sound too eager.

There's a short silence at the other end of the line. 'Listen, there's been a problem, Jo. I'm sorry but I'm not going to be able to make it.'

Chapter 38

2017

The chain coils itself around my fingers.

The blue stone catching the light winks at me like an evil eye. I don't want to believe this. But there's no denying the evidence of my own eyes. It's the same necklace Grace was wearing on the day she went missing – the one I saw in the photo that Andreas took of her that morning. So, how has it ended up in Chris's van? I thought I had everything figured out after what Dave said. But what if I'm wrong? What if she hasn't run away at all?

It's hard to breathe. The air inside the van feels as if it's been poisoned. How could he have done this to her? To us? Chris of all people.

Betrayal. It tastes like bile in my mouth and I heave, doubling over and retching. And yet, I reflect, as I wipe my mouth, trying to gather my thoughts, I should be used to it by now. It's not the first time I've been betrayed by the person I trust most in the world.

I must have imagined it. I must have imagined the necklace in the photo. Anything else is inconceivable. But the image is stamped in my mind and I can't erase it, no matter how much I try. I can see it so clearly, Grace smiling uncertainly at Andreas behind the camera, her hand to her throat, fingering the gold chain around her neck. *The one in my hands right now.* I'm certain I saw it.

I can't have seen it.

But I did.

My thoughts seesaw backwards and forwards like this. And I'm still sitting here in the passenger seat of the van, crippled by indecision and fear, when there's a sharp rap at the window. I start and stare out at Chris, his face pressed against the pane, peering in. My heart pounding out of my chest, I shove the necklace into my pocket. *Has he noticed it?* If he has, he gives no sign.

'What are you doing?' he asks as I climb out of the van.

I can't answer. I feel as if I'm about to choke. And for a moment I am overwhelmed with blind rage. I want to pound his face with my fists and demand to know why he's been lying and what he's done to Grace. With an effort of will, I pull myself together. He can't know that I know. I'm not sure how he'll react. He's never lifted a finger to me before and it's hard to imagine that he could hurt me, but then again, I never in my wildest dreams imagined that he could hurt Grace either and it looks like I'm wrong about that.

'My phone.' I force myself to smile. 'I left it in the van.'

'Oh.' He closes the front gate after us and lets Lola off the lead.

267

'I was going to ring Stella,' I continue. 'I need to go and pick up Jack.'

If I can get out of the house, I think, I can safely ring Dino without Chris overhearing me. I close my eyes, trying not to think about what it will do to Jack if his dad is guilty. *It will destroy him,* I think. But I can't worry about that now or else I'll go mad.

'Oh, didn't I tell you? Stella rang already,' Chris says casually. 'She said she would drop him back herself this evening. They've gone bowling and then she said she was going to take them to Good Burger for tea.'

'Oh, that's nice of her,' I say automatically but inwardly I'm cursing. It means I'll have to wait for another opportunity to ring the police. In the meantime, I need to appear as normal as possible.

'Would you like a cup of tea?' I ask, heading to the kitchen and filling the kettle from the water cooler. I think I'm doing a good impression of being calm but when Chris comes and stands close behind me, I nearly jump out of my skin.

'You're shaking, Jo,' he says. 'Are you ill? Here, let me. You sit yourself down.' He rubs my shoulders gently and I suppress a shudder.

'Now you mention it, I'm not feeling too good,' I say, letting him shepherd me to the kitchen table and into a chair. 'I think it's all just been a bit much. It's been a pretty stressful day – a stressful week.'

'What did Dave have to say for himself?' Chris asks, switching on the kettle.

'Oh, you know, the same old shit. He just wanted money.'

'You didn't give him any, I hope?'

'I bought him a cheap flight back to the UK. One way. I thought if I gave him money, he'd only waste it.'

Chris nods, pours the boiling water into cups and hands me one. I hold it in my trembling hands and take a sip, fighting off an urge to gag.

'I spoke to Dino about Andreas,' he says.

Shit, yes. I should have asked about that. It looks odd that I haven't. 'What did he say?'

He shrugs and frowns. 'He said he'll look into it. but I'm not sure how seriously he took it. He's still got it in for me. He doesn't say it, but I can tell by the way he looks at me.'

He sits opposite me, reaching out across the table and touching my hand. It takes all my self-control not to shrink away from him. It takes a huge effort of will not to call him out for the hypocrite he is.

'You should go to bed, Jo. You look really ill,' he says, stroking my palm with his thumb.

'Yeah, I will soon.'

He smiles wanly. 'It's going to be okay, you know. We're going to get through this together. We'll find a way to get Grace back. You and me – the A team.'

I force myself to look into his eyes, those eyes I've always trusted so much. How could I have been so wrong about him? How could I have let Grace down so badly?

'Yeah,' I smile weakly. I still can't really believe that Chris could have done this. But what alternative is there?

I withdraw my hand. What the hell am I going to do? I know the answer to that, of course. I have to tell the police about what I've found. But before I do, before I betray my husband and risk destroying my family, I need to talk to Andreas, to see the photo again to make absolutely certain that Grace was wearing the necklace that morning – that this isn't one huge mistake. But how to go and talk to Andreas without Chris insisting on coming?

Right now, I feel as if the walls are closing in on me and all I want to do is get away from him, get out of this room. After a couple of minutes, I murmur something about needing the loo, escape upstairs and lock myself in the bathroom. Sitting on the toilet lid, I turn on the tap and let the water run and, with shaking hands, I message Stella.

> *Please can Jack stay the night with you?*

She messages back almost immediately.

> *Sure. no problem. Are you okay hun?*

> *Yes, will explain later. Thank you xx*

It's hard to believe Chris would ever harm Jack, but I'm starting to doubt my own judgement in the light of the evidence and at least now I can be sure Jack will be safe for the night.

'Stella said the boys were having fun together, so Jack is going

270

to stay the night again,' I tell Chris as I come back into the living room.

'Okay.' Chris shrugs and smiles.

Now all I need to do is to wait for an opportunity to get out of the house without him noticing. But that proves easier said than done. Chris is unusually attentive this evening. He insists on cooking me a chicken curry and watches me as I force it down, trying not to gag. Then he settles down for the evening in front of the TV, right by the front window where he has a view of the door and of my car.

'Come and sit next to me,' he says, patting the space on the sofa next to him. 'Let's just try and relax for an hour or two. It won't help Grace if we both make ourselves ill with worry.'

Reluctantly, I perch on the sofa in front of the TV and stare blankly at the screen. There's some kind of documentary about earthquakes and tsunamis on. But I'm not really paying attention. The images wash over me, and the droning voice of the presenter is just a meaningless sound. I do my best to feign interest while all the time I'm feeling more and more frustrated and on edge until Chris finally suggests we go to bed.

In bed I lie awake, rigid with fear and anxiety, waiting for Chris to fall asleep. But he's restless. He tosses and turns, wrestling with the pillow and sighing loudly. It's almost as if he's guessed what's on my mind. And I've practically given up hope that he'll ever go to sleep when finally, the sound of his breathing changes subtly.

'Chris?' I whisper, just to make sure.

No answer.

Slowly, not daring to breathe, I peel back the cover and climb out of bed. Fumbling my way to the chair in the dark, I pull on the T-shirt and shorts I left there. But as I'm heading towards the door, I trip on a pair of Chris's shoes.

My heart nearly explodes in my chest as Chris gives a sudden snort and rolls over. 'What you doing, Jo?' he mumbles.

'Nothing. I just need the loo. Go back to sleep.'

In the en-suite I sit on the edge of the bath, waiting and praying that Chris will just go back to sleep. I count to a hundred in my head, trying to stop the shaking that has over-taken me. And by the time I emerge Chris is snoring gently. Glancing over at his large, dark shape in the bed, I creep past to the door. It opens with a whine which seems unbearably loud in the stillness of the night and I freeze with my hand on the handle, waiting, holding my breath. To my relief, Chris shifts a little but doesn't wake up. Exhaling slowly, I tiptoe as quickly as I can across the landing, past Jack's room and down the stairs. I've just reached the front door when I hear heavy footsteps on the landing.

Shit.

I fumble with the lock on the door and yank it open.

'Jo? Where you going?' Chris plods down the stairs, rubbing his eyes and blinking at me in surprise. 'Come back to bed.'

I don't answer. It's too late for explanations now. If I'm going to do this, I need to be quick. Heart pounding out of my chest, I escape outside and slam the door shut behind me. Then I make a dash for the car. I'm just starting up the engine as Chris comes running down the path and out of the gate.

'Jo!' he shouts, banging on the bonnet. 'What the hell?!'

Revving the engine wildly, I back up and swerve around him. And the last thing I see before I screech around the corner is Chris lit up in my taillights and the look of anger and astonishment on his face.

Twenty minutes later I'm parked outside Andreas's house. It's three in the morning and very dark. The one street lamp on the corner isn't working and the only light comes from the moon and the twinkling lights on the highway far away across the farmland opposite. I switch off the engine and sit at the wheel, trying to steady my nerves. At least Chris hasn't followed me, though he has been constantly ringing my phone. But it's not just Chris I'm worried about. I'm not sure who I want to see less right now, Chris or Andreas's brother. I glance nervously up at the house. The lights are all out and it's slightly reassuring to note that there's no sign of the brother's car outside.

I think about Yiannis, his weary, stone-grey eyes, the way he pointed the gun at Chris so casually, like he uses it all the time, and fear twists in my gut. But the fear that Chris is guilty is even greater. And even greater than that is the fear of not knowing. I try to muster my courage. *I have to do this. I have to know.*

Once my breathing has steadied, I climb out of the car, walk up to the front door and ring the doorbell. I wait for what seems like ages before Andreas finally appears, standing there in shorts and a T-shirt, his face pale in the dim light, a phone hanging limply in his hand. He looks skinny and weak and scared.

'You again!' he exclaims. 'This is harassment. I'm calling my brother.' And he starts tapping at his phone.

'Wait, Andreas,' I say hurriedly. 'Please, don't do that. I just want to talk.'

He hesitates, finger poised over the screen, then he sighs and to my intense relief slots it back in his pocket. 'Is your husband with you?' he asks, looking warily over my shoulder at the car.

'No, I'm here on my own. I promise.'

He seems to relax a little when he hears that. 'Well, what do you want?'

'Can I come in?'

He sighs and reluctantly stands back to let me in.

'What do you want?' he repeats in the living room, standing opposite me, his arms folded defensively across his chest.

'That photo you showed me of Grace, the one you took for the talent show. I need to see it.'

He stares at me. 'It's three o'clock in the morning. *That's* what you've woken me up for? Do you have to see it now?'

'It's really important. Please.'

'Okay,' he shrugs. "He takes out his phone, swipes with his finger along the screen and hands it to me. 'There. But I don't understand. Why do you need to see it?'

I ignore his question and peer at the image of Grace and a spasm of almost physical pain grips my body. I clutch the phone tightly, trying to breathe. So, I didn't imagine it. The necklace is there, around her neck, plain as day. The conclusion is unavoidable. Grace was in Chris's van at some point on Monday after I dropped her at school and he's been lying about it. And there can be only one reason why he would lie about something so serious. It must be true. He must have hurt my baby girl. I feel like I'm about to faint. My legs buckle and I sink onto the sofa.

Dimly, I'm aware that Andreas is hovering over me, long arms dangling ineffectually. 'What's wrong, Mrs Joanna? Are you okay?' he asks.

For a moment I can't speak.

'Can I get you something? A drink maybe?'

'No, no, it's okay. I'm okay.' I bat his offers away impatiently. 'Did Grace ever talk to you about anything . . .' I inhale deeply. It's hard to get the words out. Each word feels sharp and painful as if I'm regurgitating broken glass. 'Did she ever say anything about her stepfather?'

Andreas takes a step back. There's no mistaking the sudden change in his manner and my heart plummets.

'Yes, she did,' he says quietly.

So here it is. The moment of truth. There's a part of me that wants to run away, a part of me that doesn't want to hear the truth. 'What did she say?' I force myself to ask.

He frowns angrily. 'You must know. Don't try and tell me you don't.'

'Know what?' I whisper.

Andreas stares at me. 'That he was abusing her, of course.'

275

Monday, 25th September 2017

Chapter 39

2001

This can't be happening. He can't do this to me. He can't build my hopes up like this and then dash them completely as if I'm nobody. As if I'm nothing.

'So when will you come?' I ask.

'I don't know, Jo,' Hakan sighs. 'It's difficult. Helen's not very well. I can't leave her on her own with the baby. I'm not going to be able to come.'

Silence. The deafening sound of my dreams crashing and burning.

'But when she's better, you'll come?'

'I don't know. I can't really think about that right now.'

Silence.

'But you love me?' My voice rises in pitch and becomes a whine. I hate the sound of it.

Hakan gives a deep sigh at the other end of the line. 'I loved you, yes. But I have to put Helen and the kids first. Look, I'm sorry, Jo. I've got to go.'

He mumbles something vague about an appointment and rings off. I call him back immediately but there's no answer.

I punch in the numbers again, hot tears stinging the back of my eyes. Still no answer. So, I try again. On the fourth try his phone's been switched off.

'Fuck!'

With a cry of rage and frustration I fling the phone across the room and it smashes into the wall.

In her Moses basket, startled by the noise, Grace wakes up and starts crying. A low grizzly cry at first.

'Shh . . . Gracie,' I say. 'Be quiet, please, baby.' But she carries on crying, getting steadily louder until she's screaming, her little face red with fury, the sound as piercing as an electric drill. I stride angrily over to her Moses basket and pick her up, rocking her backwards and forwards.

'It's okay, Gracie,' I say as gently as I can. 'It's okay.'

But it's not okay. Hakan's not coming and he may never come. I start crying hopelessly as this sinks in. My tears seem to come from deep in my gut and my whole belly shakes. They run down my cheeks, dropping onto Grace's face and mingling with her tears. *He never really loved me*, I think. *He can't have. He cares more about Helen and Adam and his new baby than he does about me and Gracie.*

Grace carries on crying inconsolably. It's as if, somehow, she understands what's happened. I unhook my bra and try to feed her, but she refuses to latch on. Her little face scrunches up in disgust and rage and she turns away from me, crying loudly.

'Come on, Gracie, please,' I beg. 'Please stop.'

But she can't or won't stop. She carries on wailing for hours. I try everything I can to stop her. I try singing to her softly. I try burping her to get rid of wind, the way the health visitor showed me. I even try shouting at her to shock her into silence. That works for a second as she blinks at me in shock, but then her lip trembles and she screams even louder, opening her toothless mouth wide until it seems all I can see is her mouth red and raw and accusing. And finally, I can't stand it anymore, so I place her back in her Moses basket, carry her upstairs and shut the door firmly.

Downstairs I turn on the stereo very loud to drown out the sound of her wailing and I try ringing Hakan one more time. But his phone is still off the hook. It can't be a coincidence, I think. He must have left it off deliberately. *He doesn't love me anymore. He just wants me out of his life.* All the anger I felt earlier turns to despair and I take out the bottle of vodka that Tessie bought me on her holiday in Russia. I take a slug straight from the bottle. It tastes disgusting, but I can feel it numbing the pain, fogging my head. So, I drink until I can't drink anymore and curl up on the kitchen floor sobbing.

Chapter 40

2017

I knew what Andreas was going to say, of course, but it's still a massive shock hearing the words spoken out loud. Is he right? *Did* I know? Was there a small part of me that knew? I examine my conscience. There are many things I've done and not done in my life, many lines I've crossed and ways in which I am guilty. But I'm not guilty of that. I can honestly say I never suspected that Chris was hurting Grace, not for a single moment. But how could I have missed something so momentous – so horrendous – right under my nose?

It can't be true. It just can't be.

'Are you sure? She told you she was being abused by her stepfather?' I ask. 'She actually said those words?'

He thinks for a moment. 'Well, no, not those exact words. She was very upset naturally. She didn't really want to talk about it.'

'What did she say? What were her exact words?' I insist.

He frowns. 'I don't remember. She said her childhood had been stolen from her or something like that. She said she couldn't stand being at home anymore – that she'd been betrayed by the one person who she should be able to trust.'

'Do you think he had anything to do with her disappearance? Do you think it's possible that he's . . . hurt her?'

Something very subtle shifts in his manner. 'Maybe,' he says vaguely. 'I don't know.' He walks over to the window and looks out, fiddling nervously with the curtains.

I watch him carefully. Something doesn't fit, and I'm struck once again by the conviction that this boy is lying to me.

I pick up his phone and examine the photo.

At that moment I'm hit by an idea so blindingly simple I'm amazed I didn't think of it before. Glancing over at Andreas, still standing by the window, I rapidly jab the icon in the corner of the screen before he notices. Then I select 'Details'.

'Hey, what are you doing?' exclaims Andreas. And he lunges at me, trying to grab the phone, but not before I've seen enough to know that I'm right. It's all there. The size, format and resolution of the photograph. And the date it was created.

10/9/2017.

'That's my phone. It's private. You can't use it without me,' Andreas protests. I don't answer. I'm too busy thinking.

Of course. How could I not have realised? How could I ever have doubted Chris? This photograph with the necklace wasn't taken on Monday morning. It was taken more than a week earlier which means that Grace could have dropped the necklace in Chris's van sometime last week. But if Chris is innocent and he isn't the one who betrayed her trust or committed a crime . . . I turn all this over in my head, trying to order my frantic, scattered thoughts.

There's a long silence. I stare at the marble floor tiles, chipped in places, at the dust collecting in the corners of the room.

'Why did you lie?' I ask at last.

'I don't know what you mean,' he says.

'You didn't take this photo on Monday morning. You took it a week earlier.'

His eyes dart nervously from side to side. 'I must have made a mistake. Shown you the wrong picture.'

'So, where's the photo you did take?'

He scrolls through his phone, getting agitated. He knows he's not going to find it. 'I must have deleted it,' he says at last.

I think about what Maria said on Tuesday morning outside the gym. She said she thought he'd given her a phone. What if she had been right about that all along?

'You gave her a phone that morning. Why?' I say out loud. 'Did you swap it for her phone?'

He doesn't answer, just stares sullenly at the floor. And I'm gripped by another idea.

I snatch up his phone so that he can't ring his brother and make a dash for his room. I'm more than halfway up the stairs before Andreas catches up and tries to grab me. But I slip out of his grasp, pushing him away from me, and he tumbles backwards down the stairs. I hesitate for only a second, wondering if I should check he's okay.

Then I lurch into his room, shutting and locking the door. Andreas can't have hurt himself too badly because within a few seconds he's hammering furiously on the door.

'Mrs Joanna, let me in,' he demands.

Ignoring him, I make a beeline for the drawer where I found the heroin. I was so distracted the other day by my discovery, I didn't think to examine the entire contents. Now I wonder, *is there something else inside there, something I missed?* I wrench the drawer completely out and tip everything onto the floor. And there, sure enough, amongst all the junk, I find what I'm looking for.

A phone. It's just an ordinary black phone, a standard model. And one phone can look very much like another, I suppose, but Grace's has a distinctive crack like a spider's web in the right-hand corner of the screen. We hadn't got around to fixing it.

This phone has an identical crack in exactly the same place.

Chapter 41

Andreas has given up banging on the bedroom door and is slumped on the floor with his back to the wall when I finally open it.

I brandish the phone in his face.

'This is Grace's,' I say. 'Why is it in your bedroom?'

He doesn't answer but from the defeated look on his face I know that I'm right.

'She gave it to you, didn't she?' I persist, squatting down beside him on the floor. 'She knew there was no point in keeping her own phone. If she used it, the police would easily be able to track her. Did you give her a different phone in exchange? Is that what Maria saw you give her?'

Still no answer. He wraps his arms round his legs and buries his face in his knees.

'I think you helped her run away,' I say more gently. 'You know where she is, don't you? Where is she, Andreas?'

'I don't know,' he mumbles.

I don't believe him, not for a second. But it doesn't matter. I've got Grace's phone and I'm willing to bet I'll find the answers I'm seeking on it.

I press the power button and am surprised to find that it's still charged. Andreas doesn't seem worried. Maybe he's given up or maybe he assumes that I won't be able to get in because the phone is password protected.

I'm not at all sure that I will, but I'm hoping that she hasn't changed her password since I last borrowed her phone. I tap in the numbers and letters praying that I'm right.

And, just like that, I'm in.

I stand up, carry the phone downstairs, away from Andreas, and sit in the kitchen, tapping on the messages icon.

It's all there, all the calls and messages she sent in the few days before her disappearance. With a mixture of excitement and trepidation, I scroll through them backwards in time. The last was to Tom on Sunday evening at nine thirty. *Tom where are u?* she wrote.

There was no reply.

It fits with what he told us about Sunday evening, I think.

Further back, there are more messages to and from Tom. Mainly arranging where and when to meet. There's no sexting, thank God, though she has sent him a photo of herself in a bikini drinking what looks like a cocktail.

There are only two messages to Andreas a couple of weeks ago. *See you at 4pm.* And then *Thank you* with a heart emoji. I'm guessing that was when they went to see Dr Stavrides together.

287

As well as the messages to Andreas, there are lots of messages to Maria and other friends. I trawl through them, trying to make sense of the jumble of seemingly innocent, silly teenage banter. But there's nothing that gives me any clue to where she could be.

'Have you found anything?'

Andreas has come downstairs and he sits opposite me, taking out a pack of cigarettes and lighting one. He's trying to appear nonchalant, but I notice that his hands are shaking.

'Where is she, Andreas?' I ask again.

He frowns. 'I told you already. I don't know.' He stands up, stubbing out his cigarette and looking pointedly at his watch. 'Anyway, I'm sorry but I need to go to bed. I've got school tomorrow.'

I'm certain that he's lying. But how to get the truth out of him? I could threaten him with the police, I suppose, but that would mean answering some awkward questions myself.

I pick up the phone again. There must be something, something I've missed. I open her internet browser and a Wikipedia page pops up. It's about Varosha.

Of course, Varosha, I think excitedly. I click on the link and read.

> *Varosha is an abandoned Southern quarter of the Cypriot city of Famagusta. Before the Turkish invasion of Cyprus in 1974 it was the modern tourist area of the city. Its inhabitants fled during the invasion and it has remained abandoned ever since.*

I remember the day we visited the Roman ruins at Salamis and then afterwards went to the beach at Varosha to look at the empty city. Grace had been distinctly unimpressed. 'A load of old falling-down buildings, big deal,' was her grumpy teenager verdict. So why the sudden interest now? Alongside the text there are several photos of tall, empty apartment blocks and abandoned hotels. I look at them thoughtfully. They remind me of something.

'Where was your family hotel again?' I ask Andreas. He looks startled. 'What?' His reaction is so stark and obvious that I know I'm on to something. Before he can stop me, I run into the living room and snatch the picture off the wall.

I slap it down on the table in front of him.

'Your family hotel,' I say. 'It was in Varosha, wasn't it?'

His eyes widen but he stays stubbornly silent.

'Grace is in Varosha, isn't she?'

He doesn't meet my eyes. 'I don't know,' he says.

I pick up my phone. It's time to put the pressure on, call his bluff. 'Well, in that case, I'll ring the police,' I declare. 'I think they'll be interested to know what I found in the drawer in your bedroom.'

Andreas looks alarmed. 'Please don't do that . . .'

I swipe the screen and scroll through the names, slowly and deliberately. 'Here it is,' I say, my finger hovering. 'Detective Dino Markides.'

He tries to grab the phone from me. 'Okay, okay. Maybe I can help you,' he says.

I slide the phone back in my pocket. 'Look, I don't know exactly what Grace has told you,' I say more gently. 'I just want to talk to her, that's all. I'm not going to force her to come home if she doesn't want to, I promise.'

He stares at the kitchen tiles. Then he raises his head and looks searchingly into my eyes. 'You promise?'

'I promise.'

'Okay,' he says, giving a big sigh. 'I'll take you to her.'

Chapter 42

I wait in the car while Andreas gets dressed. I can hardly believe this is finally happening. He knows where Grace is. He's going to take me there. I'm so close now. I pray he doesn't change his mind.

Please let her be safe and well, I say to myself. *Please let her be safe and well*. I repeat this over and over in my head like a mantra. Right now, I really don't care about anything else.

While I wait for Andreas I fiddle with Grace's phone. I click on an icon at the corner of the screen, bringing up her internet search history, scrolling past the Varosha tab.

The list is long and comprehensive, every little search marked: Facebook login, Snapchat login, Instagram, synonym for fate. Spark notes for *Romeo and Juliet*, Wikipedia, searches for various artists on YouTube, searches ranging from Superorganism to Bob Dylan.

I scroll down further, and a search immediately leaps out at me, made at five p.m. on Saturday.

Gloucestershire Echo. 'Body of baby found in local beauty spot'.

Hands trembling, I click on the link and the article appears on the screen.

At the top there's a split-screen photo, two pictures of the same lake. One is a promotional shot on a sunny day, silver water sparkling, spring flowers and rushes fringing the banks. The other is of the same lake two weeks ago. The sky is full of dark grey clouds which are reflected in the water. The area has been cordoned off and in the foreground men in white jumpsuits are milling around.

There's a café with a terrace built on stilts over the water in the background. I stare at the dark, deep water. For a second, it feels as if I'm submerged in that water, as if I'm drowning – drowning in thick murky water.

I force myself to read the article.

BODY OF BABY FOUND
IN LOCAL BEAUTY SPOT

Fishermen at Childon Water Park made a gruesome discovery yesterday, when they found the remains of a four-month-old baby in the boating lake. The remains, which were weighted down with bricks and wrapped in a plastic bag, appear to be at least ten years old, police have revealed, but they have refused to speculate as to whether they could be the remains of baby Daisy Cooper, who went missing from outside her house in 2001, sparking a nationwide hunt.

At the time several people of interest were questioned, including Daisy's father, Gerald Cooper . . .

I can't read any more. Blackness is curling at the edge of my mind. I feel as if I'm about to faint. I hold on to the edge of the dashboard waiting for the dizziness to pass.

'What is it?' asks Andreas as he climbs into the car.

'Nothing,' I say, fighting a wave of nausea. I close the page quickly so that he can't read it and try to steady my breathing.

But it's far from nothing. This is it. There can be no doubt now. I know why Grace was reading this article and I know why she's run away.

I've buried the past for so long I'd almost let myself forget what happened all those years ago. But, if I'm honest, a part of me has always known that this day would come. It's the day of reckoning, the day I have to face the terrible things I've done. And I can't shake the feeling that I'm being punished. I'm being punished, and the punishment is almost biblical in its ferocity. An eye for an eye, a tooth for a tooth. A child for a child.

Chapter 43

'Have you got your passport?' Andreas asks.

I try to gather my shattered thoughts. 'Er, yes, I think so,' I say shakily. I rummage in my bag and find the passport still in the front pocket from my visit to the North a few days ago. 'But Grace didn't have her passport with her. We checked.'

Andreas shrugs. 'We didn't use the border crossing. She knew the police would easily find her if she did.'

I start up the engine and drive out towards the main road, thinking about his front yard, the shabby tarpaulin.

'Of course. Your boat. You went around the coast by sea.'

'Yes.'

'But how exactly? There are guards posted at the beach.' I'm not sure if there are guards on the Greek side of the border but I remember seeing one in the North when we went to Famagusta beach a few months ago. A bored-looking Turkish soldier, not much older than Grace, standing in a sentry box, staring out to sea.

Andreas taps his fingers on the dashboard. 'I met her on the beach near the power station. There's never anyone there. We sailed far out so the guards wouldn't see us and then came in again when we were safely on the other side. It was easy.'

We're on the motorway now. The road is virtually empty, just a couple of other cars on the road, drunk drivers crawling home. We drive on through scrubby farmland, the skeletons of old farm machinery lit up by our headlights. I think about them sailing out at night and I think about the marina in Ayia Napa, all the boats with women's names.

'*Marilena*. It's the name of your boat, isn't it?' I say with a sudden flash of understanding.

Andreas stares straight ahead at the road. 'What? Oh, yeah, we named it after our mother.'

'So that's why Grace had *Marilena* written on that piece of paper,' I murmur, more to myself than to Andreas.

Andreas doesn't answer. I don't think he's really listening. Our headlights light up the billboards at the side of the road. Adverts for fast food restaurants and university courses – pictures of bright-eyed, clean-cut young people wearing mortar boards.

'Why did you help her?' I ask.

'She's my friend and anyway, I couldn't let him keep hurting her.'

He means Chris, I suppose.

'It was you who told the newspaper that Grace was afraid of her stepdad,' I realise.

He nods. 'Yeah. I could have said more. I wish I had.'

'Grace's dad was not abusing her,' I say firmly. 'When we see her, she'll tell you that herself.' I drive on, battling a queasy mixture of emotions. On the one hand, I'm relieved that I was right about Chris being a good man, a good father. On the other, I'm angry with Grace for letting Andreas believe something so terrible. But underlying both these feelings is a deep vein of guilt. And I'm appalled to contemplate what Grace must be going through, to think that letting Andreas believe Chris had abused her was preferable to telling the truth.

We drive the rest of the way to the border in silence, each lost in our own thoughts. When we arrive, I park and climb out to show our passports to the border official. If the guard thinks it strange that an unrelated middle-aged English woman and a Greek teenage boy are travelling alone in the middle of the night, he shows no curiosity.

'Just carry on straight towards Famagusta,' says Andreas as I get back in the car.

Grey light is just beginning to seep into the sky as we drive past the thick stone Venetian walls that surround the old city centre of Famagusta. We reach a roundabout and pass a huge bronze statue of Atatürk's head and then take the turning to the beach.

We park near the beach opposite a closed-up kiosk with spades and inflatables outside and look up at the abandoned tower blocks.

'What kind of place is this for a young girl?' I shiver. I'm thinking of the stories I've heard of poisonous snakes thriving in the long dry grass and of packs of wild dogs prowling the area.

'It was Grace's idea,' Andreas says. 'It's the only place she was sure she wouldn't be found.'

'But aren't there lots of Turkish soldiers here? There's a barracks, isn't there?'

Andreas shrugs as he climbs out of the car. 'If you're careful, you can easily avoid them,' he says, heading for the barrier.

The whole area is fenced off and barricaded with rusted-up old oil drums. There's a red sign with a picture of a soldier that says 'Entry forbidden' in four different languages.

Ignoring the warning, Andreas ducks down and crawls through a gap under the fence.

'Come on,' he hisses, holding the wire up for me. I hesitate, worried that someone will see us, but it's early morning and there's no one about, so I scramble through after him, scratching myself on the fence in the process. A trickle of blood runs down the back of my leg. I ignore it and look around.

Row upon row of tower blocks stand empty and crumbling, looming over us in the early morning light. Their windows gape silently like wounds as we walk down the old, potholed road. Weeds nudge their way up through the cracks and rusted-up cans are strewn amongst them. Something scuttles through the grass. I try not to think about what it could be.

'How much further?' I ask Andreas. He's walking fast, striding ahead of me, and I'm struggling to keep up with him as we wind our way through a maze of streets further back from the beach. Most of the houses here are older, colonial buildings made of sandstone, shutters hanging off at angles.

'Here,' says Andreas suddenly. And I look up and find myself staring at the same tall building I saw in the photo at Andreas's house. It has the same curved balconies and above the portico a couple of the letters have fallen off but it's still recognisable as the Grecian Bay Hotel.

The door swings open easily – which means, I hope, that someone has been here recently. The reception area is dark and smells musty; wallpaper is hanging off the walls and covered in mould. Rubble and broken glass crunch under our feet as we pick our way down the hallway.

'Grace?' Andreas calls out.

There's no answer. He opens a door on the right into what appears to have once been a large bar. It's been left pretty much as it must have been in 1974. There's a disembowelled sofa, the springs poking out, and there's a dark wooden bar with beer pumps attached. There are even a couple of glasses still intact.

And there, curled up on the floor, asleep, is Grace.

Chapter 44

She's alive.

In this moment nothing else matters. I forget it all. I forget Andreas standing awkwardly in the doorway. I forget the reason she's here in the first place. She's alive and everything else pales into insignificance.

I run up and crouch down beside her, tears of joy streaming down my face.

'Gracie?' I whisper.

She doesn't stir, she's so deeply asleep. Her hair falls lankly over her face, and her narrow chest rises and falls with her breathing. She's wearing just a bra and shorts and a dirty-looking sleeping bag is twisted in her arms. I'm aware of Andreas watching from the doorway so I untangle the sleeping bag from her arms and cover her with it.

'Grace?' I say more loudly and shake her by the shoulder.

Her eyes open and I see her struggle between sleep and consciousness. For one blissful second, she blinks at me sleepily and her eyes light up. It's a look I remember from the past, the way she used to look at me when she was a little girl, an instinctive reaction to the sight of her mother – the love of a baby, borne of dependency. Then just as quickly as it appears, the light is gone. Her face snaps shut and she's teenage Grace again. Fully awake. She sits up, her blue eyes dull with hostility.

'Grace.' I kneel next to her and wrap her in my arms. She feels limp. I can feel her skinny shoulders, her heart beating fast under her ribs and her breath is sour with sleep and neglect.

'Grace, we've been so worried about you,' I murmur.

I let go of her and sit back, looking at her. She looks awful. There are dark shadows around her eyes and her hair is dirty and tangled. She looks as if she's lost weight and it's not as if she had that much spare to lose in the first place.

She stares back at me warily, reminding me of a stray cat, backed into a corner, back arched and hissing.

'You shouldn't have come here,' she says. 'How did you . . . ?' Her voice is hoarse like she hasn't spoken to anyone for a while. She glares at me then up at Andreas, noticing him for the first time and pulling the sleeping bag up around her chest. 'You!' she sneers. 'I should've known I couldn't trust you.'

Andreas shuffles uneasily. 'She promised she wouldn't make you come home,' he says.

'Don't blame him. He didn't tell me, I guessed.'

I gaze at my daughter. This is a Grace I don't recognise. Somewhere inside is the Grace I love, I'm sure, but right now she's hidden well. She looks so thin and drawn. I wonder what she's been eating. How has she been living?

'Are you hungry? Thirsty?' I ask. I wish I'd thought to bring some food. At least I have my water bottle with me. I offer it to her, but she bats it away.

'No.' She sighs heavily, stands up and pulls on a T-shirt over her dirty bra. Andreas looks away, embarrassed.

'Have you got a cigarette?' she asks him coolly.

'Sure,' he says, eager to please. He rummages in his pocket, produces a packet and hands her one.

She lights the cigarette, staring at me defiantly, and takes a drag. I think how beautiful she looks in this moment, despite everything. I think how resourceful she must have been to live like this and I'm proud of her and I love her so much but I'm also terrified. Terrified of what she knows, what she must be going through and of what she might do. I look down at her belly. It's still flat but is there life in there, growing right now inside my girl, who's still not much more than a child herself?

'Andreas, I'd like to talk to Grace alone if you don't mind,' I say.

'Well, er . . . is that okay?' He looks over at Grace who shrugs.

'I should probably go anyway,' he says. 'I've got school. They'll wonder where I am. Are you going to be okay, Grace?'

She looks at the floor, barely acknowledging him.

'How will you get home?' I ask.

'I'll get a taxi to the border. Then phone my brother to come pick me up.'

I nod. I don't really care what he does. It's better if he's out of the way.

I wait until he's left the room and is out of earshot.

'You can't stay here, Grace, it's illegal. What will happen if the soldiers find you?' I say. 'We've all been so worried. The police are looking for you. Your dad, Jack . . . They're devastated . . .'

She shrugs and stares at a cockroach scuttling across the floor. Then slowly, deliberately, she takes her shoe and crushes it.

'You should have thought of that.'

I don't ask what she means.

'You'll get ill if you stay here.' I pinch the skin on her arm. 'Look, there's nothing there, no flesh. You're so skinny. What are you even eating?'

No answer.

I take a deep breath. This subject is not easy, but it has to be broached. 'Grace, I know about the baby . . . Maria told me. You need medical attention . . .'

She laughs then, a short, bitter laugh, and turns her face away.

'Oh, Grace, sweetheart . . . I'm so sorry. It'll be okay. We can deal with this together, like we always deal with everything . . .' I reach out and try to touch her hand.

But she snatches it away. Her eyes are burning flames of anger and hatred.

'Grace . . .'

'Don't call me that,' she spits.

'What?'

'Don't call me Grace, when it's not my name.'

Her voice is like ice.

'What do you mean?' I whisper. Though, of course, I know what she means.

She stands up, her blue eyes blazing.

'Grace is dead, isn't she, *Mother?*'

Chapter 45

2001

I'm lying in my bed and sunlight is flooding in through the flimsy curtains. I must have crawled up here sometime last night, but I don't remember when or how; I was so drunk. I drank to help me forget but it hasn't helped. I haven't forgotten anything. Hakan doesn't love me and he's not coming. He probably never will. Tears of self-pity roll down my cheeks. My head aches and I feel nauseous. My breasts are painful, swollen with milk.

I roll over and look at the clock by my bed. Eleven o'clock. *That's weird. Why hasn't Gracie woken me?*

I pull myself to the other end of the bed and peer down at her Moses basket. The stand broke a couple of weeks ago and I can't afford a new one, so for the moment the basket is just on the floor by my bed. By your bed is the safest place for her, the health visitor said. But looking down now, I see to my horror that a pillow has fallen on top of her during the night. Suddenly fully awake, my heart pumping, I snatch the pillow up and look down at her. She's lying perfectly still, her little hands clenched above her head like she's hanging on to something. I reach down and touch her cheek tentatively.

It feels cold.

'Gracie, wake up!' I grab her and shake her frantically.

She doesn't move.

She's stiff and still like a doll. She's not breathing.

No, no, no, NO, NO, NO!! Please God, NO!

I pick her up, lie her on the bed and kiss her on her cold, empty mouth, trying to breathe air into her lungs. Then I pump her chest desperately with the base of my palms. I've seen people do this on TV, but I can't remember how many times you're supposed to do it or exactly where.

Nothing.

I stand up and shake her, slapping her cheeks.

'Wake up, Gracie! Wake up!'

Nothing.

Time and space stand still. Somewhere someone is screaming. My knees buckle under me and I collapse on the floor, rocking her backwards and forwards, sobbing uncontrollably. There isn't enough room in my body to contain this pain. It rages inside me, a monster of grief. *Please let this not be true,* I pray. *Please God, let this not be true.*

Nothing.

The silence is deafening.

Chapter 46

2017

I sink backwards, rocking back on my haunches. 'I don't know what you're talking about,' I say shakily.

'Yes, you do. Don't lie to me,' Grace hisses. 'You're such a liar.'

'Grace, I——' As I reach out and try to touch her, she gives a cry of rage and frustration and leaps to her feet.

'Get away from me!' she hisses. Then, before I can stop her, she's run out of the room into the foyer.

'Grace, wait!' I scrabble to my feet and dash out after her just in time to see her racing up the stairs, taking them two at a time. I have no choice but to follow her.

'Grace, stop! Where are you going?' I shout, struggling up seemingly endless flights of stairs. 'It's not safe.'

In places the concrete has crumbled and there's no handrail but Grace carries on regardless until we reach the top of the building and she ducks out of the door. I hesitate a moment, gasping for breath and gripped by fear, before I climb out after her onto the roof.

Outside, a vicious sea wind is gusting across the open space. I cling to the wall, feeling dizzy, vertigo already kicking in.

'What are we doing up here?' I say.

'Well, I *was* trying to get away from you.'

She turns and smiles at me – if you can call it a smile. It's a grotesque imitation of a smile that makes me shudder. Her eyes are glittering in her unnaturally pale face and I'm so very afraid for her.

Then my heart is in my mouth as she saunters right up to the edge and leans on the low parapet.

'Come back, Grace. It's dangerous.'

The sun, an angry, fresh red wound, has appeared on the horizon and is rising rapidly, bleeding into the sky.

'You're too close to the edge. You'll fall.'

'Every day I look down and think about what it would be like to fall. Would it be like flying? What do you think?'

Terror constricts my throat. I can barely speak. 'It'll be okay, baby. We'll sort it out together . . .'

'Will it? Just how exactly will this be okay? In what universe is this okay?' She turns on me and stares at me with so much hatred my knees buckle. 'It's too late,' she says. 'I know the truth. I know what you did, *Mother*.'

The wind whips across the rooftop and there's a loud roaring in my ears. I stagger back and slump against the wall, landing on hard concrete. The air is suddenly toxic and it's difficult to breathe.

'Grace . . .' I gasp.

'But why am I calling you that, when you're not really my mother?'

'Of course I am,' I manage with conviction because it's true. I've fed her, cared for her, taught her, loved her since she was a baby. If that doesn't make me her mother, I don't know what does.

'Bullshit.' She walks towards me, her face twisted with anger. *At least she's moving further away from the edge*, I think, as she squats beside me. 'I didn't want to believe it at first,' she says. 'When Grandad Dave came to the house last week and started dropping hints, I told myself it was just Dave being an arsehole as usual. After all, it's pretty unbelievable, isn't it? But there were things, small things, that gnawed away at me after Dave left, like I always felt, you know, that I didn't quite belong in our family – that I was different . . .'

'Everyone feels alienated when they're a teenager.'

'And then when I met Hakan he showed me the photo of Grace as a baby. In the photo she had brown eyes . . .'

'You were a baby then. Babies' eyes change colour.'

'Yeah, from blue to brown, not the other way around.'

'Sometimes . . .'

'And then there's the small matter of my birthmark.' She lifts her T-shirt, swings around and shows me the large strawberry-shaped mark on her back. 'Birthmarks can fade, I guess. Maybe they sometimes even completely disappear. But they don't just appear, do they? That's why they're called *birth*marks.

Because you have them from birth. The baby in that photo doesn't have one.'

'I must have photoshopped that photo. I'm pretty sure I did,' I say feebly.

Grace lets out a cry of rage. 'Stop lying! You've done nothing but lie to me my whole life.' She stands up. 'I really don't want to speak to you anymore. I can't stand the sight of you. You disgust me,' she fires, turning and walking back to the edge of the roof.

Then, without warning, she climbs up onto the parapet.

'Grace. Don't be an idiot. Get down, Grace. Please, let's talk about this. Just get down from there, *please*.'

She laughs. 'Only if you stop lying. There's no point in denying it. I can always do a DNA test.'

'Okay, okay. I give in. You're right. I'm not your real mother.'

Chapter 47

2001

How long do I lie there with Gracie wrapped in my arms? I've no idea. All I know is that it's getting dark by the time I finally let go of her and stumble downstairs.

I'm not sure what I'm doing; I'm demented with grief. I only know I need to deaden this pain somehow. On the kitchen worktop is the bottle of vodka I was drinking last night. I drink some more, as much as I can stomach. But the pain doesn't go away. It just seems to grow inside me, until my body can't hold it anymore. I let out a wail and bang my head against the wall. Maybe I can cancel one pain with another. But it doesn't help. I thought I knew what sadness was until this moment, but nothing – nothing – has prepared me for this.

I pick up the phone. *I need help. Maybe I can get help*, I think vaguely. But who should I call? Not an ambulance. There's nothing anyone can do for her now. I'm sure about that.

I'm still holding the phone when it rings, and I stare at it blankly, watching it vibrate in my hand. Hakan's number flashes up on the screen and I automatically press 'answer call'.

'Hi, Jojo,' he says cheerfully. And his voice seems to be coming from a whole different world – another universe; a place where Gracie still exists. 'How are you?'

'I . . .'

But he doesn't wait for an answer. 'I've got some good news. I'm coming to England after all. I should be there next Monday. I'd like to finally meet my daughter. Is that okay?'

I can't speak. *Why this? Why now?* I wonder.

'Jo, you're very quiet, are you okay?'

'Yes . . . I'm okay.' My voice comes from far away. 'What time do you think you'll be here?'

'About six . . .'

'Okay.'

'And how's little Gracie?'

'She's fine.'

'I can't wait to see her.'

I hang up. Time passes. I'm not sure how long. I fall asleep on the kitchen floor and I wake again, writhing like a worm on the cold tiles. My breasts are bursting with milk, which I squeeze out and watch as it splashes onto the floor. My head feels muddled and there's a hole in my chest where my heart should be – a hole the size of a planet. *Grace is gone*, I think vaguely. *But where? I must find her. Hakan's coming. He'll want to see his daughter. If I don't have Grace, I'll lose him too.*

I pull on a coat over my nightshirt, put on a pair of trainers and head outside. The sun is shining brightly, blinding me. I shield my eyes and head down the road in the direction of town. An elderly couple shuffle past me along the road and a woman pushing a pram gives me an odd look, then looks away quickly when she catches my eye. She senses it, I suppose. She's senses the wrongness inside of me and she's afraid. She's right to be afraid. I'm carrying a black hole inside me and it's threatening to suck everything into it.

I turn into Church Street. I've no idea where I'm headed. I've got no plan at all. I'm just walking, one foot in front of the other, propelled onwards by an awful dark energy. And I find myself in the old part of town. The houses here are posh, Victorian semis with well-tended gardens and BMWs parked outside. In a driveway a man cleans his shiny new car. In a garden, children bounce up and down on a trampoline, shrieking and giggling. The noise hurts my head.

But that's when I hear something miraculous. Over the noise of laughter there's the sound of a baby crying drifting in the air. The sound hooks into me and pulls me towards it. *Grace,* I think. *Grace.*

The crying is coming from a black SUV parked in the street. The boot and the back door are both wide open, and she's strapped in her car seat, her face red and wrinkled with crying, gasping for breath between sobs. She's not Grace. I know that. At least part of me knows that. But why have they left her here all alone? It's not right. Who would leave a baby alone like this?

I can't stand the sound of her crying and I find myself unclipping the straps and pulling her out of the seat. Weighing her tenderly in my arms, I kiss her soft cheek and smell her pure baby smell. She looks up at me then and stops crying.

'Gracie,' I say, and she smiles.

It was meant to be.

Chapter 48

2017

The sun is rising rapidly in the sky, an angry red ball. Grace balances on the parapet, her hair whipping around her face.

'Grace . . . please . . .'

'I told you not to call me that. We both know I'm not *Grace*, don't we? It was her in the lake, the baby they thought was me, wasn't it?'

I nod. 'Yes, you're right, but come back downstairs. We can talk there. *Please*.'

'But I like it up here.' She walks further away along the wall and opens her arms wide like she's being crucified. For a heart-stopping second, she teeters on the edge. Then she sighs and sits down, facing me with her back to the drop.

'How could you do it?'

'You don't understand. I was so young. Not much older than you are now . . . and I was so scared and alone. At first I think I believed you were really her.'

'You let me believe Hakan was my father. All those years I kept that stupid doll, thinking it was from my father.'

'It was you,' I realise. 'You cut up the doll.'

She looks at me directly. Her eyes are dripping poison.

'What did you do with the real Grace? Did you kill her?'

'No, of course I didn't!' I exclaim. 'What do you think I am?'

Grace gives me a cold, assessing stare. 'I don't know. You're not a normal human being, that's for sure.'

'Maybe not.' I sit down next to her on the wall, keeping my weight firmly on my feet, trying not to think about the huge drop behind me.

'How *did* she die then?' Grace demands.

The truth is, I can't be sure. There are fourteen hours, fourteen hours that I can't remember – a huge black hole in my memory. Most likely I dropped the pillow on her in my sleep but how can I be sure that I didn't smother her in a drunken rage? I only know that I loved her and that, in a normal state of mind, I would never have hurt her. But then I wasn't in a normal state of mind that night, was I? There's no point in telling Grace that, though. She doesn't need to know. Instead I tell Grace the same story I've told myself all these years.

'It was cot death. It happens sometimes. Babies just die for no reason. There was nothing anyone could have done.'

Grace kicks her legs against the wall. 'How do you know that? Did you call an ambulance? Was there an autopsy?'

'No. I was only eighteen. I was half mad with grief and I didn't know what to do. You'll understand when you have your own children. There's nothing so bad as losing a child.'

315

Chapter 49

2001

Everyone's talking about it. It's in all the newspapers and on the TV all the time.

I sit in the living room with Grace feeding in my arms and we watch the press conference together. The mother and father are both there, flanked by two grave-looking police officers. Her parents both seem bewildered, blinking at the flash from all the cameras. They don't cry; it's worse than that. They look hollowed out, devastated. The mother tries to say something but breaks down halfway through the first sentence. The father isn't much better, but he manages to splutter out the bare facts of the case – that they left her in the car outside, just for a couple of minutes, and when they came out to get her, she was gone. The police appeal for anyone who knows anything to come forward and the parents stand there looking shattered, clutching the hand of their little boy. At four years old does he have any idea what is going on? You would have to have a heart of stone not to feel sorry for them.

I don't have a heart of stone. I know right from wrong. I know that what I've done is wrong. I know that this baby is not really my Gracie. Twice, I dress her and get her ready to go out. I even put her in the car seat and drive to Church Street, but the house is surrounded by reporters and, even though I could probably smuggle her round the back, I can't go through with it. It would be like ripping out my heart all over again. They shouldn't have left her like that, I tell myself. Her father lied when he said they left her just for a couple of minutes. It was more like ten minutes at least. They weren't looking after her properly. They don't deserve her.

Grace starts crying in the back seat, so I put a dummy in her mouth and drive back home. At home, I curl up in bed with her in my arms and we drift off to sleep together.

After a while I forget she was ever not mine. It seems like she's always been my Gracie.

But the nursery is starting to smell. The postman commented on it when he delivered a parcel this morning – another present for Grace from Hakan: a rattle, with an apology note. It turns out he's not coming after all. Strange how I really don't care anymore.

'Jesus. You got a dead rat in there, love?' the postman said, holding his nose. 'You want to get something done about that.'

I need to do something. I have no choice, unless I want to

risk losing Grace. So, I wrap the body in brown paper. When it's wrapped it's pathetically small and light. *It probably wouldn't cost very much to post*, I think. I could post it to Hakan – a kind of revenge. But it would never work. They'd soon realise who sent the parcel and why. And then I would lose Grace.

Instead, I put the parcel in a large plastic bag, along with some bricks that I grab from the building site down the road, and I tie the whole thing tightly with duct tape.

The moon is swollen and high in the sky as I pull up, tyres crunching on frosty gravel. I kill the engine and switch off the headlights, letting my eyes adjust to the darkness and my heart rate slow. The baby is still asleep in the back, thank God. She'll be okay for a few minutes. I hate leaving her alone, even for a second – but I don't have much of a choice.

I look round furtively as I open the boot, but the car park is empty. No one around for miles. The package is in the back tucked under a blanket and wrapped in so many layers of paper, plastic and duct tape that it resembles a sort of sick pass the parcel. I lift it out and, carefully locking the car door, carry it to the fence as fast as I can. In my rush, as I squeeze through the gap, I snag my jumper on a piece of wire and wriggle there for a moment, terrified, like an animal caught in a trap.

'Don't panic,' I soothe myself, unhooking the jumper with trembling hands. 'Everything's okay.' But, of course, it isn't okay. Everything is about as far from okay as it can be.

The package is heavy because of the bricks, and when I finally reach the water's edge I'm panting, my breath clouding in the cold air. But at least the rowing boat is there, tied to the jetty. I place the parcel in the bottom and clamber in after, trying to keep my balance as the wooden craft creaks and pitches.

Fitting the oars in their slots, I head for the deep water. The last time I rowed a boat I was about eight, with Dad – my real dad, that is, not Dave. We were here, at the lake. It was the last time I saw him in fact. And it's tricky at first, but after a couple of false starts I soon have the hang of it, digging in on one side with the oars if I veer off course. When I reach the centre of the lake I let go and the boat drifts.

It's unforgivable what I'm about to do. I know that. But I've already gone so far, there's no turning back now. Even so, my fingers clamp onto the package and won't let go as I hold it over the side of the boat. I'm frozen with fear. It's only the sound of something – a night-time creature maybe – rustling in the bushes that finally startles me into action. With one swift motion, I fling it into the lake and the black water swallows it whole.

For a while I sit in the boat, watching the lake shiver in the moonlight, feeling sick and shaky.

When I get back to the car the baby has woken up and is crying, a sort of steady, hopeless grizzle that suggests she's been crying for some time.

I scoop her up in my arms and crush her to my chest.

'I'm so sorry,' I say, tears rolling down my cheeks. 'I'm so, so sorry. Mummy's here now, Grace.'

Chapter 50

2017

'There's no excuse for what you did,' Grace says. 'You stole my life from me. You stole my family, my mother . . . my brother . . .' On the last word her voice breaks and my heart breaks along with it. All her life, all I've ever wanted to do was protect her from pain. But now I'm the cause of it.

I watch, feeling helpless, as she starts crying uncontrollably.

'You stood by and let me . . . let me fall in love with him,' she wails between sobs.

What? I stare at her, confused. 'What are you talking about?'

She wipes her eyes and a smile, a horrible, contorted smile, spreads across her lips. 'Don't try to tell me you don't know.'

'Know what?' I say, battling a deep feeling of unease.

'Last Saturday, Tom told me he had to go back to England to be with his mother. Do you know why?'

'Uh . . .' I try to collect my muddled thoughts, thinking back to the conversation I had with Tom down at the marina. 'Yes, his mother had received bad news of some kind.'

'You could say that.' Grace gives a short, humourless laugh. 'They'd just found the body of a baby in Childon Lake and the police had originally thought it might be Tom's baby sister, Daisy.'

'But I don't understand . . .' The truth is, I don't want to understand. Every part of me is rebelling against understanding. But something from the back of my mind is oozing to the surface. Something unthinkable.

'Don't you? Really?' She stares at me with those ferocious blue eyes.

I close my eyes, reeling. *It's impossible. It can't be. Please God . . . let it not be.* 'But your name was Daisy *Cooper* . . . I — I saw it on the news. Tom's surname is Mitchinson.'

Grace sighs and says in an unnaturally calm voice, 'Tom's real father's name was Cooper, yes. But he killed himself shortly after he lost his daughter.'

I rub my face. 'Yes, Tom told me about his dad, now I remember, but I don't see—'

'Tom took his stepfather's name when his mother remarried. They thought it would help him avoid all the publicity. They wanted his upbringing to be as normal as possible.'

There's a long silence as what she's saying sinks in.

'But Tom's sister died. He told me himself,' I say finally, clinging on to this fact like it can save me from being swallowed up by the blackness.

'Because that's what his parents told him. His mum only told him the truth when they found the baby in Childon Lake – that his sister was abducted and never found.'

I clutch my stomach as if I've been physically punched. I see it now – the complete, devastating truth; all the horrific consequences of what I've done.

'No . . .' I whisper. 'I had no idea. I could never have predicted . . . I would never have . . .'

'It doesn't matter what you knew. Tom is my *brother*,' she says, shaking her head. I stand up and stagger forward. Nausea curls in my belly. Doubling over, I retch out the contents of my stomach. Because I haven't eaten much in the past few days there's not much for me to bring up, just a bitter, watery bile spilling onto concrete.

'I didn't know, I swear,' I say.

Grace eyes me dispassionately. 'It makes no difference. The damage is done. I'm pregnant with my own brother's baby.'

'Does he know?' I whisper.

Her face twists with pain. She shakes her head and looks away. 'No. I've tried to spare him all this . . .' She looks back at me, eyes welling up. 'You have no idea how hard it was to break things off with him without being able to tell him why. It broke my heart.'

She chokes out the last words and flings her head into her hands, sobbing hopelessly, her whole body convulsing with tears.

I sit there, unable to move, still reeling with shock. How can this have happened? Grace and Tom. Brother and sister. It's like a cruel, horrible joke.

'How could I have known? How can I make this right?' I say, looking over at Grace. She's stopped crying now and is staring straight ahead at something I can't see. I crawl over to her and attempt to put my arm around her.

'Grace . . . my love . . .'

She shakes me off savagely. 'Get away from me, you fucking bitch,' she spits, scrambling to her feet.

And I watch in helpless horror as she climbs back up on the parapet.

Trying to gather my scattered wits, I make a last desperate attempt to salvage the situation.

'Grace, we can sort this. We'll go back to England. You can get an abortion. No one needs to know. Just get down from there, please.'

She looks down at me. She looks so small and fragile. A sudden gust of wind could blow her over the edge.

'I don't have to do what you say anymore. I think you've lost the moral high ground, don't you?' she says. 'You were always so controlling. You made out it was because you loved me, but you don't love me, not really. You couldn't love me and do what you've done to me . . .'

'Grace, get down. Think about Chris and Jack. If not for me, do it for them.'

I see her wavering. Jack is the ace up my sleeve. She's always been close to Jack. But then she turns and walks away along the wall, balancing like a tightrope walker.

She's teetering on the edge. I feel dizzy, so terrified that my heart is thumping out of my chest. I take a step towards her slowly, cautiously.

'If you take one step closer, I'll jump,' she says.

'Come back to us,' I try desperately. 'We can talk about what to do together. You could meet your family – your other family, I mean. You could stay with Chris and Jack. I would leave if you wanted.'

For a moment, I see it there in her eyes, the possibility, the future. Then her face snaps closed.

Tuesday, 26th September 2017

Chapter 51

'Why? That's what I don't understand.'

Chris has ordered a double vodka. He downs it in one and looks at me across the table. Tears are streaming down his freckled cheeks. He looks lost and bewildered. In the past few days he seems to have shrunk to about half his original size.

We're in Nicosia, in a pub near the embassy, where we've just been to see about repatriating Grace's body. Everybody's been incredibly efficient and kind. They've already completed her inquest – a verdict of accidental death – and have booked her onto a flight to England. The whole thing is not as expensive as I expected. We've got a sort of package deal. Just three thousand pounds to dispatch a life. It doesn't seem like much, does it?

'I just don't understand.' Chris stares into his glass as if the answer can be found there. 'I mean, she was happy, wasn't she? We did all we could for her. How could we have missed this?' His face scrunches up and he's crying properly now, huge sobs that shake his whole body.

It looks all wrong to see him crying like this – a big strong man like him. Usually he's my rock. I guess I'm going to have to be his for a while now.

'I suppose she just couldn't handle being pregnant,' I say feebly. Chris will never know the truth about who Grace really was and what happened on that rooftop. And it's best that way, I think. There's no point in dredging it all up now. Who would that help? Certainly not Grace.

'Did she tell you whose baby it was? Was it Tom's?' he asks. I nod. 'I believe so.'

'I'm going to kill that fucking shit.'

'Leave him be,' I say. 'Tom didn't mean to hurt her. He must be pretty devastated.'

Chris snorts. 'I'm sorry but I'm not going to lose too much sleep over what he's feeling.'

'No,' I sigh. 'It's Jack I worry about. What's all this going to do to him?' Jack has refused to speak about Grace since her death and seems to be in denial. I'm afraid that if he buries his emotions too deeply, the long-term effects of her loss will be more damaging.

We stare out at the traffic crawling past the window. I have to focus on Jack now. Jack and Chris, my little family. They're all I have left.

'Oh Jesus. What are we going to do?' says Chris, putting his head in his hands.

I feel strangely calm. I suppose it's the shock. Everything seems muffled, as if nothing is real, as if nothing really matters.

'One step at a time,' I say. 'We go back to England for the funeral. We'll have to tell all Grace's friends in England and my mum. God knows how she's going to take this – and Dave . . .'

Chris winces and looks away. 'Joanna, there's something you need to know. I didn't want to tell you this, with all that you've gone through already, but I don't want you to read it in the paper or hear it from someone else.'

'What?' My heart thuds dully. But there's nothing that can really hurt me. Not anymore. The worst has already happened. Twice. And I'm still alive.

'They found Dave in his hotel room in Larnaca. He overdosed.'

'Oh . . . Is he okay?'

'I'm afraid he's dead, Jo.' Chris rubs his eyes and looks at me searchingly.

But I feel nothing. How could Dave's death make any impact next to the grief I feel for Grace. It's nothing but a small gust of wind compared to a tornado. No, not even a gust, more of a breath. On the whole, I think the world is a better place without Dave.

'Well,' I shrug. 'Considering he was a heroin addict for years, he was lucky to survive as long as he did.' I take a sip of wine.

My hand is shaking slightly as I bring the glass to my lips. But Chris doesn't notice, or if he does, he just puts it down to shock.

Chapter 52

Three days earlier

'She said you weren't her mother,' Dave whispers in my ear. 'And she was right, wasn't she?'

I recoil, gripping my chair tightly. It's as I feared. He *knows*.

'I've no idea what you're talking about,' I say as lightly as I can.

'Oh, I think you do.'

'You're lying. She didn't say that. You never even saw Grace in Ayia Napa – you're full of bullshit.'

'Haha, okay, okay! You caught me. I might have imagined it. Like I said before, I think I'm going a little senile in my old age.' He leans back with a smile. He's sitting opposite me in the restaurant. Mayonnaise has dribbled out of his mouth and is caught on the stubble sprouting from his chin. It makes me seethe with disgust.

'Here. Wipe your face,' I say, handing him a serviette. 'You're worse than a baby.'

He takes the napkin, rubs his chin and smiles at me ingratiatingly. 'I need more money, to get home,' he says. 'Your mother needs me home. All my money was stolen. Did I tell you?'

'Yes, you told me,' I say wearily.

'Have you got any cash, Joanna?' he wheedles. 'Just a bit of cash for your old dad.'

'We haven't got any more to give you . . .'

'Oh?' His eyes narrow. And just like that the ingratiating manner vanishes, and he sits back and stares at me balefully. 'Well, in that case,' he says, 'maybe I'll have to sell my story to the papers. I think they'll be very interested in that little granddaughter of mine. Stolen as a baby. It's quite a story, isn't it? I think the police might be interested too.'

If I had any doubt about what I'm about to do, he's just erased it right there. This is necessary – like exterminating vermin.

I lean forward, my heart hammering, and try to smile.

'I haven't got any cash, Dave, but I've got something else – something I think you'll like.'

'What?' He looks alert suddenly. The instinct of the addict kicking in.

I pat my bag, which is hanging over the back of the chair. 'It's in here,' I say.

'What is it?' He tries to grab the bag, but I snatch it away, out of his reach.

'I can't show you here.'

'Okay,' he grins. 'Let's go to my hotel.'

So, I pay the bill and we make our way along the seafront to

331

the place where he's staying. As we walk Dave gabbles away, full of nervous energy, as if there's a part of him that knows what's coming. As if he's walking towards this willingly.

'This had better be good, Joanna,' he says. ''Cos I ain't fucking around anymore.'

'How did you know?' I ask curiously. 'You must have only seen baby Gracie once before she was four months old.'

'I figured it out, didn't I? Not as daft as I look, am I?' He chuckles, absurdly pleased with himself. 'A couple of weeks ago your mother added Grace on Facebook. She started showing me all the photos Grace shared. You know how girls are these days, all these selfies and pictures of themselves they like to post.'

'Yes, I know,' I say impatiently. 'Just get to the point.'

'Well, there was one picture Grace was tagged in. It was a snap someone had taken of her in a bikini playing volleyball on the beach. There was something about it that didn't sit right with me. At first, I couldn't work out what it was, but then I realised it was that huge ugly birthmark on her back. Your mother's got a photo of baby Grace on her mantlepiece. She's lying on her front in her nappy. I must have seen it every day for the past sixteen years. And the baby in that photo has no birthmark.'

The photo I sent to my mother. I should have got rid of it. I thought about it many times over the years, but, somehow, I couldn't bring myself to do it.

'But it wasn't just that,' Dave continues. 'It was the way you were with Grace when she was a little kid. You were so secretive. And you always refused to take her to the doctor's. I always thought it was weird, but I never really put two and two together until I saw that birthmark.'

He breaks off as we cross the road and turn into a shady back street.

'When I saw that, I knew for sure there was something fishy going on. Then it was on the news, about how they'd found a baby's body in the lake. They thought it was the body of Daisy Cooper, that kid that went missing all those years ago.'

'I remember that,' I say weakly. 'But I don't see what that's got to do with Grace.'

Dave stops and grins at me.

'Come on, Jo. There's no point in pretending anymore, is there? I know what I know. Where was I? Oh yes. They did one of those DNA tests and found out that it wasn't Daisy. It was another baby that'd been put there roughly the same time as the Cooper kid went missing – a baby they couldn't identify.'

He turns and carries on walking. 'That made me think, I can tell you. So, I did a bit of research – looked at some old newspapers online. Do you know what I found?'

I don't answer.

'I found out that Daisy Cooper would've been sixteen if she was alive – the same age as Grace. It was all there – how she had a strawberry-shaped birthmark on her back and how she'd gone missing from outside her parents' house not far from where you used to live.'

When we reach his hotel there's no one on the desk at reception. *Good*. It feels like it's meant to be, like the universe is giving me its blessing. 'So that's why you came to Cyprus,' I say bitterly. 'You came to tell her, so you could ruin my life – or was blackmail the idea? Was it all just about money?'

He shrugs and grins. 'There was a cheap flight online. Just fancied a bit of a holiday, didn't I? I didn't know it was going to be such an interesting trip.'

'Did you tell Grace what you know?' I ask as we wait for the lift. I'm trying to sound nonchalant. I don't want to give him the satisfaction of seeing how afraid I am of his answer.

He smirks at me, enjoying my discomfort. 'No, course not. But I think I might have mentioned something about her birthmark. I wouldn't be surprised if she'd worked it out.'

Once we're in his room, I hang the 'Do not disturb' sign outside his door, then I lift my bag onto the bed, open it and display the contents.

His eyes light up and he rubs his hands together, chuckling like a pirate that's discovered gold. 'You clever little girlie. Where'd you get all that?'

'I bought it from a friend of Grace's.'

The truth is, I slipped a couple of the little bags into my handbag the day I found the heroin in Andreas's room. I thought it would be useful as a bribe to get Dave out of my hair, out of my life. But I know now that it won't work as a bribe – that unless I do something decisive, he will always be in my life, threatening me and leeching off me.

'This is good shit,' Dave says, dipping his finger in and licking it. 'Old school.'

It doesn't occur to him to ask why, after years of hating his habit even more than I hate him, I'm suddenly so willing to help him. He doesn't care, I suppose. He has the tunnel vision of an addict.

'You're a good girl, Joanna,' he says, handing me a tourniquet and needle. He lies back on the bed as I heat the heroin the way he taught me when I was a kid. I know the correct dose off by heart, I did it so often. He trusts me to get it right. He doesn't check to see what I'm doing. If I give him a slightly higher dose than is safe, he'll never know.

I tie the ready-made tourniquet around his arm and squeeze until the vein pops. I hesitate just for a second, with the syringe in my hand. I know with what I'm about to do I'm crossing a line, but I've crossed so many lines already. What's one more?

Taking a deep breath, I dig the point of the needle into his flesh.

'You do it,' I say, feeling suddenly queasy. It will be useful to have his fingerprints on the needle in case there are any questions raised when they find him.

'Okay.' Dave takes hold of the syringe and injects the heroin into his own arm. Then he lies back, a beatific smile on his face.

'Thanks, Joanna,' he says.

'You're welcome,' I say.

And I watch him drift in and out of consciousness. Until I'm confident that I got it right.

Tuesday, 3rd October 2017

Chapter 53

It's stopped raining as we arrive at the crematorium, but the sky is still grey and heavy. The ground is saturated, the grass swamped, the trees bedraggled and dripping. How appropriately grim, I think – as if there's not enough world to soak up all our sorrow.

There's a large crowd gathered outside, spilling out from the waiting area, shaking their umbrellas, talking in subdued voices. Lots of Grace's old school friends have turned up and even some of her friends from Cyprus have made the journey. I spot Maria and her parents talking to one of Chris's friends, and Andreas is here as well, with his brother, standing apart from everyone else, looking out of place and uncomfortable. Chris's relatives have turned out in force too and he's soon whisked away in a crowd of Appletons, leaving me standing alone. The only representatives from my own family are my brothers and my mother sitting huddled together in a corner of the waiting room. Mum catches my eye through the window and half smiles, raising her hand. But I pretend I haven't seen her. I've already had the sob story from her about how much she misses Dave and how lost she is now without him, and I don't want to hear it again. It's complete crap. She's much better off with him out of her life, and she knows it.

'I'm so sorry for your loss. Words can't express . . .' says a man I don't recognise, patting my arm.

I nod automatically. 'Thank you,' I say and stare over his shoulder at a woman just outside the waiting room talking to one of Chris's relatives. She's cradling a small baby in her arms. *Who brings a baby to a funeral?* I wonder. But I find that I can't look away. I gaze at it, mesmerised. The way it's staring up at her with its big, innocent eyes and trying to grab her earring with its tiny hands reminds me so much of Grace when she was that age. My self-control dissolves and the tears start flowing. *Grace, forgive me*, I beg silently. *Grace, my love, I'm so sorry.* But perhaps I'm thinking of the other Grace – the one I gave birth to. I get them muddled in my mind sometimes.

'Mrs Appleton.'

Someone taps me on the shoulder. I wipe my eyes and turn to see Tom standing behind me.

'Tom,' I say. I knew he would be here, of course, but it still comes as a shock seeing him.

'Can I ask you something, privately?' he says gravely. He's wearing a black suit and his long hair has been cropped. It makes him seem much more grown-up and serious than before and I wonder with a twinge of unease if he knows something.

'Er, yes, sure.' I glance over at Chris who's talking to his sister, Katie, Jack clinging to his hand. Good. I don't trust him to be civil to Tom and I don't want Grace's funeral ruined by a scene. I watch Chris and Katie embrace each other and Chris's big shoulders shake as she wraps him in her arms, and I usher Tom away around the corner to the car park.

'What do you want to know?' I ask as we huddle under a dripping chestnut.

He stares at me. Opens his mouth, then closes it again.

I wait patiently for him to build up the courage to ask what he wants to ask. Something about him has changed. It's not just his hair. It's his eyes – there's a kind of hardness to them that wasn't there before. More than ever they remind me of Grace.

'The police said she was pregnant. Is that true?' he finally blurts out.

I nod. 'I'm afraid so.'

He stares, stricken, at the ground and his shoulders slump. 'Is that why . . . ?'

'I don't know.' Part of me wants to spare him but the other part thinks, *Let him feel guilty. He should feel guilty. None of this would've happened if he hadn't got involved with Grace in the first place.*

'Maybe in part,' I say.

He winces. 'I don't understand. I would've been there for her. I wanted to marry her, you know, eventually.'

I don't answer.

'We were so similar, me and Grace,' he says. 'There was something so familiar about her from the moment I met her. It felt like coming home, like we were made for each other.'

Maybe one day he'll realise why, I think. It wouldn't take much for him to put two and two together and what then? But it's too late to worry about that now. What's done is done.

'I really loved her, you know,' he says as we head back towards the crowd of mourners.

'I know. Me too,' I sigh.

I rejoin Chris as we file into the crematorium and, sitting down, pick up the booklet the undertakers have left on the seats. There's a photo of Grace on the front, beaming at the camera. Above the picture it says *In loving memory of Grace Appleton* in curling black letters.

I did love Grace, even at the end, and did my best for her, I tell myself, as the coffin vanishes behind a screen. I loved baby Gracie more, of course, but nonetheless, a mother's love doesn't just die – it fades a little over the years, whittled away by a million small ingratitudes and insults. But it never completely dies, and I know I'll be grieving for both Graces for as long as I live.

But it's not just grief I feel. I'm haunted by a memory – a nightmare vision that won't leave me. Every morning when I wake up and every time I close my eyes at night, I see her.

Grace.

She's standing on the parapet with her arms outstretched. She looks beautiful and wild. Her dark hair is blowing in the wind, whipping around her face, and her eyes are glittering in the morning light.

'I hate you,' she says. And her voice drips in the air like poison.

342

'Grace, please . . .' I take a step towards her.

'I mean it. If you take a step closer, I'll jump.'

I'm thinking about Jack and Chris. I'm thinking about what it will do to them, my fragile little family, if they find out what I've done. I'm thinking about the huge mess I've created. And I'm thinking that Grace is part of that mess – that maybe it would all be simpler if she wasn't here. And if I'm totally honest, isn't there a moment, just a split second, when I wish her out of the way? It's just a thought – a fleeting firing of neurones. I only think it for a second but in that second . . .

I take another step.

And watch, frozen in horror, as she turns and throws herself from the rooftop.

Acknowledgements

Thank you to the brilliant team at Quercus. First and foremost, to my fantastic editor Rachel Neely, who has played a huge part in whipping this story into shape. A big thank you also goes to Natasha Webber for her gorgeous cover designs, and Ella and Hannah for all their hard work.

I'm grateful, too, to my friend Soulla Sophocli for reading the first three chapters and the useful and encouraging comments she made and to all the friends I've made in Cyprus, this country that I've grown to love and think of as home.

And last, but definitely not least, to Jim Lodge. My love and gratitude always.